◇◇◇◇◇◇◇◇◇◇◇◇◇◇◇◇◇◇◇

A Clue For Adrianna

A Captain's Point Story

By

Charlotte Kent

◇◇◇◇◇◇◇◇◇◇◇◇◇◇◇◇◇◇◇◇◇◇◇◇◇◇◇◇◇

Charlotte Kent is the pseudonym used by Annie Acorn and Juliette Hill when writing their collaborative contemporary women's fiction series Captain's Point Stories

You may contact and/or follow the authors at:
charlottekentromances@gmail.com
@CharlotteKent20

For my favorite couple, Joe and Susan,
who have provided so much inspiration and
encouragement to me
Annie Acorn

To my husband, John, the love of my life
Juliette Hill

This is Max's second starring role in a work of fiction.
The true story of his actual rescue can be found in Annie Acorn's cozy mystery novel
Chocolate Can Kill

CHAPTER I

Viewing the tarmac beneath her, Adrianna Montgomery could see Chicago's Midway Airport's ground crew loading last minute luggage and truly relaxed for the first time since her arrival home to her condo in Seattle the previous evening.

"Is this seat taken?" a shy, cultured voice asked from the aisle to her right.

Turning, she found herself looking into a pair of worried blue eyes. Reflexively, she straightened the seat belt and lowered the armrest that would separate them as she replied, "No, it's free. Help yourself."

"Thank you." The elderly woman joined her. "I don't often fly, and I've been dreading hours spent aloft beside a crying child." With the toe of a tiny shoe, the newcomer pushed a large patent leather handbag beneath the forward seat before fastening her seatbelt.

A light fragrance of honeysuckle wafted its way towards Adrianna, reminiscent of early childhood summers spent playing in the gazebo behind her great-aunt's seaside mansion, breezes blowing off the Atlantic lifting her dark curls. Despite her parents having left her behind as they had traveled the world in search of archeological treasure, those had been happy times.

But then, she had grown old enough to accompany them, and the summer visits had ended. As promised, she had written to her great-aunt of her travels, her childish script filling pages with stories of her adventures – a camel ride in Egypt, a mosaic at a dig in Turkey, a Minoan vase her mother had uncovered on a Greek isle – the list had gone on and on.

"My name's Edwina Foster." Her traveling companion broke through her thoughts. "I'm flying to visit my grandson and his wife."

"This trip is strictly business for me," Adrianna replied.

"Actually, it's more than a visit." The blue eyes now twinkled. "They're in their mid-thirties, and Ginny is expecting their first child. Jason has to attend a long conference in New York and didn't want to leave his wife alone this close to her due date. They've just moved to Captain's Point, Maryland, and haven't had time to make friends."

"Captain's Point?"

"Do you know it? I hear it's lovely."

"I haven't been there for any length of time since I was seven – almost twenty years ago, but I liked it back then. The town was full of little shops, but my favorite memory is of looking for shells on the beach."

With a start, Adrianna realized she had just lied. Her favorite memory had nothing to do with the beach, but rather with the wind-tossed woods behind the giant house.

One day during the early part of her last summer visit, she had found an old butterfly net stuffed between the croquet sticks and badminton racquets that were stored in a deep closet beneath the staircase. Not wanting to disturb her great-aunt's pre-dinner nap, she had gone outside to play with it, neglecting to tell the housekeeper where she was going. Happily chasing a bevy of yellow and white butterflies, she had left the manicured lawn and entered the cool quiet of the woods.

Other paths covered in pine needles had crossed, joined and then separated from the one that she had followed, and as the sun had set, she had realized that she was lost. A twig had snapped sharply somewhere behind her, and she had started to run, her way partially revealed through the leaves of the trees by a full moon rising overhead. Inevitably, she had tripped on a root and fallen to her knees, her right one striking the corner of a sharp pebble as she had let out a cry.

"Who is it?" A voice had called out up ahead.

"Adrianna," she had responded, forgetting her great-aunt's careful instructions about speaking with strangers.

"Stay where you are," the voice had commanded. "I'm coming."

A light rounded the bend ahead and came towards her, at first blocking her view of the boy who was carrying it. "What are you doing out here?" He had dropped a backpack onto the ground. "Miss Martha will be fit to be tied."

"You know my great-aunt?"

"Everyone knows Martha Montgomery." He had shrugged, calmly pulling a first aid kit from his pack and cleaning the cut on her knee with water from a Boy Scout canteen. "These woods aren't safe at night for a little girl."

"You're here," she had pointed out.

"But I'm older, and besides, I'm collecting specimens for my merit badge."

At the time, she hadn't known what a merit badge was, but it had sounded important. Silently, she had watched as he had applied an adhesive bandage to the cut by the light of his flashlight.

"I'll walk you back." He had held out his hand, and she had taken it gladly.

As the aircraft's engines roared to life, Edwina's voice broke through Adrianna's long ago memories. "I'm sure I wasn't the first person my grandson called on, but still, it's nice to be needed," Edwina admitted.

"I know they'll appreciate your help," she assured her traveling companion.

Turning towards the window, Adrianna watched as the runway flashed by, wondering if she had ever been needed by anyone – certainly not by her bright, shining parents, who had left her at a Swiss finishing school just two weeks before they had plunged to their deaths from one of the infamous curves along the Amalfi coast. And yet, here she was, flying from one end of the country to the other in response to two letters – one that had been more a command than a request and one that had broken her heart.

CHAPTER II

An additional bit of thrust lifted the aircraft from the pavement, and the sun soon reflected off the white fluffy clouds beneath them. Exhausted from lack of sleep the night before, Adrianna felt her eyelids grow heavy and rested her head against the fuselage's inner wall.

Had it been only hours since she had discovered the letters waiting at the concierge's desk in her building - the one having arrived through the mail, the other having been delivered by hand? If she hadn't opened the one postmarked Captain's Point first, she might not have read it, tossing it aside at the end of a horrible day and forgetting it. Instead she had saved the one she had thought best for last.

Settled at the kitchen table, she had opened the thick cream envelope with care, revealing a single sheet of paper and a cashier's check. The name Sheffield, Sheffield, Chesterton and Sheffield, Attorneys at Law, was printed on the letterhead.

Dear Ms. Montgomery:

Please accept our firm's condolences for your recent loss of your great-aunt, Martha Chesterton Montgomery. As the recipient of a bequest from Miss Montgomery, it is imperative that you make yourself available to our firm here in Captain's Point no later than April 30 of this year.

We have enclosed a cashier's check that should be sufficient to cover the cost of your airfare and normal travel expenses for one day. If you will advise us of your flight's arrival time, you will be met at BWI, driven to Montgomery House and provided with appropriate transportation for your use during your stay in Captain's Point.

We look forward to being of service to you as we have been to your family for many years.

Very truly yours,

Chase Sheffield
Attorney at Law

CC: File

Who did Chase Sheffield of Sheffield, Sheffield, Chesterton and Sheffield think he was, sending her a demanding letter like that? She had thought at the time. It wasn't as if she could switch gears and fly to Captain's Point just because he commanded it. But then, she had remembered the exit interview in Human Resources that day.

The expression on the other woman's face had been apologetic. "We're sorry to have to terminate your employment. Your work has been excellent, but we're downsizing."

Four months' severance pay, insurance benefits, 401K rollover, the words had barely entered her head as the young woman had droned on. Thank goodness, she had put a little aside from each paycheck for emergencies.

With no picture forming in her mind of the sender, she had carefully read Chase Sheffield's letter through once again. With the time difference between the west and east coasts, his office was already closed. She would give him a call in the morning and try to learn more about her great-aunt's estate before she agreed to a cross-country trip. Surely they could read her the will over the phone or through their computers.

For a moment, she had been saddened by the news of her great-aunt's death, forgetting how she had been treated in more recent years. After all, now she was the last surviving member of the Montgomery family. Captain Jebediah Montgomery, patriarch of them all, was probably turning over in his own grave at the mere thought of it.

Rising from her seat, she had taken her mug of tea and the second letter into the main room, prepared to receive another romantic gesture from her fiancé, Brad. As the sky outside her condo's large windows had reflected mauve, rose and pink from the setting sun, she had slit open the plain white envelope with her name written on the front in his familiar scrawl. Nothing could have prepared her for the message sealed inside.

CHAPTER III

The key to Adrianna's condo that had fallen into her lap as she had removed Brad's note had been the first indication that something was wrong. A sick feeling settling in the pit of her stomach, she had placed the small piece of metal on the end table beside her and then unfolded his letter:

Adrianna –

Life doesn't play by our rules. Passion overtakes us, weaknesses appear, and we must cope and pick up the pieces.
I have fallen in love with someone else - a nurse at the hospital. By the time you read this, we will be on a sun-drenched beach in Mexico.
Please don't hate me. You kept me going through the tiresome classes, labs, rounds and endless studying. Live your life now. You never needed me, and you will go much further alone than we would have gone together.

Brad

How could she have been so stupid? There must have been signs, but somehow she had missed them. Her mind had filled with a series of images - Brad's face in various poses, Brad catching her as she had slid on a rock, almost plunging into one of Mt. Rainier's glacial streams, Brad's eyes as he had leaned towards her in flickering candlelight.

What a fool she had been! It would be a long time before she would allow another man to hurt her like Brad had.

She would meet with Mr. Chase Sheffield, Attorney at Law, and see what he had to say about her great-aunt's estate. Then she would have a good think. Perhaps, settling in Seattle hadn't been her best idea. All those years struggling to pay her way through Stanford and then graduate school for her MBA hadn't exactly paid off in spades.

Sensing increased activity around her, Adrianna straightened.

"Jason will be picking me up at the airport," Edwina said, providing a welcome interruption to her previous thoughts. "Is someone meeting you, too?"

"Yes, they are," she replied with more confidence than she felt.

As requested in Mr. Sheffield's letter, she had left a message on his firm's voicemail detailing her flight's arrival time at BWI, but she had no idea what arrangements would actually be made for her transportation southward along the Maryland coast to Captain's Point. Not that it made any difference. She was perfectly capable of renting a car.

"You're exactly like that Italian mother of yours." Her great-aunt's words came back to her now. "You're always flitting from here to there on the spur of the moment without thinking ahead to the consequences."

While she recognized that the statement hadn't been true to her nature when uttered seven years ago, her actions since the arrival of Brad's letter proved it might be true now. What had made her flee from Seattle at the drop of a hat? Flying across the country wouldn't make him come back.

Perhaps it would be best if she didn't stay at Montgomery House as isolated as it was at the end of Captain's Point, the bluff that had given the town its name. Then again, there had always been something about the sea that had spoken to her – a little bit of Jebediah Montgomery running through her veins to the last.

Above Adrianna's head, the Fasten Seatbelt light flashed on once again.

"We're arriving at BWI right on schedule," the pilot's voice came through the intercom as the plane banked sharply to the left and began its descent, passing over water.

"Isn't this exciting?" Edwina's pert little face beneath her gray curls glowed with anticipation.

Adrianna sent her new acquaintance - possibly the only friend she would have in Captain's Point - the smile required by good manners, surprised when the older woman asked if they could exchange phone numbers with an eye to meeting for lunch in a day or two.

But then, the plane touched down, and Adrianna felt herself filled with a great sense of dread.

CHAPTER IV

Off to Adrianna's right at the baggage claim area, a family of four chatted about sightseeing plans. On a bench along the wall, a man sat with his arm around his young wife as both of them gazed at the baby she held in her arms. Suddenly, she felt very lonely.

"Adrianna!" A tall, grizzle-haired man hurried towards her. "Is that you?"

For a moment, she hesitated as she took in his plaid flannel shirt and worn jeans, but then she met his twinkling blue eyes and recognized him. "Otis? Oh, I'm so glad they sent you!" She had just enough time to shift her computer out of the way, before she felt herself embraced in a bear hug.

"Let me get a good look at you." Her great-aunt's property manager held her at arm's length, obviously pleased with what he saw. "Point out your suitcases, and we'll get on our way." He released her, referring to his wife in his next breath. "Penny can't wait to see you!"

Clicking her seatbelt closed a few minutes later, Adrianna watched as he rounded the front of the car, remembering how large a portion of her visits to Montgomery House had been spent in either Penny or Otis Plunk's company, her great-aunt having been busy entertaining this committee or that group of friends. How many hours had she spent in that large square kitchen with Penny, helping to slide cookies onto a cooling rack or icing a cake?

But Otis had been her true summer friend, allowing her to follow him around like a stray puppy. Otis had set her atop her first pony, and Otis had taught her to swim. Together they had nurtured the kitchen garden and pruned the roses. During her last summer visit, he had even taught her to row the small dinghy. How could she have so easily forgotten about him?

She studied his face, pleased that the years had been good to him, merely adding a few laugh lines to his eye area and lengthening his dimples until they were now more like creases. As he started the car, she realized he must be in his early sixties, his wife in her late fifties, as all the years since they had parted fell away.

What would become of the Plunks now? Their whole adult lives had been spent serving her great-aunt's needs and maintaining Montgomery House. Where would they go? What would they do?

Adrianna straightened in her seat. These were the questions she would ask Mr. Chase Sheffield. When they got to Montgomery House, she would start a list - quite possibly a long one.

With the skill of practice, Otis merged their car into the stream of vehicles heading south on I-95. "It won't be long now." He broke their comfortable silence. "Things haven't changed as much as you have."

"Well, you couldn't expect me to still be a teenager."

"No, but you sure were a charmer, both then and when you were a little girl. Penny and I have a picture of you riding a camel on our mantel. I imagine that was a lot different than riding Silver Queen," he referred to the Shetland pony on which she had been taught to ride.

"Now there was a beautiful animal," Adrianna said. "I was upset when I had to leave her that last summer."

"I bet she'll remember you. Offer her a sugar cube, and you'll see."

"Silver Queen's still at the farm?"

"Sure. Shetlands can live thirty years. Your great-aunt never said anything about selling her, and I kept feeding her. Penny's nieces and nephews used to ride her when they came to visit, but they're all grown now."

"Is the gazebo still there?" Adrianna pictured her favorite play spot in her mind.

"Of course, I wouldn't let anything that lovely go to rack and ruin." For a moment, Otis's attention was diverted as he negotiated their way onto the highway that would take them to Captain's Point.

Adrianna turned to the window and watched fields of Silver Queen corn as they rushed by. Gradually, her eyelids grew heavy again as she remembered the first time she had ridden her pony. Soon her memories merged with her dreams, as she and Silver Queen once again trotted around the long field and a tall, slim, dark-haired boy cleaned her cut knee and then reached out his hand.

CHAPTER V

"Almost there now." Otis's soft spoken words woke Adrianna as he steered the car between the tall gateposts that marked Montgomery property. In the gathering dusk, Montgomery House revealed its grey granite façade and octagonal tower, dark against the pastel colors of the sunset.

Otis had barely brought the aged Lincoln to a halt when the massive front door was opened to reveal Penny Plunk's plump figure.

"We have arriven." Otis stated the obvious without a care for his tenses and disembarked.

Adrianna followed suit, only to find herself embraced in her second hug of the day.

"You made it!" Penny held her at arm's length. "Haven't you turned into a beauty? You're the spitting image of your mama, although you've got the Montgomery mouth. Let's get you settled in." The older woman led the way.

Once inside, Adrianna surveyed the foyer, surprised that it seemed almost as large as she had remembered it. To her right, an archway opened into the front parlor that filled the bottom floor of the tower. Straight ahead she glimpsed the formal dining room. A hallway passed along the right of this room, leading to the kitchen beyond.

To her immediate left the second parlor led to the library - her favorite childhood haunt. Behind these two rooms sprawled, she remembered, the Captain's study as well as the morning room that overlooked the back gardens and, in the distance, the sea.

A broad stairway rose to the second floor, where an open walkway separated her great-aunt's tower suite on the right from the other bedrooms on the left, and it was to this that Penny headed.

Adrianna followed, glimpsing herself in the large gilt-framed mirror that hung between the second parlor's door and the bottom of the stairs. Her dark waves coursed wildly around her head, not surprising since she had fallen asleep in the car, and her dark eyes seemed tired.

Reaching the landing, Penny steered her to the right.

"But that's Great-aunt Martha's room," Adrianna objected.

"Martha stipulated that you were to make that suite of rooms yours while staying at Montgomery House, according to Mr. Sheffield," Penny explained. "I've given it a thorough cleaning, and the mattress has been exchanged with a new one. Besides, you could hardly stay in the old nursery now, could you?"

Remembering the youth bed she had slept in during her childhood visits, Adrianna had to agree. Still, if Otis and Penny had gone to all of this trouble to obey her great-aunt's orders, then she supposed it would be churlish to not go along with them.

Obediently following the housekeeper - Otis and her luggage bringing up the rear - Adrianna straightened her shoulders, wondering if a vestige of her great-aunt's powerful personality would still remain in the room. Passing through the heavily carved arch that led into the suite, she shivered in the small hallway from which a narrower stairway led to the upstairs sitting room with its wonderful views of the ocean.

Penny flipped a switch, and the large bedroom was illuminated against the darkening panes of three bay windows.

Straight ahead stood the massive half-tester bed, its carved mahogany and rosewood frame showing dark against the cream walls. More open than its heavily curtained predecessor, it appeared approachable, comfortable and inviting - its rose damask duvet and lace-enclosed pillows softening the prospect of slumber.

An Aubusson carpet in soft pastels covered the floor, providing a welcome contrast to the dark furnishings. Crystal and gold sconces adorned the walls, a testament to a bygone era of stunning opulence. Two Queen Anne chairs upholstered in cranberry-colored velvet provided seating on either side of the hearth, and Adrianna spotted her great-aunt's knitting basket positioned for another project.

A portrait of Jebediah Montgomery as a young man hung over the mantel, and she remembered how as a child she had felt his eyes following her as if watching for her to misbehave. Now, though, she noted a hint of laughter and a warm welcome.

"We'll leave you to freshen up," Penny suggested. "I thought we'd have supper informally in the morning room, this being your first night back."

"I've left your luggage in the dressing room." Otis rejoined them through a door to their left. "I'm sure you remember that you access the bathroom through it. Penny took care of soaps, towels and the what-nots you ladies need."

"Supper in the morning room sounds perfect," Adrianna agreed, suddenly realizing she was quite hungry. "I won't be but a few minutes."

"Welcome home, love." Penny gave her another quick hug and then followed her husband from the room, closing the door behind them.

Left alone, Adrianna strode to the nearer bay window, through which she had a clear view of the back gardens below, a broad expanse of mowed grass leading to the cliff's edge and, finally, the sea – now shimmering pink, silver and gold in the last remaining rays of the sun. Setting her purse and computer on the window seat, she recognized the lights of water craft in the distance as they made their way to Baltimore or New York.

Home…

Penny had referred to this as her home, but Montgomery House had never been that. Suddenly, Adrianna recognized that her condo in Seattle had never been a true home either, feeling more like a custom designed hotel room as had all the other residences of her lifetime.

As the world outside darkened, she watched her reflected face in the panes of the window tighten as she realized two things – she felt lonely without Brad and Chase Sheffield now seemed to control even the smallest details of her life.

CHAPTER VI

The next morning found Adrianna ensconced in a leather visitor's chair across his desk from Mr. Chase Sheffield, Attorney at Law, just as that hallowed being had requested, at precisely ten o'clock. The mahogany wainscoting, finely crafted seascapes and deep plush carpet that filled the over-sized room denoted both power and money. To say that she would have preferred not to have been there would have been one of the world's greatest understatements.

Anyone who had not known them both would have speculated that they were brother and sister, his being the older of the two by five or six years. Both sported dark wavy hair, fine complexions and sat ramrod straight in their chairs, but here the likeness ended - his nose being slightly more patrician than hers and her eyes being darkest brown to his deep blue ones. For a moment, they eyed one another before he broke the silence.

"I appreciate your coming so quickly, Ms. Montgomery. Your great-aunt has left the disposition of her estate well-ordered as had all of her predecessors. On the other hand, she has also followed their tendency to deviate from the norm."

"Your letter didn't leave me much choice." Adrianna met his steady gaze. "While I didn't find it easy to travel cross-country on a whim to a place I had not visited for seven years, it seemed the expedient course. You need to understand, Mr. Sheffield..."

"Please, call me Chase," he interrupted her, "and it might be better if you would permit me to address you as Adrianna, since we will be working together for some time."

"If you think that best." Adrianna, preferring to pick her battles, acquiesced. "As I had started to say, though, I won't be staying long, so anything you can do to speed up the settlement process will be appreciated."

"I'm afraid you don't understand." The attorney sent her a cool smile. "Your great-aunt's instructions will require your presence here for some time."

"And if I'm unwilling to remain beyond say a period of two weeks, what then?"

"Perhaps it would be better if we went through the terms of the will from beginning to end, and then I'll answer any questions you have."

Unwilling to start off on the wrong foot with someone who controlled a great deal, Adrianna settled into her chair. "Let's get started then."

"First, there is a letter from your great-aunt that you must read," he stated.

As if on cue, a light knock on the office door preceded the entrance of a red-haired secretary, bearing a complete beverage service that she placed on a credenza.

"Coffee or tea?" the woman asked.

"Tea, please." Adrianna felt as if she had fallen down Alice's rabbit hole.

"Lemon or sugar?"

"Sugar – one lump."

"I'll have my usual, Bridgette." Chase Sheffield rose from his chair, took Adrianna's teacup and handed it to her before accepting his own. "I'll let you know if you're needed."

His secretary now gone, the attorney lifted a sealed envelope from his desk blotter and handed it to his new client, who noted her name written in her great-aunt's flowery script.

"Take your time." The lawyer took a sip of his tea.

Torn between anger at his presumptive nature and appreciation of his calm attitude, Adrianna picked up a sterling letter opener from the desk and slit the envelope, expecting to find another typed letter like the one she had received from Mr. Sheffield inside. Instead, the scent of her great-aunt's Lilies of the Valley toilette water assailed her, evoking memories of years past, as the missive had been written on Martha Montgomery's signature blue stationery. Quickly, she read:

Dear Adrianna –

*If you are in possession of this letter, then one of Life's truths
has occurred, and I am now dead. As my father and his father
before me have done, I am relying on the firm of Sheffield,
Sheffield, Chesterton and Sheffield to take care of my estate. I
am sure that you will find Augustus Chesterton to be most
helpful to you at this time.*

*As the last living member of the Montgomery family, it would
appear unseemly for me to leave Montgomery House and my
estate to anyone but you. Unfortunately, I am unsure that you
are up to the task, concerned as I am that you have taken more
after your flighty mother than your only slightly steadier father.
You remain unmarried, have accumulated no wealth of your own
and, even though you have taken steps to secure employment at a
high level, have failed to do so.*

*I will leave it to Mr. Chesterton to explain the provisions of
my will. I hope that at least some of the attributes I saw in you
as a child have followed you into womanhood. Don't disappoint
me. I'm counting on you to live up to the Montgomery legacy
that Jebediah envisioned for his family.*

Martha C. Montgomery

Still feeling jet-lagged and somewhat intimated by the
attorney's haughty reception of her, Adrianna wished both to
laugh and cry. Three days ago, she had felt in control of her life
as Brad's fiancée and the holder of a promising management
position. Now her life was being tossed to and fro by a series of
letters that were becoming more bizarre as first one and then
another appeared.

Carefully folding her great-aunt's note, she returned it to its
envelope before looking up and asking the first question she
wanted answered. "Why is Mr. Chesterton not here?"

CHAPTER VII

"Mr. Chesterton?" Chase Sheffield put down his pen, surprise reflected on his face, the first true emotion he had shown since Adrianna's arrival.

"This letter indicates that he will be handling her estate." She met his gaze.

"Ours is an old firm," the lawyer explained. "The first two Sheffields were my great-grandfather and my grandfather, my father having chosen medicine as his profession. Augustus Chesterton was your great-aunt's cousin and a cousin by marriage to my grandfather. Unfortunately, Augustus predeceased Martha by a few weeks, leaving me as the only remaining senior partner to oversee the handling of her estate per the terms of her will."

"And will you be able to give the matter the attention it deserves as short-handed as you must be?"

"The firm is in the process of bringing on a new senior partner, not that it pertains to the matter at hand," he assured her. "In the meantime, our associates will handle anything that would preclude me from doing my duty to your great-aunt's estate."

What a stick-in-the-mud! Adrianna pushed down a laugh. 'Doing his duty?' How stiff a person was he?

"So what exactly are the provisions of my great-aunt's will?" she asked.

"You may want to take notes," the attorney suggested and indicated a leather portfolio on the table beside her that when opened revealed a legal pad and a shiny gold pen.

Thinking she might as well humor him in an effort to get the meeting behind her, Adrianna held the pen poised over the pad.

"First and foremost, you must reside at Montgomery House for a period of one year beginning three weeks from today, allowing you time to return home to Seattle and make whatever arrangements are necessary for you to comply."

"Live here? For a year?" Adrianna couldn't believe what she was hearing. "Was my great-aunt suffering from some sort of dementia?"

Mr. Sheffield held up his hand. "Let me make this perfectly clear before we go any further. There is no question whatsoever of your great-aunt not having been of sound mind, and her doctor is willing to say so under oath."

For a moment, the room filled with a pregnant silence, but then Adrianna let out the breath she had been holding, made a note on the pad before her and looked up prepared to hear more.

"During the year of your residency, you will live in Montgomery House proper, sit in the Montgomery pew during the main service three Sundays out of every four unless I excuse you from doing so, and act as General Manager of the Montgomery holdings here at Captain's Point."

"Won't Otis object to that?"

"No, Otis will remain Property Manager and continue his duties as before. As General Manager, you will fill your great-aunt's role as his employer within reason and with my approval."

"In other words, I can't start a commune." Adrianna rolled her eyes.

"Exactly." A hint of a smile flitted across the lawyer's face, but quickly disappeared. "At least, not during the first year. You will be paid a salary reflective of the position, and you will be able to access estate funds as needed for reasonable property expenses and development as well as other expenses – all to be approved by myself."

"And at the end of one year?"

"If you have met Miss Martha's expectations, the deed for Montgomery House and her various properties will be signed over to you. You will also inherit what is left of her estate after we finish paying out two sizeable charitable bequests and the sum of $100,000 to Otis and Penny Plunk that is contingent on their remaining throughout your one year."

"And that estate will amount to?"

"Somewhere in the range of twelve million dollars, not including the properties," the lawyer stated. "Your great-aunt was an astute businesswoman."

Adrianna hoped she had not revealed her surprise at the size of the estate. "And if I am unable to meet her expectations?"

"If you have lived in the house, attended the services and attempted in good faith to fulfill your role as General Manager as I see fit, then you will receive $250,000 on top of the salary that will have already been paid to you. All of the estate's assets, including Montgomery House and the farm will be liquidated, and the proceeds will be divided equally between the two charities."

"What exactly are my great-aunt's expectations?" Adrianna looked up from the notes she had written and met the attorney's gaze.

"They will be revealed to you by me when you achieve them."

"Now that is nuts!" Adrianna clicked the pen closed. "How can I achieve these so-called expectations if I don't even know what they are?"

"It was your great-aunt's hope that you would grow into them – her words, not mine. In the meantime, I am to give you a clue." The lawyer handed her yet another envelope. "If you will let Bridgette know your plans for flying home and back, she will arrange for your tickets. In the meantime, if you have no further questions…?"

"None at all," Adrianna stated, her eyes flashing as she gathered her belongings and stood. "You have just turned my entire life upside down. Why in the world would I have any questions?" And with that, she took her leave of Mr. Chase Sheffield, Attorney at Law.

A few moments later, a striking, blonde-haired woman wearing a well-cut business suit entered the room. "So how did it go?" she asked.

"About as I expected." Chase sent her a grin. "Martha Montgomery was a shrewd woman, and I'll enjoy fulfilling whatever wishes she indicates to me from beyond the grave. In the meantime, it will be interesting to see how much of her has been inherited by her great-niece."

"Well, Adrianna passed round one as far as I'm concerned, since she didn't storm out of here." She handed him a thick legal document before dropping into the chair that his new client had so recently vacated. "All signed, sealed and delivered."

He flipped through the pages, here and there placing his own initials and signature as required. Finished, he stood and rounded his desk, before he paused and indicated his office door. "Now that all of that has been settled, Miss Susan, may I escort you to lunch at Montgomery's in celebration of our new partnership?"

"Yes, you may, Mr. Sheffield." She rose and joined him, slipping her hand through the crook in his offered arm as she laughed. "Sheffield, Sheffield, Chesterton, Sheffield and Chesterton. I'm afraid our fine old firm is beginning to sound a tad bit repetitive."

CHAPTER VIII

Once home, Adrianna headed straight for the inviting kitchen as had been her childhood habit. Here Penny received an almost imperceptible nod from her husband that indicated all was not well.

"Why don't you eat your lunch in the breakfast room and enjoy this bright spring day through the windows. The garden is really coming into its own," the housekeeper suggested. "I'll have your place set in a jif."

"Sure," Adrianna agreed not wishing to appear churlish, despite having no desire whatsoever to eat.

Penny's light chatter as she served the meal lightened her mood considerably, and Adrianna surprised herself by consuming an excellent luncheon of Cobb salad, fresh fruit and a slice of the housekeeper's homemade bread. Neither of the Plunks quizzed her about her meeting with the attorney, for which she was grateful as she wasn't sure of their feelings towards their own part of the affair. Excusing herself, she made her way to the master suite that she still couldn't think of as her own.

Here she changed into a pair of faded jeans, an old T-shirt and trainers, believing she would do her best thinking if she were comfortable. Then she positioned herself where she could work with a view - ensconced on the window seat, the portfolio given to her by Chase Sheffield resting in her lap, the gold pen in danger of falling from her fingers to the floor as lightly as she held it.

Movement below drew her attention to the lap pool that had been added by an earlier Montgomery. Quickly she identified the culprits as two squirrels who were chasing one another up, over and around the marble benches placed alongside it.

Her eyes wandered to the rose garden exhibiting its full glory directly beneath her window before traveling across the lawn to the sea. Somewhere beyond the horizon, she thought, Brad was laughing with his nurse at this very moment, their position overlooking much bluer water than that seen from her window. Well, good riddance to bad rubbish as the old saying went.

Her focus remained where it was, though, as she reviewed her meeting with the lawyer that morning. Granted, the terms of her great-aunt's will were surprising, but given the fact she was unemployed, meeting the requirements was doable. So much of her life controlled by someone as stiff and remote as Chase Sheffield might not be pleasant, but it would, after all, only last for one year. Either way, at that point, she would come out a winner, and she had handled any number of men just as pedantic as he was in the course of her work.

Tightening her grip on the pen, she began making a list of things that would have to be done in Seattle, surprised by its short length since she wouldn't be moving. Her clothes would need to be packed and shipped, arrangements would have to be made with the concierge for her plants to be watered, and the cleaning service would need to be limited to fewer visits. Arranging for her mail to be forwarded would take care of the rest. How empty, she realized, her former life must have been!

Flipping the page, she wrote Chase Sheffield's name along the top and then added 'one-way ticket' beneath it. With a smile, she wondered what his reaction would be when he discovered that it was her intention to drive her car back from Seattle, not that it mattered. It would do him good to realize that while she was somewhat constrained under the terms of her great-aunt's will, she was by no means hindered from following her own mind.

Therein, though, lay the problem. Losing her job, Brad's letter, the will – it had all happened too fast. Did she even want Montgomery House and all that it entailed? While her childhood memories of the property were wonderful, they had certainly been eclipsed in recent years by her great-aunt's cold-hearted refusal to assist her with her education after her parents' death.

What would her life be like if she decided to remain at Captain's Point as a permanent resident? She couldn't just live here in isolation being waited on by the Plunks hand and foot. She had worked too hard to attain her degrees only to vegetate in an old mausoleum. On the other hand, the house and its surrounding property were too expensive to maintain merely as a weekend residence if she were to secure a position in D.C.

Thrusting the portfolio aside, she rose and picked up a photo of her parents resting in a silver frame that she had placed on the bedside table before going to bed the previous evening. "What should I do?" she asked their smiling faces, before she returned the frame to the table and picked up the envelope she had placed there on returning from the attorney's office.

"So what is your perspective on all of this?" she asked Jebediah's portrait. "What do you think of me now that I'm here? I promise you neither Brad nor Mr. High-and-Mighty Chase Sheffield are going to get the better of me, even when it comes to meeting the latter's expectations."

For a moment, she thought his eyes had taken on an even brighter twinkle as they looked down, but then she recognized it as reflection from the sun streaming through the large windows. Dropping into one of the Queen Anne chairs, she slit open the envelope in her hand with a knitting needle from her great-aunt's work basket. Once again the scent of Lilies of the Valley toilette water wafted towards her, as she removed a sheet of folded paper from which a photograph fell into her lap.

Turning it over, she discovered herself front and center, playing in a large sandbox that Otis had built for her in a corner of the walled kitchen garden so many years before. On a folding chair to her right, her great-aunt sat reading a children's classic aloud, while she attempted to dig her way to China with a plastic shovel that land having figured in her bedtime story the previous evening. What had hardened her great-aunt's heart so much as the intervening years had passed by?

Placing the photo on a leather-topped wine table, she lifted the sheet of paper and unfolded it to be greeted by a single sentence in her great-aunt's flowery hand.

The answer is in the garden, it read.

CHAPTER IX

Two weeks later found Adrianna returned to Montgomery House from Seattle and the Plunks sitting across from one another at the kitchen table, relieved that their charge had arrived safely the night before.

"Have you glimpsed her this morning?" Otis raised a mug of black coffee to his lips.

"Haven't heard a peep out of her." His wife looked up from buttering her toast. "I imagine she'll sleep in. That was a long drive."

"Made even longer by the route she took, given the postcards she sent us."

"How did she seem to you last night?" Penny exchanged her knife for the jelly spoon.

"Tired, but then it was ten o'clock when she got here." Otis began systematically cutting a link of kielbasa into bite-sized pieces. "But there was something more..." He met his wife's worried gaze. "Determination."

"Exactly. When she first arrived, there was a sadness about her that made me wish she were still a little girl. I wanted to take her upon my knee, wipe away her tears and tell her everything would be okay. For a while, I wondered if she was grieving for Martha, but somehow I don't think so. After all, they hadn't seen one another since her parents' funeral, and that was seven years ago. Still, it was there, as if she was only partially with us, but last night it was gone."

"Martha was wrong treating Adrianna that way." Her husband kept his eyes on his plate.

"Why Otis Plunk, I believe that's the first negative comment I've heard you utter in the thirty-odd years that you've worked here." Penny looked up, surprised. "But I must say I agree. I never did understand Martha's being so spiteful. It wasn't like her."

"No, but we all have our moments."

"What did Chase have to say when you spoke with him yesterday?" His wife rose and took her plate to the sink.

"Not much. He wanted to know if our girl had asked me for any funds, and I told him that as far as I knew she hadn't discussed money with either of us. I got the impression that he had expected her to have her hand out to him immediately."

"She's never mentioned money to me." Penny opened the dishwasher.

"Anyway, a new day has dawned, and the young woman our little girl has become has our future sitting smack dab in the palm of her hand." Finished with his breakfast, her husband pushed his plate away. "I'd be surprised if Adrianna doesn't sleep until noon. I'll stay somewhere on the property, and if you need me, call my cell." He pulled his wife, who had returned to the table for his empty plate and mug, down towards him and planted a kiss on her lips.

"Behave yourself!" She sent him a smile. "But I'll bet you another one of those that our new Miss Montgomery will be down here and raring to go much earlier than you think."

Unbeknownst to either of them, the object of their conversation was throwing back the covers on the half-tester bed at that very moment, preparing to win Penny's bet for her. Pulling back the chintz drapes from the window seat, Adrianna exposed the morning sun and expertly executed a series of Tai Chi moves.

Satisfied that it was going to be a lovely May morning, she headed for the dressing room where the night before she had discovered the boxes of clothes and belongings she had shipped eastward neatly stored. Pulling a pair of jeans and a soft cotton top from her suitcase, she turned and then paused, her gaze having taken in the cream-colored bank of drawers and small doors with their old-fashioned glass knobs that ran along one wall.

Curious, she reached out her hand to a slightly larger door that was placed waist high in the center of the wall, remembering that this had held special books and rainy day toys during her childhood visits – items that had kept her busy and quiet while her great-aunt had knitted. When opened the storage nook revealed an array of stuffed animals and storybooks, coloring books and paper dolls stored in an old shoe box. Surprised to find them still there, Adrianna wondered why a woman who had treated her so coldly during the past seven years would have kept them.

Once dressed, she ran a brush through her dark waves and then gathered them into a ponytail and secured it. Ready for her day, she reentered the bedroom, where she at once noticed Jebediah's twinkling eyes smiling down at her.

"Glad to have me back?" she asked the portrait, striking a pose. "Well, you needn't have worried. One way or the other, I've said my goodbyes to Seattle."

Crossing to the half-tester, she made up the bed with a few quick motions of her hands. Whether it was memories from her childhood, the toys discovered in the wall cabinet or merely the lovely furnishings and décor, she couldn't have said, but the room felt like home, which boded well for the time she would be spending in it during the coming year.

"Oh…," she paused and addressed the young Jebediah's portrait again, "You might be interested in knowing that I've had a good think and I've made a few plans. Mr. Chase Sheffield, Attorney at Law, will wonder what he's gotten himself into by the time I get done with him, and the first thing I'm determined to show him is that we Montgomerys don't waste any time."

And with that said, she left the large, pleasant room behind her and headed to the kitchen where she surprised Penny.

"After breakfast, I plan to take a thorough tour of the gardens," Adrianna announced, giving the older woman a quick hug. "Then I'd like to meet with Otis and you. It's time that we three put our heads together and make some decisions."

CHAPTER X

Adrianna consumed a croissant accompanied by a wedge of cantaloupe, then took time as she enjoyed her coffee to glance through a morning newspaper she had discovered neatly folded beside her place. Soon tiring of wars and bloodshed, she moved forward through the pages, glancing briefly at an article about the rise of small businesses.

Reaching for the next section, she enjoyed a piece on the artists' colony that was rapidly developing in the Captain's Point area before returning the paper to its original state. It was time to get on with her day, she thought as she left a thick spiral notebook and pen that she had brought downstairs with her ready for her upcoming meeting.

Glancing at the retro, black and white cat clock hanging on the wall over the kitchen table, its tail swinging back and forth in time with the seconds, she completed a quick calculation and then turned to Penny who was rolling out pie dough on the counter. "I won't be too long," she said. "Would it work for the three of us to meet in the breakfast room around ten?"

"Sure." The older woman paused in her work. "Otis usually stops in for a second cup of coffee about then anyway."

An uncomfortable silence hung in the air as Adrianna struggled for words that would convey her feelings given their new relationship. "I appreciate all that you two are doing for me." She heard the words flow from her mouth in a rush, remembering her father's simple motto that truth always served one best. "My memories of my time spent here when I was younger have always been special to me."

"And ours of you." Penny sent her a bright smile. "We're both looking forward to hearing about your plans as, I'm sure, is Chase Sheffield."

"Well, Mr. Sheffield will have to wait a bit longer." Adrianna laughed as she headed towards the mudroom, where she grabbed a large straw hat from a hook before swinging open the back door.

Once outside, she paused for a moment, enjoying the sun on her face and the scent of salt air carried by the breeze from the ocean. Then she plopped the hat on her head and looked around her at the large kitchen garden. Backing onto the house, it was contained by three additional granite walls in an effort to protect the produce contained within from unwanted animals.

Directly to her right, Adrianna recognized the herbs that made Penny's meals sing – the smaller plants arranged within paving stone paths nearest to the kitchen door, the large rosemary bush at the far back, a fair-sized potting shed taking up most of the corner. Next came the lettuces and behind them the tomato plants, already enclosed in their cages. Along the wall to her left, small fruit trees were espaliered, and two cherry trees filled each of the far corners.

Neat and well organized, its beds either raised or surrounded by paving stone paths, the garden had always been a pleasant place in which to sit, somewhat protected as it was from the ocean breezes. Still, Adrianna was surprised to see that her sandbox remained in the near left corner surrounded by a small patio area. A stone bench large enough to accommodate four had replaced the chair her great-aunt had formerly used, but otherwise the area was unchanged from the way it appeared in the photo she had been given along with the clue.

Changing her initial plan, she headed to the sandbox and lifted its lid, greeted by nothing but a small plastic bucket and shovel readied for play. Disappointed, she replaced the lid and returned to the main path that led from the kitchen door to one in the far wall of the garden.

Reaching the second door, she paused and took a last look around, confirming her original impression. Unless it was buried in the ground, tied to a plant, hidden in a crevice in one of the granite walls, or tucked away in the potting shed, there was nowhere anything could be hidden in the kitchen garden. At least now, she knew how to organize her search.

This decided, she proceeded through the door into the formal gardens, following the path along a short walkway that skirted the kitchen garden wall and into a tunnel that was covered in flowering vines. Here she almost tripped over a cat, who sat in the dappled shade grooming a black and white coat that mimicked the example on the kitchen clock inside.

"Meow!" It let out an exclamation when she failed to pass around it, as if to make clear that she was the interloper.

"Excuse me," she laughed as it resumed its grooming. "I'm sorry to have bothered you."

At the sound of her voice, the cat lowered his hind leg and gave her his full attention, examining her from her feet to her face.

"May I ask if you're part of my supposed inheritance as well, or are you just passing through?" She met the animal's gaze.

As if to answer, the cat rose and approached, rubbing the side of his face against her ankle.

"I see you've made friends with Nip." A young man, whose muscular shape now blocked the other entrance to the walkway, took a step forward and held out his hand. "Jeff Stuart. I help Otis out around here as my class schedule at the local college permits. You must be the new Miss Montgomery I've heard about."

"Guilty as charged." Adrianna took his offered hand, feeling the deep calluses in his palms as they shook. "But if you call me Miss Montgomery, I'll have you banned from the property. My name's Adrianna."

"I can live with that." He laughed as he turned and walked with her into the sunlight.

"Tell me, Jeff, if you were going to hide something in one of the gardens, where would you put it?" Adrianna asked.

"That's a no-brainer. I'd dig a hole and bury it somewhere against one of the granite walls where it wouldn't be disturbed." He shaded his eyes against the sun. "Why do you ask?" His eyes narrowed further.

"Just wondering." She shrugged, not wishing to reveal her mission to someone she had just met, although recognizing she might have to call on him for assistance in the future. "So what's your major?"

"Long term I want to go into journalism. At this point, I'm concentrating on the general curriculum."

"Well, I wish you the best," Adrianna said, realizing the sun was higher now than when she had left the house. "I'm sure we'll see a lot of each other, but right now I'm late for a meeting."

And with that, she turned on her heel and headed back through the kitchen garden accompanied by Nip. How many more people were now her employees? Obviously, Otis and she would have to spend some serious time together, a single thought having haunted her drive back to Captain's Point.

Her great-aunt hadn't just left her an opportunity. She had also left her with a great deal of responsibility, much more than she had previously encountered. The question now was did she have enough knowledge and experience to rise to the occasion in the time allotted?

CHAPTER XI

Chase Sheffield turned the document he had been reading over and viewed his new work partner where she sat on the other side of his desk. The sun streaming in the office window highlighted her blonde hair as it fell around her shoulders, producing a pleasant sight.

"Do you need me?" Feeling his gaze, Susan glanced up.

"Not at this moment, but I'm glad that you're here. You're going to make a difference to the firm."

"High praise indeed from the most senior partner." She laughed. "I thought for a moment that you were serious."

"I've never been more serious in my life." He relaxed against the back of his chair. "Augustus was a great lawyer, and I enjoyed working with him. Still, in recent years, he hasn't been that motivated. You've already brought new clients into the fold, you're skilled and you improve the look of the place."

"Okay, you had me going until that last bit. What a sexist you are!" A twinkle in her eyes took the sting from her words.

"You did well to come here," he assured her. "Captain's Point has benefited as more D.C. and Baltimore residents have searched for weekend getaways, and I intend to make the most of the opportunities. The question is do we rely on the Montgomery property as our starting point, or do we cast our nets a bit further afield."

"Now that you've spoken with Adrianna, what are your feelings?" Susan asked.

"Honestly, I don't know. Martha Montgomery didn't think much of her abilities and backbone, but then she hadn't spent time with her great-niece for years."

"And I don't care how shrewd a businesswoman she was, Martha may not have been that great a judge of Adrianna's character," his partner interjected. "Occasional reports from private investigators don't give one all that much information as to someone's untapped potential."

"I agree."

"So what are our new client's plans?" Susan set the papers she had been reading on the table beside her and gave him her attention.

"As far as I know, she doesn't have any." He shrugged. "She flew to Seattle, which I had expected, but then she took her time and drove back, taking a fairly circuitous route according to Otis. Frankly, I'm not all that impressed. Martha would've hit the ground running."

"Aren't you being unfair?" his partner asked. "Adrianna has had her life flipped upside down. Perhaps she needed some time to sort out her thoughts."

"Perhaps…" Chase's face remained a blank canvas.

"How much have you advanced her so far?"

"Not a dime beyond her plane tickets and her original travel expenses, which were negligible."

"Then the estate hasn't been harmed, and you've done your duty," Susan pointed out. "On the other hand, you haven't been able to bill it much for your services."

"Spoken like a true partner." Chase sent her a slow languid smile.

"Is that worrying you?"

"Not billing the most possible for the firm from my representation of a client always worries me."

"That's not exactly what I asked you, but we'll leave it at that." She retrieved her papers from the table and flipped them to the page she had been studying. "Given what you've just told me, my answer to your original question would be that we continue to look upon the Montgomery properties as a reasonable starting point for development at the end of one year. At the same time, since Adrianna's abilities remain such an unknown, we investigate other possibilities in the area. I agree with you that neither of us should let opportunities pass us by."

"If that's what you want." Chase picked up his pen and bent to his work, his face once again a blank slate.

Susan pretended to continue her reading, but her thoughts were somewhere else. In many ways, she saw herself and

Adrianna as being in the same boat, each having had their lives flipped upside down – hers by an embarrassing divorce, leaving her with a young son, and their client's by her great-aunt's strange will. What would she be doing if she were in Adrianna's shoes? Would she have hit the ground running?

Perhaps not. Returning to Captain's Point to seek solace and support from those people and places that she had loved as a child wasn't exactly a sign of great inner strength on her part. Still, Daniel would be better off being cared for by her mother after preschool, and Chase would certainly be there for her.

For a moment, she studied her partner from under her lids and wondered how well she really knew him. They had played together as children and dated on and off through their teens, but it had been years since they had really shared confidences, keeping connected only through her holiday visits. She had been surprised when he had approached her about joining his firm, although in the short time she had been here she had made a difference he obviously appreciated. Was it possible that he had merely pitied her?

She straightened her shoulders. Whatever his reasons, she owed him her best, and she was grateful for the opportunity to start over. She would leave him to manage the Montgomery estate, and in the meantime, she would scope out the area. Then, with her mind settled, she firmly pushed thoughts of Chase Sheffield aside and turned back to her work.

CHAPTER XII

Back at the house, Adrianna discovered an empty kitchen and made quick work of investigating something that had bothered her since her arrival at Montgomery House. Her suspicion confirmed, she returned to the breakfast room from which the aroma of brewed coffee now emanated.

"There you are!" Otis placed a plate of oatmeal raisin cookies in the middle of the table on which awaited three cheerful mugs, then took a seat.

"Did you have a nice walk?" Penny asked the younger woman as she joined them, a large French press coffee pot in her hand.

"I did, thank you." Adrianna reached for a cookie. "I met Jeff Stuart and a rather haughty hanger-on named Nip while I was out there."

"I imagine the cat made it clear to you that he owns the place." Otis chuckled, but then his expression sobered. "Perhaps that was a poor choice of words."

"No, it was very appropriate." Adrianna added some milk to her coffee. "Right now, he's the only one who can honestly claim a clear title."

"Otis and I want to say right off the bat that we don't understand why Martha worded her will like she did," Penny said. "It just isn't fair. Not what she did for us, you understand, but Montgomery House should have been left to you outright. After all, you're the last surviving member of the family."

"Yes, but I'm not deserving." Adrianna heard bitterness running beneath her words as an uncomfortable silence fell over the room. "But enough of that." She forced a smile. "I'm assuming that you're aware of the terms as they pertain to me."

"We are." Otis sat back in his chair.

Adrianna flipped open her notebook and picked up her pen. "So what are your thoughts, specifically pertaining to anything that we need to address right away?" She looked up expectantly.

"The farm's in pretty good shape." Otis's voice took on a business-like tone. "The house is rented to a nice young couple, Ron and Judy Ladner. They're both from around here originally, so they'll probably stay a while."

"Sounds like a good arrangement." Adrianna made a note. "What about equipment? Is most of it new, or are you to the point of having to replace it?"

"We'll probably need a new tractor in a couple of years, but right now, everything's running fine." Otis reached for his mug. "Martha always kept the farm's budget separated from the other properties, and it's self-sufficient."

"I confirmed just now that Montgomery House has no TV." Adrianna's gaze traveled from one of them to the other.

"Your great-aunt wouldn't have one in the house," Penny explained.

"Well, I'm not an old woman, and I have no intention of cutting myself off from the real world. Is there any reason why we can't have it here at the house?"

"None whatsoever," Otis assured her.

"Then, after lunch, please take me into town so we can select the TVs." Adrianna made another quick note. "Three of them will get us started – one for me in the tower sitting room, one for the Captain's study where I intend to set up my office and a small one for the kitchen. If you'll make the arrangements for the installation I'd appreciate it, and I'm also going to need internet and Wi-Fi access going forward."

"Your great-aunt's probably turning over in her grave," Penny stated, "but I think it's about time the new millennium came to Montgomery House. I can't say that I won't enjoy catching a show while I work or seeing the weather radar from time to time."

"Especially when a big storm is coming up the coast," Otis agreed.

"So how do we pay for it?" Adrianna was embarrassed to have to ask. "Are there operating funds we can draw on?"

"Enough to cover a couple of TVs." Otis sent her a grin.

"Excellent." Adrianna met his gaze. "I feel like we're making progress. What about the house, the dependency and the other outbuildings? How would you describe those?"

For a moment, an awkward silence fell over the room as the Plunks exchanged meaningful glances.

"The news isn't as good there," Otis said. "Your great-aunt was ill for the past three years, not to mention that she was in her mid-eighties. I've kept up with the smaller repair jobs, but while this is a fine old house, it is in need of some major upgrades."

"For 'fine' and 'old' substitute 'expensive' and 'decrepit,'" Adrianna suggested.

"Exactly," Penny agreed. "There've been times when we've joked that Martha should've bought a duct tape factory, so that Otis would have had an unlimited supply to wrap around everything."

"The slate roofs and copper gutters all need major attention, if not out and out replacement." Otis counted them off on his fingers. "The boiler here at the house needs to be replaced, both to save money on repairs and from the standpoint of energy efficiency."

"And you don't even want to know about the wiring," Penny carried forward the list, "and the kitchen could stand to have new appliances for the same reasons."

"You're talking about a lot of money," Adrianna pointed out, a worried look in her eyes. "How much would it actually cost to get everything back to ship shape?"

"Honestly, I don't know." Otis shrugged. "Every time I've tried to put together an overall plan, I've given up. It's a relief to have a fresh viewpoint on board."

"Obviously, we've got to get started – the sooner the better," Adrianna stated. "The overall key is to get the main house and the surrounding property as self-sustaining as the farm, and I have some ideas. When we get back from town, we'll sit down and make a comprehensive list of what's needed and compare it with the funds we currently have on hand in the operating account. I'll also need the name of my great-aunt's broker."

"That would be Larry Chesterton," Penny said. "I can give you his number, but you and Otis would be welcomed if you dropped in to see him when you're in town this afternoon. If you like, I can set up an appointment."

"Sounds like a plan." Adrianna made another entry in her notebook. "That will let me really assess the situation, before I have to explain everything to Chase Sheffield – something I'm not looking forward to doing."

CHAPTER XIII

After lunch, Adrianna chauffeured Otis into the town of Captain's Point, so that she could begin learning her way around.

"Let's get the TVs out of the way first," she suggested. "I want my mind clear for our meeting with Larry Chesterton."

"You'll want to turn right at the end of the drive. Our best bet will be the discount store out on the highway," Otis explained. "I think you'll enjoy working with Larry. He's very laid back, but don't let that fool you. He's also sharp as a tack."

"I'm glad he's on our side then." Adrianna negotiated her turn, surprised at the traffic that was flowing back and forth on the two-lane highway.

An hour later, they were back in the car and headed for the town proper, their shopping having taken longer than either of them had anticipated by the time they had made their selections, arranged for delivery and paid for the TVs.

Here and there, Adrianna recognized a landmark recalled from her earlier visits. A farmhouse she remembered was now surrounded by a cookie-cutter subdivision. A Mom and Pop grocery shared their parking lot with an apartment complex.

"Growth has definitely come to Captain's Point," she commented.

"And not all of it to the benefit of the community."

"You don't think so?" She was surprised by the vehemence running beneath her property manager's words.

"Don't get me wrong. Change is inevitable, but a little zoning here and there wouldn't hurt as far as I'm concerned." Otis shifted in his seat in order to face her. "You might want to go to some of the town meetings."

"Do you?"

"Penny and I usually attend."

"Then let me know the next time one is scheduled, and I'll join you," Adrianna agreed.

"Park in the free lot by the Post Office," Otis suggested. "It's one block along on this side."

Adrianna found a spot for her Elantra with an ease that surprised her after Seattle. They both disembarked, and the property manager led the way to the local hardware store where he needed to pick up an order.

Preferring to enjoy the sunshine and light breeze as opposed to doing more shopping, Adrianna took a seat on a rustic bench outside the store, content to watch those passing by.

"Why look who's here!" A woman's voice exclaimed as a shadow fell across her. "This is the gal I was telling you about."

"Edwina!" Adrianna greeted the older woman with a smile. "And this must be Ginny."

"Ginny Foster," the obviously pregnant young woman introduced herself.

"Adrianna Montgomery. I hope you two have been having a nice visit."

"We're having a wonderful time, but Ginny will be glad when the baby arrives," Edwina filled her in.

"Just one more week, if the doctor's right, and I do wish she would come early," the mother-to-be stated. "The nursery is ready, neither Jason nor Edwina will allow me to lift a finger, and I'm about to go stark-raving mad."

"Why don't you both come for tea at Montgomery House tomorrow afternoon?" Adrianna suggested, suddenly desiring the company of someone more her own age. "I'd love to show you the house, and Penny's scones are delicious."

"That would be lovely." Edwina sent her a grateful look. "Would three o'clock be okay?"

"Perfect." Adrianna reached for her notebook so she could draw them a map, and then realized she wasn't sure how to give them directions. "Oh, good, here's Otis." She was pleased to see her property manager coming through the hardware store's entrance. "He can show you the way." She passed him her notebook and a pen.

"Ginny and Edwina will be joining me for tea tomorrow afternoon," she explained. "Edwina and I sat together after she boarded my flight to Captain's Point in Chicago."

"It's about time you had friends come to visit," Otis stated. "Now where do you ladies live?"

Ginny gave her address, and Otis drew them a map.

Then the property manager checked his watch. "We had better be moving along, unless we want to be late for our appointment."

"See you tomorrow then." Adrianna gave Edwina a quick hug before hurrying to catch up with Otis, who was sauntering along acknowledging first this person and then that one. How long would it be, she wondered, before she would recognize people that she passed?

A good looking couple exited a shop up ahead, and she noted how happy they seemed. With a start, she realized that the dark-haired man, who strolled along beside the laughing young woman, was none other than Chase Sheffield. As he placed his hand on the small of his companion's back and guided her through the doorway of a cozy-looking restaurant, Adrianna felt a pang of jealousy.

Don't be silly, she chided herself. It's just that you're lonely and still missing Brad Williams, Jerk Extraordinaire. After all, it had only been a matter of weeks since all of her dreams had been thrown in the trash. No wonder she had found it hard to watch someone else's happiness.

"Here we are." Otis's words broke through her thoughts, and she saw he was holding open the brokerage firm's door.

Passing from the sunlight into the cool, business-like interior, Adrianna felt her hand taken in a strong grip and, surprised, gazed into the smiling, tanned face of a blond, blue-eyed man who she took to be her ex-fiancé before her eyes adjusted.

"Larry Chesterton," the grinning Adonis introduced himself. "Boy, am I glad to see you!"

CHAPTER XIV

At their moment of meeting, Adrianna had almost expected the words 'Where have you been all my life, Gorgeous?' to issue from her new broker's mouth, but after a few minutes in his office, she had changed her mind about him. Once they had been seated at a small meeting table, he had commenced to deal out bottled waters and printed portfolios all around.

"Let's get right down to business," Larry had started the conversational ball rolling, addressing his newly met client. "Penny explained that Otis and she had apprised you of the situation only this morning, so I imagine you have a few questions. Why don't you look over the documents I've set before you?"

He had then excused himself for a few minutes, leaving Adrianna to comfortably follow his advice.

"It's too bad that so many of the investments came due at the same time," she pointed out to her property manager when she had finished her review.

"Larry will agree with you on that, and your great-aunt was too sick to bother with what did come due during the past year," Otis replied.

"Ready for me yet?" Their broker reentered the room.

"Ready as we'll ever be," Otis said, as Adrianna turned to a fresh page in the notebook that was fast becoming her constant companion.

"A couple of things strike me." She met the broker's gaze head on. "One is that I would prefer to stagger the due dates going forward, and the second is that saving money can sometimes mean more in bad economic times than making money."

"Go on." Larry pulled a legal pad from beneath his own portfolio and prepared to take notes.

"Otis has pointed out items, such as the heating system at the main house, that need expensive repairs, but would be more energy efficient if they were replaced," Adrianna continued, "and I believe we should consider ways we can make the house and its surrounding property self-sufficient – the same way as the farm."

"Penny didn't mention that you've inherited your great-aunt's forthright nature and quick-off-the-mark mind." The broker sent her a smile.

"I'm not sure about all that." Adrianna blushed. "I do think, though, that a multi-faceted approach might be best. I would suggest we go ahead and replace those things that will save on operating costs, since we already have realized cash available. I have some ideas for generating income from the property that Otis and I will discuss first thing tomorrow, after which I will draw up a cost outline, she proceeded to list her plans. Once the funds for development have been put aside, then you and I can discuss reinvestment of the rest."

To her surprise, Larry Chesterton threw back his head and laughed. "Delightful," he said as he pulled an additional three sheets of paper from his own portfolio, passing one each to Otis and Adrianna. "As you can see, Miss Montgomery, we are on the same page. I almost have to ask if you peeked."

Printed across the top of the sheet were the words Plan for Retaining Montgomery Properties, and it only took a glance for Adrianna to realize that she had just stated Chesterton's proposed plan almost verbatim.

"In all good consciousness, I feel duty bound to tell you that your great-aunt wouldn't have agreed." The broker's face sobered. "In her book, capital was sacred. Unfortunately, times have changed, and the property isn't in good shape. By opening up to development potential that Martha wouldn't have considered, investing in cost savings and underwriting your own swing loan, you may manage to save Montgomery House for future generations, and I may still have a client."

"Well, we wouldn't want him to lose a client now, would we?" Otis sent his employer a proud smile as Larry stood, bringing their meeting to a close.

Wishing she had shipped her thin leather briefcase east along with her clothes, Adrianna gathered her notebook, the portfolio and her purse, then followed their host to the outer office where they all agreed on a luncheon appointment for the following Tuesday.

A few minutes later as she turned their vehicle onto Captain's Point's Main Street, Adrianna felt herself panic. What had she gotten herself into? She had talked the talk – certainly. Matching her broker's plan line by line proved that, but was she knowledgeable and experienced enough to walk the walk?

In her mind, Jebediah's eyes twinkled at her from the portrait of him as an older man that still hung in his study. The key, she felt he had been telling her all along, was to enjoy the journey - something her life in Seattle proved she had so far failed to do. Good, bad or indifferent, she had committed to one year at the end of which no one, including Mr. Chase Sheffield, was going to say that she hadn't given saving Montgomery House a good try.

"Did you see his face when you were outlining your plans?" Otis's words broke through, once they had gained the main highway. "No wonder he thought you had peeked."

"I was a bit taken aback when he started laughing." She smiled at the memory as they passed between the gateposts onto Montgomery property.

"You've made a conquest there, no mistake about it, and Larry Chesterton has been highlighted by the Chamber of Commerce in their Most Eligible Bachelors Calendar for the past seven years."

"Don't be ridiculous." Adrianna sent him a look.

"No kidding," Otis shot back. "Chase Sheffield and he toss November and December back and forth like a tennis ball. It's quite a rivalry."

"Well, they can just keep it up," she stated firmly as she brought the Elantra to a stop and threw open the driver's door.

"She was amazing!" Otis called to Penny who had come onto the porch at the sound of the car's approach.

"Can't say that I'm all that surprised." His wife grinned. "Wait till you see what arrived a few minutes ago." She led the way through the front doorway, where a huge floral arrangement greeted them from atop the octagonal foyer table.

"How lovely!" Adrianna took the small green envelope that had accompanied the flowers from Penny's hand, wondering what had possessed Larry Chesterton to make such a gesture, but when she withdrew the card, she received a surprise.

Would like to hear your plans for going forward. Dinner Saturday evening? I'll call you.

Chase Sheffield

CHAPTER XV

"You would've been proud of her." Otis smiled at his wife across the kitchen table where they both sat enjoying a mug of coffee, Adrianna having left them to take a walk. "Our little girl came across like a true professional. Larry was really impressed."

"I told you she would do fine." Penny reached over and patted his hand. "Perhaps, you'll quit worrying so much now."

"It has been a long couple of years," he admitted. "I could get another position somewhere if need be, but frankly, I don't want to leave here."

"Neither do I, and from what you've been telling me, I'd bet we won't have to," his wife reassured him. "Our job now will be to make Adrianna's way going forward as easy for her as possible, and I'm pleased that she's asked some friends over for tea tomorrow. It's a sign she's settling in."

"They both seemed like nice women," Otis agreed as he took his mug to the sink. "I'll be in my office, putting together the comprehensive list that she's asked for, if you need me. Unless…" He glanced down at his phone that had started to ring. "This ties me up here."

Meanwhile, Adrianna was making her way through the floral gardens, pleased that Nip had joined her as soon as she had passed through the doorway in the kitchen garden wall.

"I wondered if you would speak to me again," she said to her feline companion as she changed direction and strode onto the grass. "After all, I'm a mere interloper."

The cat failed to acknowledge her words, but still matched his steps with hers, and she welcomed his company.

"The wind has picked up today," she commented as they neared the cliff's edge at the point where a wrought iron handrail and steps led down to the narrow strip of boulder strewn beach below, to which Nip let out a 'Meow!' as if to agree.

As a child, Adrianna had been denied the beach as too dangerous a play area, and once she reached the sand, she quickened her pace barely noticing the large whitecaps on the waves, eager to explore this once forbidden territory. As she approached the water's edge, though, movement to her left caught her eye.

"Hold still!" She called as she ran towards a large boulder to which a metal ring was attached for tying up boats. "I'm coming!"

Struggling to get free, a small dog was suspended, one circle of a plastic six-pack holder forced around the ring, while another encircled the animal's neck. His hind feet barely touched a flat rock lying horizontal at the boulder's base, and Adrianna wondered how he could breathe.

"Who would do such a thing?" she asked as she scooped up the dog, disregarding his sand and dirt encrusted brown coat as he sagged against her arm.

Above them on the boulder, Nip stood guard, his black tail swishing back and forth rapidly.

Unable to stretch the plastic circle back over the ring, she turned her attention to the circle around the dog's neck, avoiding his fear-filled eyes and the memories that had washed over her at the sight of them.

Moving around as her parents and she had, pets hadn't been an option, but as a child she had never given up hope. One spring, in a small town near a promising Minoan site, she and her tutor had been followed by a similar mixed breed during their afternoon walk. Enchanted, Adrianna had stopped and petted the animal, crying when she had been told she could not give it a home.

The next day the dog's carcass had lain in the middle of the road where it had fallen victim to one of the area's crazed drivers. "Don't worry. We're going to make this right," she assured the frightened animal who now shivered in the crook of her arm, recognizing that this time no one could tell her not to keep him.

Suddenly, she felt her trainers fill with water as Nip let out a loud, "Meow!"

The tide obviously coming in, Adrianna searched frantically for a sharp-edged rock that she could use to cut the plastic away from the ring, even as the next wave crashed further up her calves. Stepping onto the flat rock, so as to avoid the shifting sand, she was surprised to feel strong hands on her shoulders.

"Let him go!" Chase Sheffield yelled at her above the increasingly noisy surf. "You'll get yourself killed."

"I'm not going to leave him to drown," she refused to release the animal as the attorney reached into the front pocket of his jeans and drew out a Swiss Army knife, grabbing the dog from her.

"I said go! I can't deal with two of you!" He thrust her away as he worked to cut the plastic circle from the ring.

Realizing there was nothing more she could do, Adrianna headed for the steps, glad to see Nip several treads up from the beach. Fighting to keep her long waves from her eyes in the much stronger wind, she felt a chill as the sun disappeared behind a bank of low-hanging dark clouds that were rapidly blowing in.

Reaching the top of the cliff, she turned to find Chase right behind her, the dog tucked under his arm.

"Whatever made you go down there at this time of day?" He thrust the dog at her, his eyes flashing. "Don't you know there's a huge storm coming our way?"

"How would I know that?" She shot back at him. "I haven't seen the news since I returned." She held the dog close as she blinked back tears of relief.

"Well, see that you turn on a radio." He started towards the house. "He needs to be taken to a vet. He favored one of his hind legs when I first released him."

"Otis and I will see to it." She had trouble matching her attorney's long strides as they approached the kitchen garden wall and he threw open the door. "Thank you for your quick response." She paused in the doorway and looked up at his expressionless face. "We owe you, and thanks for the flowers, too. They're beautiful."

"Beth's Buds always does a great job," he stated, and Adrianna found herself wondering how many women he had sent flowers to over the years. "As for my rescuing you, I'm glad I walked over to confirm our dinner engagement, instead of calling like I had intended. You might check with Otis or Penny before walking along the beach until you're more used to the area."

"I might."

"Around seven Saturday for dinner?" He searched her face.

"I'll be ready," she agreed and turned towards the house, the exhausted animal now asleep in her arms, the plastic holder still hanging from his neck.

Chase Sheffield, she thought as she heard the garden's door shut behind her, was in for a surprise when she unveiled her plans to him over supper Saturday evening.

CHAPTER XVI

"I'm keeping him," Adrianna announced a few moments later when she entered the kitchen, a loud clap of thunder accompanying her announcement.

"Of course, you are," the Plunks agreed in unison from where Otis was helping his wife rehang a kitchen curtain.

"Laundry room." Penny opened the door that led to the home's basement. "We'll give him a bath."

"And I'll contact Jim Laidlaw," Otis called after them, referring to the veterinarian that serviced the farm.

"I don't know what I would've done if Chase Sheffield hadn't come along and cut him loose." Adrianna felt as if she were babbling. "Someone had left him hanging from the boat ring on the beach at the bottom of the cliffs."

"You shouldn't have been on the beach with the storm coming in." Penny removed the plastic holder from the dog's neck with a pair of utility scissors and then turned on the water in the laundry room sink, before reaching for animal shampoo that stood ready on the shelf above. "I keep this on hand, so I can occasionally hose down Nip," she explained.

"Chase said the same thing about the storm." Adrianna handed the little guy to the housekeeper and then brushed the dirt and sand from her shirt into a trash can. "I had no idea a storm was coming. How am I ever going to learn everything that I need to know?"

"You'll catch on soon enough, and I wouldn't beat yourself too badly over this mistake," Penny reassured her as she reached for a beach towel that hung ready next to the sink. "One of us should've told you." She proceeded to give the new member of the family a good rubdown, before wrapping him up snuggly and giving him a hug. "What a sweetheart you are!"

"I caught Jim at his office." Otis called down the stairs. "He's going to wait for us if we want to come now."

"Please," Adrianna replied. "Chase said he's favoring one of his legs."

"We'll be there in just a few minutes." Otis's words carried back to them as Penny handed the rescue to Adrianna.

"Let's hope he's housebroken," the housekeeper said, "but he doesn't look or act as if he's a wild animal."

"No, but someone had deliberately hung him from that boat hook and left him to drown," Adrianna stated, "and whoever it was isn't going to get him back."

"I should think not," Penny agreed as they headed upstairs.

A few minutes later found Otis and Adrianna headed for the vet's, the rescue shivering within his beach towel cocoon despite the warmth of his new owner's arms wrapped around him, as a torrential downpour lashed the red pickup truck they had chosen for the trip.

"Do you think he's sick or just scared?" Adrianna asked, sending her property manager a worried glance.

"I imagine he's just scared, either way we're here now," he replied as he turned into the parking lot of a converted house, where a sign announced Captain's Point's Veterinary Hospital. "Wait a second, and I'll bring the golf umbrella I keep in the back around for you."

Appreciating the gesture, Adrianna kept her seat, not really believing that the umbrella would make much difference given the windswept rain.

"Pop out, and we'll make a run for it," Otis shouted as he opened the passenger door.

Dashing towards the small covered porch, Adrianna noticed the door to the house was opening and immediately she felt the little dog's tail begin to wag inside the towel – a good sign since it had remained between his legs most of the time he had been with them.

"Max!" A tall, lean man wearing a white doctor's coat held out his hands and took the now squirming animal from her. "What kind of trouble have you gotten yourself into little fellow?" Tucking the dog under his left arm, he held out his right hand to Adrianna. "Jim Laidlaw, animal quack." He sent her a broad grin.

With his close-cropped auburn hair, blue eyes and slightly freckled complexion, she liked him immediately. "Adrianna Montgomery." She felt his firm grip for a moment, before he moved aside and let them into the building, which had obviously undergone an extensive renovation, now presenting a highly professional appearance.

"Let's use #3." The vet indicated a small examination room. "If you'll keep him on the table, I'll pull up his chart." He rebooted a laptop computer that stood ready on a side counter.

"You called him Max, and he obviously recognized you," Adrianna said.

"He should've." Dr. Laidlaw's hands traveled slowly along the dog's body. "I've been treating him since Mabel Spooner first brought him in as a puppy."

"Ah…" Otis murmured from the seat he had taken in a corner. "Mabel passed away the week after your great-aunt did."

"I told that grandson of hers to bring him to me, and I would find him a home." The vet peered in first one and then the other of Max's ears. "I guess he couldn't be bothered."

"I found him suspended by a plastic six-pack holder from a boat ring on our private beach," Adrianna explained.

"Sounds like the kind of stunt Billy Spooner would pull." Dr. Laidlaw again tucked the dog under his arm. "I'd like to take a quick x-ray of his back right leg, if you don't mind, but I don't really think that it's broken."

"Sure," she agreed. "Whatever's best."

"I'll give him a flea and tick chewable while we're back there as well, just in case he didn't get his last one, although I didn't see any evidence of infestation when I examined his underbelly." The vet headed into the lab area of the hospital to be greeted by a few hopeful barks from a kennel area that obviously lay beyond.

"Why would Billy Spooner have done such a thing?" Adrianna addressed her property manager once they were alone.

"Probably to get back at me." Otis shrugged. "I took him on as a farmworker a few months back at Mabel's request, but then some of the small tools came up missing. All of the other staff had been with us for some time, and I knew Billy had been caught shoplifting a few years ago."

"So you laid him off."

"It was winter by then, and I told him we didn't need him anymore, which was partially true." Otis met her gaze. "One of the guys at the farm told me last week that Billy was planning to leave town. This was probably his parting gesture."

"I would've done the same thing you did." Adrianna reached out for Max as the vet rejoined them.

"Give me a sec to read this, and then we'll have you on your way." Dr. Laidlaw brought the x-ray he had taken onto the computer's screen. "Everything appears to be okay." He looked up and sent Adrianna a smile. "Otis said you're planning to keep him. Do you have everything you need?"

"Not really," her property manager spoke up.

"You can put him down out here, and pick out what you want." The vet led them into the waiting room and grabbed a bag of dog food from the retail area where it waited off to the side. "He'll need a medium-sized harness, and I'll give you a rabies tag."

"How old is he?" Adrianna asked as she chose a hunter green harness and leash.

"Almost three. His mother was a large Chihuahua, and Mabel thought his father was a beagle," Dr. Laidlaw replied. "His shots are up to date, but you'll need to give him a flea and tick chewable every month. Are you planning to stay at Montgomery House?"

"At least for a year." She pulled out a credit card and prepared to pay for the stack of treats, bowls and toys that she had accumulated and Otis was now loading into the truck.

"I'd love to show you around, if you're agreeable," the vet said as he handed her a receipt. "I could pick you up around five on Saturday, and we could do dinner afterwards."

Adrianna was surprised to receive her second request for a date in as many hours. "I'm afraid I already have plans for that evening," she stated as she slung her purse over her shoulder. "Perhaps another time."

"I'll hold you to that." He took her rejection well as he held open the hospital's front door, revealing that the rain had subsided to a mere mist. "After all, I have to keep track of my patient now, don't I?"

CHAPTER XVII

Adrianna gave Max a tour of his new home and ate her supper, then entered the library where she located a Jane Austen novel and took it upstairs to read in her room, her furry friend tagging along at her heels. Here he settled into his new bed where she had placed it in front of the hearth, promptly falling asleep and remaining so for some time while she sat in one of the Queen Anne chairs reading.

As soon as she turned out all but the bedside lamp and donned her pajamas, though, he jumped onto the half-tester and burrowed his way under the covers. Not sure that she wanted their friendship to go quite so far, Adrianna pulled him out and placed him back in the dog bed.

"I don't know what your previous owners allowed you to do," she stated, petting him as she spoke, "but we each have our own beds here."

Leaving him, she crossed the room and turned out the lamp, but as soon as she had settled beneath the covers, she heard a rustle and then felt his weight as he again jumped onto the bed. Loath to shut him out of her room, she saw nothing for it but to let him remain, at least for the one night.

Closing her eyes, she knew nothing else until a large clap of thunder awoke her to the odor of the dog's breath in her face as he now huddled beside her panting and shaking. Realizing he was frightened of the storm, she gathered him into her arms, turned the bedside lamp onto low and carried him to the bay window, where she pushed aside one of the drapes.

"We're okay," she assured the shivering animal. "It's only a storm. You're okay."

Outside rain lashed against the panes as yet another bolt of lightning lit up the night sky and the cherry trees that were being tossed by the wind, despite the relative protection of the kitchen garden's thick walls. The mantel clock softly chimed three, drawing Adrianna's attention to the fireplace just as another bolt shot across the sky, illuminating young Jebediah's portrait in such a way as to make him appear as if he were stepping from his canvas.

Reflexively, Adrianna took an answering step backwards only to feel like a fool, the room having returned to normal and her ancestor once again smiling down at her. "Now you have me overreacting," she chided the dog in her arms, even as she held him closer.

"I think we've seen enough for one night." She drew the drape across the window and dropped Max back onto the bed before once again turning off the lamp and drawing the covers close around her, suddenly feeling uncomfortable in the knowledge that only the large empty house lay about them.

Used to living alone in Seattle, she hadn't previously experienced this particular sensation, although she had developed the habit of turning the old key in the lock of the master suite's door each night as she prepared for bed. "This is your fault," she directed her comment at Jebediah's portrait through the darkness. "You shouldn't have scared me like that."

Once again her furry friend burrowed beneath the covers, and she pulled his shaking body to her in much the same way as she had held her teddy bear during her childhood. "I'm probably spoiling you rotten." She held him close with one arm, glad of his company. "Montgomery House is your home now, and there's certainly room in this big, old house for both of us."

Gradually, the storm outside abated, the rain settling into a steady patter against the panes as the thunder moved farther and farther into the distance. Beside Adrianna, Max let out a long sigh, and she drifted to sleep, secure in the knowledge that the dog would alert her to any real danger and a button that would summon the Plunks from the gatehouse was positioned right by her bed.

A few hours later, she was awakened by Max pulling away from her. "Good morning," she addressed her new roommate. "Sleep well?"

Dropping her legs over the side of the bed, she placed the dog on the floor before she crossed to the bay window and pulled aside the drapes, revealing low gray clouds hanging over the debris-strewn gardens below.

"What a mess," she advised her furry companion as she caught sight of Jeff Stuart already at work in the floral gardens, where he was rapidly filling a wheelbarrow with small limbs, leaves and petals. "And I was so looking forward to showing Edwina and Ginny the flowers."

Slipping into casual clothes, she headed downstairs with Max at her heels, clipping the hunter green leash to his halter before opening the mudroom door and letting him out.

In the garden... Her great-aunt's clue came back to her as she took in the drenched scene before her, many of the plants beaten to the ground by the previous night's pelting rain. Two of the tomato cages had been overturned, and one section of espaliered fruit had pulled partially away from its support wall.

"Definitely a mess," Adrianna confirmed her previous comment, and then headed back inside to feed Max, who seemed content to return to his new home.

Sounds of a vacuum cleaner at work greeted them from the front of the house, and Adrianna strode to the formal parlor, planning to discuss plans for her tea with Penny. Instead, she discovered a round-faced, middle-aged woman, who turned off the machine as she entered.

"I'm Adrianna Montgomery," she introduced herself, "and this is Max." She indicated her furry companion who was already approaching the newcomer, his tail wagging, obviously having wolfed down his food.

"Maggie Daniels. I help Penny on a come as needed basis," the woman said. "No one can say that you didn't land on your feet, now can they?" She bent and petted Max's head. "Somewhere Mabel's glad to know that you've found nice folks to love you."

"We took him in yesterday," Adrianna filled her in.

"Well, you won't be sorry." Maggie unplugged the vacuum. "He has a sweet disposition, and he was devoted to Mabel. I used to stop by and clean up a bit for her from time to time as part of our church circle's outreach program, and he hardly left her side."

"I had forgotten how beautiful my great-aunt was as a young woman," Adrianna commented, her eyes drawn to a full-length portrait hanging over the marble mantel that depicted Martha Montgomery in a white gown, suspended over her left shoulder by a wide sash, its flowing skirt shot with silver. One toe of a satin slipper peeked from beneath the gown's hem, again giving Adrianna the impression of a portrait's subject being ready to step from their canvas.

"That was her coming out gown, but of course, you know that." Maggie guided the vacuum towards the foyer.

Wondering how many employees she had left to meet, Adrianna tagged along behind the maid, who continued into the second parlor.

"I'm entertaining some ladies for tea later this afternoon, and I think we'd be more comfortable in this room," she observed, her gaze approving the overstuffed, chintz-covered matching loveseats and comfortable chairs.

"Martha would've used the formal parlor," Maggie chuckled, "but I'm with you. The brocade-covered chairs in that room sit hard as rocks. Your friends will thank you for showing them into here."

"There you are," Penny addressed Adrianna from the arched doorway. "Jeff is in the mudroom wondering if he could have a word with you."

"Sure." She turned back to Maggie, before following Penny from the room. "It was nice to meet you."

"It's nice to know there's a Montgomery still here." The older woman sent her a smile.

"I'm sure you've been busy this morning," Adrianna greeted Jeff a few moments later.

"That storm was a doozy." He sent her a grin. "Hope I didn't interrupt anything important, but I remembered you asked me where I would bury something in one of the gardens and well…" He held out a small, plastic-wrapped parcel from which clung traces of wet soil. "I discovered this when I reattached the espaliered fruit tree that had pulled loose."

"What is it?" She took it from him and, holding it over a trash can, tore the wrapping away from a rusty metal box that still showed traces of blue paint. "I'm afraid it's stuck." She struggled to open it.

"Let me try." Jeff opened a utility drawer from which he removed a small screw driver. "I think if I wedge this just so…" He pressed upward against the lip of the lid. "Yep, that's done it." He handed her the box.

For a moment, Adrianna couldn't believe her good fortune. Was it possible that a freak storm had revealed her great-aunt's clue to her in only a matter of a few days? Opening the lid, she removed a plastic travel soap container and emptied its contents onto the counter – a Mickey Mantle baseball card, an article detailing the launch of Sputnik, an advertisement for a hula hoop and a faded newspaper photo of Eisenhower and Nixon.

Unfolding a sheet of 3-ring notebook paper, she revealed a note written in a childish scrawl and read aloud to her gardener:

Congratulations!

If you are reading this, you have discovered my 1957 time capsule. My name is Walter Jebediah Montgomery, and I'm ten years old. All of us in my scout troop are burying one of these somewhere. I wonder what year it is now. I'm hoping that it's at least 2957 and that you're somebody special, since you now own one of my two Mickey Mantle cards.

Your friend,

Walt

Blinking back tears, Adrianna lifted her eyes and sent Jeff a smile. "You have uncovered a treasure," she said. "Walt was my father, and I think he would be happy, knowing that we were the ones who discovered this so many years later."

CHAPTER XVIII

Adrianna shared Jeff's find with Penny and then breakfasted on whole wheat toast slathered in the housekeeper's homemade lemon curd, before snapping on Max's leash and going in search of Otis.

"You'll probably find him in his office," his wife had told her, so it was to the carriage house that the twosome headed with her spiral notebook.

"Just in time," Otis greeted them when Adrianna tapped on the doorframe. "I've finished detailing your repair and maintenance needs and their approximate costs."

"Great!" She took the stapled pages from his hand. "Whew! This is quite a list."

"Now you can understand why I got so depressed over it, but I think you're heading in the right direction by prioritizing the needs and doing what you can to save us in operating costs first."

"We have to do more than that, though, if we're going to make the property self-sufficient," Adrianna restated her position. "We also have to bring in regular, measurable income. Do you have a minute?"

"For you? All the time in the world."

Moving a stack of papers to clear a place, she plopped into the single visitor's chair, noting that Max took a seat beside her, an expectant look on his face. "How many buildings are there on the estate proper?" She opened her notebook and sat with her pen poised.

"Quite a few, there's the dependency, which was originally the old kitchen and cold storage as well as the cook's quarters." Otis began counting them out on his fingers. "Then there's the carriage house, which now contains my office and four finished garage spaces."

"What are they currently being used for?" Adrianna asked.

"The Lincoln, the pickup, the riding lawnmower and your little car." Otis seemed surprised by the question. "Of course, the remaining carriage bays and the stable area are still unfinished down at the other end," he continued. "Then there are the old smoke house, the spring house, two large equipment sheds, and the caretaker's cottage that Martha's old school friend lived in until she died about ten years ago."

"What shape is the cottage in?" she asked.

"Fair to middlin'. It could use some upgrading and roof repair." Otis rested his arms on his desk blotter. "Where are you going with all of this?"

She sent him a grin as she flipped to a clean page and placed her notebook on the desk in such a way that he could see the plans she was drawing. "If we put a garage here, we could swing a new drive to the carriage house from about here."

"Why a six car garage?" Otis asked.

"Because I'd like to rent out the dependency as a two-bedroom home – adults only, and that would provide a space for the new tenant," she explained. "Once we've cleared everything but your office from the carriage house, we could upgrade it into a series of small retail or studio spaces, hoping to attract members of the artist community. If we provide the right amenities and advertise it correctly, I think it would work from what I've read in the paper."

"You're right!" Otis's face brightened. "Why didn't I ever think of that?"

"Probably because you were too close or knew my great-aunt wouldn't go for it," Adrianna said. "I'd also like to construct a pavilion in this area." She added a rectangle to the map some distance away from the other structures. "It would be hidden from the main house and would be large enough to accommodate a wedding or outdoor concert of up to 200 people."

"That'll cost money," her property manager pointed out.

"I'll need estimates from you as soon as possible." Adrianna met his steady gaze. "Sometimes, you have to spend money to make money. We'll start with the caretaker's cottage and dependency first, since part of the work is already done."

"I can give you rough estimates by close of business Friday," he promised.

"Fine! What do you think of my plan overall?"

"I think it's about time."

Unbeknownst to the two planners, Chase Sheffield would've agreed. "It's about time she does something other than play around," he was saying to his new law partner at the same moment. "First she takes a leisurely trip across the country, then she purchases several televisions and installs Wi-Fi, after which she nearly drowns herself rescuing a dog – none of which addresses the estate's problems."

"Don't you think you're being a bit harsh?" Susan looked up from some documents she had been studying. "The girl's only been here a few days."

"That's exactly the problem." Frustration filled her partner's face. "Adrianna Montgomery isn't a girl on vacation. She's an MBA with experience, who has been handed a mess and a great deal of responsibility, and time, my dear friend, is running out if she's going to make a success of what she seems to perceive as some sort of adventure."

"Ah…"

"What do you mean, ah…?"

"It sounds to me like you've allowed this young woman to get under your skin," Susan stated.

"I promise you that I haven't." He met her gaze, his face once again a blank slate.

"You forget that I've known you since grade school." Susan stood and gathered her papers, preparing to leave. "And I'm afraid. Yes, I'm very much afraid that you have."

CHAPTER XIX

A few moments later, Susan departed, and Chase strode to the large arched window in his office that offered him a clear view three floors down of Captain's Point's Main Street. Here he stood, oblivious to the pedestrians strolling back and forth below, his thoughts in an uproar.

It wasn't often that someone penetrated his carefully courted reserve, and Susan's having done so disturbed him. Maybe he should have brought on a new partner that didn't know him so well. Not that Susan had been completely right in her insinuations, because she hadn't been, he assured himself.

True, Adrianna Montgomery's presence in Captain's Point had gotten under his skin, but not for the reasons most people might assume, the real problem having begun its never ending growth spiral a long time before her arrival. He returned to his desk, where he addressed a photo of his father that filled one side of a double frame on the credenza behind it as expected by his clients. "Did you know what a mess you were leaving Mom and me?" he asked. "Did you care?"

It had been fifteen years now since his father had dropped dead of a heart attack while playing golf in D.C. with his mistress on the hottest day of the year, strictly against his cardiologist's orders. His father's affair becoming a public spectacle had been bad. The mountains of debts left behind had been worse - his medical practice in a shambles, his patients' balances uncollectable, his life insurance premium left unpaid in a drawer and his widow's heart broken.

"If it hadn't been for Augustus Chesterton paying my way, I couldn't even have gone to law school." He swiveled his desk chair around, turning his back on the photo.

Thank goodness for Augustus, who had attacked the mess left behind, squeezing out every nickel and dime until it became possible for the grieving widow to remain in her home.

"Were you in love with her?" Chase asked the portrait of his dead partner that now hung on the opposite wall, having been moved from the office that had been given to Susan. "Or did you do it all out of pity?"

Whatever Augustus's motives, he had certainly saved the day, although it hadn't been until his senior partner's death that Chase had learned the true cost when he had taken over the handling of the older man's estate. A quick run through the accounts had given a clear enough picture. It had mainly been Chesterton money that had kept his mother's home going until her death from cancer two years before, at which point her son had relinquished his bachelor apartment and moved into the old home himself.

Now he was stuck with the burden of upkeep on the big house, the same burden that his father had ignored and his partner had suffered. Part of him loved his childhood home, passed down through the generations by his family, but part of him was quickly coming to hate it, recognizing it for the money pit that it was.

With her inheritance, Adrianna Montgomery had now landed in the same position, and where he was fighting for his survival, she was playing. Attorney's fees paid by Montgomery business had always formed a large part of the firm's profits, and if the heir apparent didn't get herself into gear soon, he would find himself in the position of merely being another one of her bankruptcy creditors. And if that wasn't enough, the woman was leaving her stamp everywhere.

"Thanks for sending Adrianna my way." Jim Laidlaw had slapped him on the back as he waited for a table at Chester's crab shack the evening before. "What a looker!"

In return, he had mumbled something about not having noticed.

"Adrianna and Otis came to see me." Larry Chesterton had sent him a sly grin when they had met for beers at Patrick's. "That woman's smart as a tack, although I imagine Martha's turning over in her grave about now."

The broker had then paid his part of the tab and left, leaving him worried as to what exactly his new client's plans were. Suffering from a bad night's sleep and too much caffeine, he had further exacerbated the situation by ordering the bane of his existence a huge floral arrangement and asking her to dinner, thus committing himself to an evening spent with someone who had almost drowned herself for a dog.

What had he been thinking? Was it any wonder that he was frustrated? Of course, the woman's presence had gotten under his skin. Too much was riding on her success or her failure.

A light tap broke through Chase's thoughts as Bridgette opened his office door and announced his next appointment. "Captain Reb is here to see you about Montgomery Marina as scheduled," she announced.

"Glad you could fit me in." A man with a ruddy complexion, whose six-pack abs had long since morphed into a keg, strode in behind her - dressed in jeans, a striped golf shirt and a belligerent expression. "I'd like a word with you."

"My time is your time." The attorney directed him to take a seat in one of the visitors' chairs, where the captain accepted a bottled water from Bridgette and then waited pointedly for her to leave them.

"I'll get right down to it." Reb leaned forward, resting his wrists on Chase's desk. "I'm madder than hell!"

"About something I've done?" The attorney's left eyebrow rose slightly.

"Not exactly. It's more like what you haven't done. Everyone in town is talking about Martha Montgomery's great-niece – what a looker she is, how smart she is, how nice she is. They all want to know what I think of her, and I haven't even met her – me, skipper of Montgomery Marina." The marina's manager unscrewed the cap from his water and took a long swig. "Now I ask you, is that fair? I should have been introduced official like, and you should have seen to it."

"The girl's only been here a few days." Chase realized he had just fallen back on the very words that Susan had said to him a short time earlier. "And I have every intention of introducing you to her Saturday evening. I'm bringing her to dinner at

Montgomery's. Sue Ellen's already reserved us Martha's regular table."

"The weather's been lousy with the storm passing through." Captain Reb became chatty. "Boat charters are way down."

"Not surprising."

"Of course, I can't be held accountable for the weather."

"No, you can't." Chase stood and offered the captain his hand and then ushered the marina manager to the door.

"Sorry if I seemed a bit gruff back there, but Martha let things slide for a long time." The captain paused in the doorway.

"Don't you worry," the attorney assured him with more confidence than he felt. "We'll soon have things sorted out."

Closing the door behind his last appointment of the day, Chase once again strode to the arched window, this time taking in the smiling faces of the pedestrians below him. Adrianna Montgomery, he thought, was fast becoming too large a part of his life.

CHAPTER XX

"Frankly, I hadn't thought much beyond mugs in the morning room," Adrianna admitted, closing yet another cabinet door in the large butler's pantry.

"Your great-aunt just turned over in her grave." Penny pinched a tiny dead leaf from a small round floral arrangement that the two women had pieced together from the offerings Jeff had delivered to them from the storm-ravaged rose garden.

"Again…" Adrianna sighed. "I feel like she's been in perpetual motion since I arrived."

"Now you mustn't think that," the older woman stated firmly. "Otis and Larry Chesterton are both thrilled with your ideas."

"I'm not at all sure that Chase Sheffield will be," Adrianna pointed out, but then decided to move on. "I've narrowed it down to these two." She indicated two cups and saucers on the counter. "They would tie in with the arrangement."

"Old Country Roses by Royal Albert and Rosalinde by Haviland – they're both good choices," Penny agreed. "Either one will go well with the Old Master sterling. Which one do you prefer?"

"I'm leaning towards the Old Country Roses. The flowers are a little more vibrant and will go better with the real roses."

"You know, that's you and your great-aunt in a nutshell," the housekeeper pointed out. "Martha liked both patterns, but she always favored the Rosalinde. It's as if you are walking on different sides of the same path, but in the end, you'll both reach the same destination."

"Do you think so? Really?" Adrianna's face filled with pleasure. "I've felt so bad about her these last few years. She was wonderful to me as a child, and then she hurt me so badly by refusing to help me get through college. In some ways, this test she has put before me seems like my last opportunity to please her."

"Otis and I never did understand that." Penny's mouth drew into a thin line. "She didn't care for your mother, but frankly, neither of us ever felt that was related to you. It was more that she perceived your mother as having taken Walt away from her because of their working overseas, but that wasn't true. He would have buried himself in various archeological digs anyway. Martha just needed someone to blame. We thought she would move Heaven and Earth to get you to make this your home after the accident, but then, she didn't."

"Oh, I was free to make this my home," Adrianna corrected, "but only if I gave up furthering my education. I told her that was ridiculous this being the new millennium, and we both said things that we shouldn't have the evening after my parents' funeral."

"And your pride and her pride never allowed for a reconciliation."

"I wish now that I had swallowed mine. She was an older woman and the last member of my family on my father's side." Adrianna felt the prick of tears. "Jeff's having found Dad's time capsule this morning really pointed out how much my stupid pride cost me – all the stories my great-aunt could've told me."

"Otis and I are here anytime you want to ask us," Penny said, "and most of them are probably documented in a photo album or keepsake somewhere in this big, old house. The next rainy day, you should spend some time exploring."

"I intend to." Adrianna returned the unwanted cup and saucer to the cabinet and began loading a tray with the serving items that would be needed to set up the second parlor. "Things are going to look pretty." She held the swinging door open, so that the housekeeper could bring up the rear with the arrangement, Max slipping through the doorway with her.

"And the food will be good," the older woman assured her. "We made plenty of cucumber sandwiches, and I'll pop the scones in the oven just before they're due to arrive."

"Your strawberry preserves will finish those off," Adrianna pointed out, "and we have your lemon curd mini-tarts as well. If that's not enough for three women, we're in trouble."

Together the two of them made quick work of arranging everything on Great-grandmother Serepta's marble-topped buffet, the roses from the garden already having found a home in the middle of the mahogany coffee table.

"You get dressed in your party clothes." Penny shooed the younger woman away. "I'll set the dishes of spiced nuts and wrapped chocolates on either side of the arrangement. Everything else should stay covered in the fridge until the last minute."

"Thanks for your help." Adrianna gave the housekeeper a quick hug. "You're a peach!"

A few minutes later in her room, she took a last glimpse of herself in the long dressing room mirror, having slipped into a pair of beige linen slacks, a light green blouse and a pair of low heels. A small gold locket that had belonged to her mother and simple gold stud earrings were her only decoration. "That should do it," she told herself, just as the front doorbell chimed that her guests had arrived.

Max immediately jumped up from his dog bed in front of the hearth, running first to her and then to the suite's doorway as if he were unsure of his role.

"You wait and go down with me," Adrianna stated firmly, pleased when he paused by the doorway.

"Miss Adrianna will be right with you," she heard Penny announce as she headed for the upstairs walkway. "Won't you come in here and be seated?"

Surprised at how nervous she felt about her first attempt at entertaining since her arrival at Montgomery House, Adrianna took her time on the stairs, not wanting to appear flustered when she made her entrance.

"How lovely everything is!" Edwina's soft voice found its way to her.

"And yet so welcoming," Ginny added as Adrianna entered the room with Max beside her like a small shadow and Penny rejoined them carrying a teapot on a tray.

"I'm so glad you could make it," their hostess greeted them. "This is Penny, who has been keeping everything in order here for many years and can probably answer any questions about the area that you might have. Penny, this is my travel buddy, Edwina, and her grandson Jason's wife Ginny."

"It's nice to meet both of you," the housekeeper acknowledged the introduction. "May I pour you each a cup of tea? Adrianna thought decaf English Afternoon."

"Yes, thank you." Ginny accepted a cup. "That was thoughtful of you to think of decaf."

"Please try a scone while they're still warm." Adrianna indicated the plate of pastries.

Soon Penny excused herself, everyone having selected goodies from the buffet and found a seat.

"How have you been feeling?" Adrianna addressed Ginny.

"Spectacular!" The mother-to-be grinned. "For an older first-time mother, I've done really well, and I've been so full of energy the past few days that I can't stand it. Edwina says it could mean the baby will come a day or two early, and I certainly hope so."

"One thing is for sure, she won't come one second earlier than she chooses," the older woman advised. "They never do, although I will be glad when it's over for you." Then she turned to their hostess. "So, how many people live here?" she asked. "And would it be terribly forward of me to ask for a tour of this lovely old home?"

CHAPTER XXI

"Max and I are the only ones who actually live at Montgomery House," Adrianna said, indicating her furry companion who was now fast asleep, curled in a ball by her foot.

"You live here by yourself?" Surprise filled Edwina's kind face.

"Rattle around here might be a better way of putting it." Adrianna chuckled. "I'm used to living by myself, so most of the time it doesn't bother me, although it did feel a little lonely when the storm woke me last night. I only rescued Max yesterday, but I found I was glad of his company. Penny and her husband live in the gatehouse. There's a security alarm, of course, and my great-aunt had an emergency button that connects to the Plunk's home installed when she found herself living here alone."

"Is it your intention to stay here permanently?" Ginny asked.

"At least for a year." Adrianna noticed that while the mother-to-be had chosen several items from the buffet, she had actually eaten very little, merely crumbling a bit of her scone and trying a bite of one of Penny's dainty lemon curd tarts.

"How did you come to rescue your little dog?" Edwina changed the subject.

Adrianna told them the story of Max's dramatic rescue, struck by Chase Sheffield's quick thinking under pressure as she did so.

"You were lucky that man came along when he did." Ginny gave up any pretense of eating and set her plate on the coffee table. "The tides and currents around here can be deadly during a storm."

"Max and I were both lucky," Adrianna agreed. "The big wave that hit me almost took my feet out from beneath me. Would either of you like some more tea?" she asked as Edwina took a last sip and replaced her cup in its saucer. "No? Then let me give you a tour of the house. This room we refer to as the second parlor." She stood, making sure that she pointed out the miniatures of Jebediah and his wife that were displayed in a small curio cabinet to the right of the room's fireplace.

Slowly, the women made their way through the downstairs rooms, commenting on the well-stocked library, the pleasant sunny nature of the breakfast room, and how beautiful Great-aunt Martha had been in her youth as portrayed by her portrait in the main parlor. Leading the way up the broad stairway, neither of the other women noticed that Ginny's hand tightened on the stair rail for a moment as she followed slowly behind them.

"And this is my bedroom." Adrianna led the way into the tower suite.

"What a beautiful view!" Edwina hurried to the window seat straight ahead.

"It's even more magnificent from the sitting room upstairs," Adrianna mentioned, "and this, of course, is Jebediah as a young man." She pointed out the portrait over the fireplace.

"I love your half-tester." Ginny looked longingly at the bed with its rose-colored duvet.

"You should've seen the one that my great-aunt replaced." Adrianna laughed. "It was massive and hung with thick curtains all around to keep out the drafts. I was quite scared of it the first summer that I came to visit as a child."

The small group moved on to the dressing room and ensuite bath, Max leading the way as if he were an experienced docent.

"Look at the storage!" Edwina was clearly enraptured by the dressing room cabinets. "And I love these tiny crystal knobs."

"Do you knit?" Ginny indicated the workbasket by the Queen Anne chair as they reentered the bedroom on their way to view the sitting room upstairs.

"My great-aunt taught me when I was young." Adrianna stepped aside to let them precede her up the smaller tower staircase. "Unfortunately, I've forgotten everything that I once knew."

"Come over one evening, and we'll get you started again if you're interested," Edwina offered. "Ginny is an absolute wiz with a pair of needles."

"I do love to knit." The mother-to-be smiled shyly as she paused halfway up the stairs and turned back to face her hostess for a moment. "I've produced all sorts of things for the baby."

"I may take you up on that offer." Adrianna reached the top step, although both of her guests were now engrossed in the view afforded by the four windowed sides of the octagonal room.

"I could sit for hours just watching the ships," Ginny sank onto one of the window seats. "How do you ever leave here?"

"I certainly couldn't," Edwina agreed.

"Unfortunately, I don't have any choice," Adrianna told them as Ginny hoisted her uneven weight to a standing position. "If you're up to a tour of the gardens and outbuildings, I'll tell you about my situation and give you a clue to consider. I have a feeling that the more helpers I can rope in the better."

"Now I'm intrigued." Edwina headed back to the staircase. "I love a good mystery."

Adrianna snapped Max's leash on once they reached the mudroom, thinking she might as well give him some exercise as well. A pleasant breeze now flowing from the sea, the foursome strolled slowly through the kitchen garden and then along the paths leading past the roses and more formal floral gardens. Finally making their way through the covered walkway, Adrianna finished explaining the terms of her great-aunt's will just as they reached the dependency and came into sight of the carriage house.

"And you agreed to stay for the year." Edwina's eyes twinkled. "Good for you! You would have regretted it the rest of your life if you hadn't."

"I may as easily regret that I have," Adrianna said, "but my plan is to make the property self-sufficient." She moved on towards the carriage house, where she hoped to find Otis in his office so he could tell them about the farm.

As they approached the first bay, though, she was surprised to see an SUV approaching along the drive, her attention being torn away before she could see who was driving by Ginny's doubling over and letting out a cry from where she had lagged behind.

"Help me!" The mother-to-be sagged towards the sidewalk, the other two women catching her just in time to lower her softly onto the grass beside it.

"Otis! Jeff! Someone come help!" Adrianna shouted as the SUV pulled up beside them.

"What's going on?" Chase Sheffield disembarked and hurried to join them.

"Ooooohhhh!" Ginny let out another moan and lowered her head to her knees.

"My grandson's wife is going into labor," Edwina explained, a worried look on her face, as Otis arrived on the scene from his office in the carriage house.

"Let's get her into the car!" Chase tossed his keys to Adrianna and bent over Ginny, helping her up and continuing to support her weight as he began to almost carry her towards his vehicle. "We can get her to the hospital quicker than we can call an ambulance."

Handing Max's leash to her property manager, Adrianna hurried ahead and opened the SUV's back door. Edwina immediately hopped in, ready to receive Ginny and provide any assistance needed on the way. Once the patient was secured in her seat, Adrianna climbed into the front, and a few moments later they were heading along the drive at a fast pace.

"I can't tell you how glad I am that you came along when you did," Adrianna said, wondering what her haughty attorney must think of her. "Everything happened so suddenly."

"I imagine it did." Chase steered the SUV through the gateposts and onto the main road. "But we really have to stop meeting like this. I'm not sure that I'll have enough time to take care of all your emergencies."

CHAPTER XXII

Given Chase Sheffield's comment about his time, Adrianna was surprised a few minutes later at the hospital when he assumed responsibility for getting Ginny into a wheelchair and to the Labor and Delivery input area.

"I'll go park the car," he said once the mother-to-be had been rolled out of sight, then headed for the Emergency Room entrance where he had left his SUV.

"What a nice young man!" Edwina stated when she and Adrianna had found seats in the appropriate waiting area. "What would we have done without him? I wish I could've reached Jason on my cell phone when I tried on the way, but his flight has probably already taken off. I left him a voicemail."

"I'm sure he'll get here as quickly as he can," Adrianna assured her, "and they'll both be glad that you were with Ginny when this happened."

"Mrs. Foster?" A pretty, brown-haired woman addressed Edwina. "I'm Dr. Haygood. Ginny is settled in the Labor room now, if you would like to join her for a few minutes."

"My, how things have changed since my day!" The older woman managed to look pleased and flustered at the same time as she stood. "If you think I won't be in the way…"

"I think your grandson's wife will be glad to have your company," the doctor's calm words carried back as the two women walked away. "First babies often take their own sweet time getting here."

Left alone in the waiting room, Adrianna selected a magazine from a stack on the table beside her and began flipping through it as her attorney rejoined her.

"I picked up a couple of these on the way in." Chase handed her a chilled bottled water.

"Thanks." Adrianna marked her place with her finger. "I'm sure I'll be fine now if you would rather go home."

"I'm sure you will be." The attorney's calm exterior gave no clue to his thoughts. "But I've found over the years that older women are often reassured by the presence of a man in stressful situations. Has Edwina been allowed to visit Ginny for a few minutes?"

"Yes." Adrianna felt the implied criticism in his words.

Would she never get anything right in his view? What an ego! She couldn't help but wonder if her great-aunt would have handled things differently had she known this was the person who would determine the success or failure of her great-niece's ideas for Montgomery House and its properties.

"So what do you think of Captain's Point now that you've seen it?" Chase's words brought her back to the waiting room.

"I like it," Adrianna answered honestly. "Otis and I were on our way to see Larry Chesterton when we drove in, but there were a number of small shops and craft stores I would like to go back and visit as well as some nice looking restaurants. It's obviously grown a lot since I was last here, but the city fathers have done a good job of maintaining the small town feel, while at the same time providing ample parking and benches."

"We've put a lot of money into the decorative street lights, fancier sidewalks and oversized flower pots, too," Chase pointed out, "but it's been money well spent, since it gives people a clear choice between the downtown shops and the discount stores."

"Dr. Haygood's with Ginny," Edwina said as she rejoined them. "Jason's plane has probably landed by now." The older woman indicated with a nod the institutional wall clock that showed it was almost six.

"I need to make a quick phone call," Chase addressed the older woman. "Why don't you come with me and see if he's left you a message, since they don't want us to use our cell phones in here?"

Left to herself, Adrianna reflected on how kind her attorney was being to Edwina, someone he had only just met. A little voice inside tried to tell her that he was only looking out for a prospective client, but Edwina had told him that she wasn't a resident of the area. How odd that, in comparison, he always maintained such a stiff appearance with her, since she was a client!

With a start, she realized she would be sitting across from him at a dinner table in two days, and they had already exhausted the only logical subject of conversation that they had in common. What would they talk about? Perhaps, Penny could give her some insight into his character and interests.

"There you are Mrs. Foster," Dr. Haygood, who had entered the waiting room area, paused and waited for Edwina who was exiting the elevator along with Chase. "Ginny's contractions are a little closer together now, so I don't think it will be too much longer."

"Oh, I do hope Jason gets here in time," Edwina stated. "He started this way from the airport about forty minutes ago."

"I let Penny know that you would be a while yet." Chase resumed his seat beside Adrianna. "She said to tell you that Otis had eaten all of the remaining cucumber sandwiches and was making good headway on the scones."

"He's welcome to them." Adrianna chuckled. "Both of the Plunks have done so much for me, and they were very loyal to Great-aunt Martha."

"For which they were paid," Chase pointed out. "You don't owe them anything."

Catching sight of a tall, lanky teenager wearing a Patrick's Pub T-shirt, who had just exited the elevator, he stood before she could utter the caustic reply that had leaped to her mind.

"That didn't take long." The attorney strode forward, relieved the delivery boy of a large paper bag and handed him a ten dollar bill. "Tell Patrick I'll settle with him tomorrow."

"There are paper plates, plastic silverware and condiments in there, too," the teenager said, sending Adrianna a shy smile and then, pocketing the tip, headed back to the elevator as Edwina took a seat.

"I ordered us some sliders and potato chips." Chase set the bag on a small table and handed each of the ladies a paper plate. "Patrick's is known for them. The ones in the red wrappers are steak with a blue cheese sauce, the blue ones are crab cake and tartar sauce, and the green ones are grilled Portobello mushroom."

"You know your crab cakes here in Maryland. I'll take one of those." Edwina accepted a blue one and a bag of chips, as the elevator once again opened and disgorged a pleasant looking blond-haired man wearing a navy blue business suit. "Jason, you made it!" The older woman set her plate aside and rushed to give her grandson a hug. "Ginny is doing fine, and the doctor says it won't be long now. Things are going much faster than she would've expected. Let's tell them that you're here." She took his arm and led him to the intake desk.

Adrianna accepted a blue slider as requested and sent her attorney a smile. "This was nice of you," she said as he once again sat down beside her and Edwina rejoined them, her grandson's suit coat and tie hanging over her arm.

"Just in the nick of time." The older woman took a seat and unwrapped her crab cake slider.

"This is delicious," Adrianna commented before taking a second bite.

"We can drop in the pub after dinner on Saturday," Chase suggested. "Patrick and the others at the marina are anxious to meet you. After all, as Martha's heir, you hold their leases."

CHAPTER XXIII

Saturday evening arrived with Adrianna still dreading her dinner date with Chase Sheffield, the intervening time having been filled with alternating bouts of work and pleasure in a way that had made time fly by.

Lucy Foster had arrived weighing in at six pounds ten ounces – baby, mother, father and great-grandmother all doing fine. Adrianna had stayed with Edwina in the waiting area until Jason was able to drive them home, Chase having excused himself after their slider supper.

Friday had been a full work day as Otis had presented her with his facts and figures, resulting in many phone calls to this plumber or that roofer in order to review further options or ask additional questions. The result had been daunting and satisfying at the same time. What they were proposing to do was a huge project, but the ready cash was available to cover the cost of their higher priority objectives.

During a lull in the action, Adrianna had spent some time reviewing the personnel and payroll files for those whom she employed and had been surprised to see that this included household staff at a vacation home in Key West as well as a part-time caretaker for a cabin in Maine. Both of these homes appeared to have remained empty for some time awaiting Martha's arrival, and she had added looking into weekly rental options for the two properties to her To Do List as well.

"You don't owe the Plunks anything." Chase Sheffield's words of the night before had returned to her at this point.

Feeling like an interloper, she had glanced at their files, where she had been appalled to see how little the Plunks were paid for their efforts, even accounting for the fact that they received free room at the gatehouse and some board at the main house, resulting in another addition to her list.

"Don't tease me now!" Penny had exclaimed when she had learned that the kitchen and laundry appliances were all going to be replaced with new stainless steel, energy efficient models. "Are you for real?"

"Of course, we're for real," Adrianna had assured her. "They'll save us money in the long run."

"The thing is, Pen, we were wondering if you would give us a hand with the kitchen designs for the new construction projects," Otis had then put forward. "You've spent a lot more time in a kitchen than either of us has, and you'll better understand the layout of things."

"I'd love to help out." The housekeeper's face had lit up. "Let me know when you want me."

Wasting no time, the three of them had gone shopping Saturday morning, ordering the new appliances to be delivered on Monday. This done, the ladies had both insisted that a baby gift should be purchased and delivered to the Foster's, Lucy and her mother having gone home that morning. Otis had been agreeable and everyone had 'Ooohed' and 'Ahhed' over the baby, who Penny had declared really did look like a little girl despite being a newborn. Then the men had talked fishing, and the women had discussed knitting for another hour.

Needing to catch up on her sleep a bit more, Adrianna had decided to stretch out on her bed for a few moments when they arrived home, only to be awakened when Penny brought her a cup of tea and her freshly pressed dress several hours later.

"It's nice that you're going out for a change," the housekeeper said.

"To be perfectly honest, I'm not looking forward to this evening." Adrianna set her cup and saucer on the bedside table.

"Why not?" Surprise filled Penny's face. "You need to get out with people your own age, and Chase Sheffield is a very nice man."

"For one thing, he wants to hear all about my plans for Montgomery House, and I don't get the impression that he thinks I'm up to the task." Adrianna paused as she considered whether or not to take her housekeeper into her confidence. "And he's so haughty and reserved. What in the world will we talk about?"

"That's just his way." Penny hung the dress from the dressing room doorframe and took a seat on the end of the bed. "Has he mentioned his parents?"

"Not a word about them."

"Like you, he's an orphan," the housekeeper began and then went on to explain the details of his parents' deaths. "One shouldn't speak ill of the dead, but Chase's mother was a bright, glittery beauty whose thoughts never went beyond her designer outfits and her jewel box. Augustus Chesterton claimed that her son had spent most of his childhood cooped up in his father's library. What you see as his being haughty may be nothing more than reserve or an innate shyness."

"He was wonderful to Edwina at the hospital," Adrianna gave him credit.

"Well, he would know what an older woman expected of him the way his mother relied on him the last years of her life, especially during her final illness." Penny patted Adrianna's hand and then stood. "Maybe what both of you need is a good laugh. Otis and I have always found that a dose of humor goes a long way towards healing what's hurt us."

"Humor…" Adrianna couldn't quite see herself laughing her eyes out with Chase Sheffield, although she did feel that the housekeeper had given her a new perspective of him.

"Now you take a long soak in the tub," Penny said, indicating for Max to come with her. "In the meantime, I'm going to let this little fellow out and feed him his dinner."

Taking her housekeeper's advice, Adrianna splashed some bubble bath into the tub as she filled it, relaxing as she slipped into the warm water. Somehow the fact that Chase had lost both of his parents as well provided a tiny connection. Losing those that you had loved was hard, and yet both of them were obviously survivors.

Previously, she had rushed through her morning ablutions, but this evening she took time with her makeup and hair, enjoying the opportunity to pamper herself. Carrying the feeling forward, she picked out her prettiest lingerie, silkiest hose and daintiest earrings, before sliding into her favorite black dress and heels.

It was only then that she looked into the dressing room's full-length mirror and realized she was wearing the exact outfit she had worn the evening Brad had proposed to her. With dismay, she heard the front doorbell chime Chase Sheffield's arrival, recognizing that she had no time left in which to change.

Slipping her lip gloss into an evening bag, she draped a thin shawl shot with silver and gold threads over her arm and headed into the bedroom where she paused for a moment before Jebediah's portrait. "For better or worse, I'm on my way," she reported in to him. "I'm sure neither Great-aunt Martha nor you ever left this room feeling quite so nervous."

Laughter reached her from the foyer, and she hurried through the bedroom doorway and onto the walkway. For a moment at the top of the stairs, she paused to view Chase unawares as he bent and petted Max, the former presenting a handsome appearance in a black suit, blue shirt and tie that set off his hair and eyes. For a fraction of a second, she felt a stab of attraction, but quickly shook it away and started down the stairs, the movement causing her date to glance up.

"You look lovely," he straightened and came forward to meet her, a soft look in his eyes for once revealing real pleasure at her appearance. "Your great-aunt would be very proud of you."

CHAPTER XXIV

"I'm glad you decided to keep Max," Chase said a few minutes later as he headed his SUV along the drive.

"You know Max?" Adrianna turned sharply. "I thought you were willing to leave him to drown."

"Given the choice of saving a damsel or a dog, I'll always opt for the lady." Chase turned their vehicle onto the main road. "Still, Max deserves a good home."

"Was Mabel Spooner one of your clients?"

"I did some pro bono work for her through the Captain's Point Senior Center. Towards the end, though, she wasn't able to leave her home, and that's how I met Max."

"I'm glad you were able to help her." Adrianna welcomed yet another, softer view of her attorney's personality. Perhaps, as Penny had implied, she had misjudged him.

An illuminated sign indicated that they were now heading in the direction of Montgomery Marina, and she felt a pulse of excitement, vaguely remembering visits there with her great-aunt as a child.

"You mentioned that I held the lease on Patrick's Pub as well as some of the others." She wished now that she had opened the computer file that had carried the marina's name, when she had been waiting on Otis to complete a call the day before.

"You own the marina outright," Chase informed her. "Captain Reb is your General Manager, although he thinks of himself as its skipper. He oversees the boat house and slip rentals in addition to making sure the buildings and docks are kept in good repair. He also runs a fishing charter business of his own on the side. He's a character, but overall he does a passable job and folks like him."

"I see. What other businesses are there besides his fishing charter and Patrick's?"

"Chester's Crab Shack is at the far end," Chase continued. "Larry Chesterton owns it, and it's about what you would expect. Next comes Captain Reb's office, out of which he also runs his charter company. Martha always thought he would be more available to run her business that way."

"Makes sense," Adrianna agreed.

"Then there are two small retail stores with Patrick's Pub taking up the middle of the main boardwalk, followed by three more small retails. Finally, on the end, is Montgomery's where we're going for dinner. It's fine dining, heavy on the seafood, and you own the restaurant outright, although you may want to change that." He turned the SUV into the marina's parking lot and then into the best space from which to approach the boardwalk, a small sign indicating the spot was reserved for the Montgomery family.

Waiting for her attorney to open her door, Adrianna once again found the level of responsibility that had been handed to her a bit daunting. After all, restaurant management required specialized knowledge that she didn't have.

"What prompted my great-aunt to start a restaurant?" She asked as the two of them stepped onto the broad sidewalk that wrapped around a rough wood building that apparently housed their destination.

"Your great-great grandfather originally built the marina as much as anything to house a speakeasy in this part of the structure," Chase explained. "He supposedly had a very successful 'importing' business throughout Prohibition."

"Ah, the skeleton in the Montgomery family closet." Adrianna chuckled.

"When Prohibition ended the building was leased as a restaurant and continued that way until about twenty years ago, when an impoverished school friend of Martha's appeared on Montgomery House's doorstep."

"Is this the same one that lived in the cottage?" she asked.

"Yes." Chase glanced at her sharply, surprised that she had any knowledge at all of Maud Thornburg. "Five years after she had taken up residence on the property, Maud approached your great-aunt about a nephew who had trained as a chef in Europe and now needed a job. At the time, the restaurant space was available, the couple who had run a successful pancake house out of it having retired and moved to Florida. The two ladies put their heads together and decided that nothing would do but for Martha to open a restaurant herself and make Maud's nephew the head chef."

"What were they thinking?" Adrianna paused, giving him her full attention.

"Augustus never could figure that out." Chase laughed. "And believe me, he tried to dissuade them. In the end, though, everything worked out. John Thornburg knew his stuff, the ladies enjoyed overseeing the redecorations and designing the menu covers, and Martha appreciated that some of her favorite dinner entrees were now available locally."

"Amazing." Adrianna moved slowly forward towards the boardwalk.

"Once the newness wore off, John was pretty much left to his own devices and eventually married a local girl," the attorney continued. "He's done a good job of staying ahead of food and wine trends. If you do decide to sell out, it would be nice if you were to offer him first refusal."

They reached the corner of the building, and the ocean spread out before them.

"I had forgotten how beautiful it is." She paused again, amazed by how many slips ranged along the boardwalk and its perpendicular docks.

Straight ahead, the sidewalk ended and the pier widened to form an outdoor seating area for approximately one hundred with a small stage at one end. Thin wires wove back and forth overhead from which were suspended strings of tiny lights and occasional Japanese lanterns. The boardwalk itself ran along their right, wide enough to accommodate what Adrianna viewed as surprisingly heavy foot traffic as well as a large number of courageous seagulls intent on possible handouts.

Families sat on benches licking ice cream cones, watching the boats come in and enjoying the view. A group of laughing teenagers brushed past them, two of the young couples holding hands. The scent of salt air mingled with the aroma of grilling beef in a way that reminded her she had only eaten a small salad for lunch and that had been some time ago.

"I'm glad you like it," said Chase as, by unspoken mutual agreement, they moved towards the wide double doors that led into Montgomery's where he guided her into the restaurant.

Suddenly remembering his having executed the same move with the laughing young woman in Captain's Point, she felt herself stiffen, but then forced herself to relax as the maître d' approached.

"This way, please, Miss Montgomery, Mr. Sheffield." He led them into an elevator that sent them to the second floor, where the clink of silverware on fine crockery replaced the shrill cries of the gulls. "As you see, the table is ready." He indicated a banquette table set in an alcove that extended over the boardwalk below.

Here again, Adrianna noted a small pewter frame within which a notice read, "Reserved for the Montgomery Family."

"Thank you, Raoul," she said, having identified the maître d' from his name tag. "This is lovely."

The table for six had been set in such a way that the two place settings provided for the best view of the marina and the pink and mauve streaks that now stretched across the sky as the sun set somewhere out of sight.

"Please let John know that we're here," Chase requested as he waited for Adrianna to be seated.

"Certainly, sir." Raoul handed them each a thick, leather-bound menu and set a wine list presented as its smaller cousin in an open position in front of them.

"Is this table always reserved for the family?" Adrianna asked once the maître d' had left them. "After all, it has the best view."

"This table is held until Penny calls each evening and lets the management know that the family won't need it. There's always a waiting list for a seating upgrade."

"I imagine there is." She indicated the now glowing sky with a nod of her head. "This is truly spectacular. But still, the best parking slot and the best seat both reserved – it all seems a bit medieval."

"Such is old money in small town coastal America." Chase shrugged. "Keep in mind that the Montgomerys, Chestertons and Sheffields have owned and run most of Captain's Point for the better part of two centuries. There are some who refer to us as the royal families."

"But surely, the newcomers to the area resent that," Adrianna stated firmly. "Why should you, they probably ask, have been raised as a prince?"

With chagrin she noted the warmth disappear from his eyes. His face now devoid of emotion, he said, "Keep in mind that if I am its prince, Miss Montgomery, then you are Captain's Point's princess."

CHAPTER XXV

Adrianna did not immediately respond to his comment, but rather sat lost in thought as she gazed at the spectacular sunset that was dying before her.

For his own part, Chase found himself both surprised and pleased by her response to the idea, recognizing that most of the women in his experience would have simpered a meaningless denial, while nonetheless thrilled by the implications.

"John." He stood and shook hands with the white-coated man who approached. "Let me introduce you to Martha's great-niece. Adrianna, this is our chef for the evening, John Thornburg."

"Chase has been singing your praises." She smiled and took Thornburg's offered hand. "It sounds like I'm in for a treat."

"We'll try not to disappoint you." The chef sent her attorney a pointed look, then pulled out a chair and joined them. "What do you think of our offerings?"

"To be honest, I was enjoying the view and the sunset so much that I haven't made a selection," Adrianna apologized. "Would it be too much of an imposition for you to simply provide us with a tasting menu?"

"No trouble at all." John's face lit up with pleasure.

"With one codicil," Chase added a hint of legal terminology to the conversation. "Whatever you choose to offer us, Adrianna deserves to enjoy a cup of your cream of crab soup."

"Yes." She laughed. "I'm afraid I would have to insist on that, too."

"Your wish is my command, mademoiselle." Their chef smiled, then stood and slid the chair he had utilized back into place. "And the wines?"

"You choose this evening," Chase said as he handed him their menus.

"I'll check back with you at the end of the meal to get your feedback," John promised and, sending Adrianna a brief nod and a smile, returned to his kitchen.

"He's very elegant for a chef, isn't he?" Adrianna commented once they were alone. "I often think of chefs as being more solidly built with bad tempers that require them to throw china and give their underlings nightmares."

Chase laughed. "Maybe those are only the American ones. Remember, John received his training in Europe." Then his face sobered. "So what were you thinking about before he joined us?"

For a moment, Adrianna busied herself spreading her napkin across her lap, but then met his gaze. "I was thinking about the enormous responsibility it all brings." She made a dismissing gesture with her right hand. "Not the royalty thing, you understand, I don't really accept that. A generation or so ago maybe, but not now. It's all the people relying on me for their bread and butter – the shop owners whose leases I hold, the caretaker in Maine, Captain Reb's business and even this restaurant. They're all looking to me."

Again Chase was impressed. There was more of Martha in her great-niece than he had imagined. Certainly, she had dug deeper into her inheritance than he had thought if she had learned about the cabin in Maine.

"Miss Montgomery, Mr. Sheffield." The sommelier interrupted the attorney's thoughts, as he offered a buttery California chardonnay wrapped in a white napkin for examination. Once the wine was approved, he then opened and poured it into their waiting glasses with a flourish.

"Perfect," Chase pronounced, once he had taken a sip.

"Excellent." The sommelier beamed. "Enjoy your meal." He stepped back, allowing a waiter clad in black pants, a white shirt and black tie to place cups of creamy soup garnished with fresh parsley in front of them, followed by a basket of warm rolls and cornbread sticks tucked within a cloth napkin.

Left alone, silence reined over the table for a few minutes as both diners gave the soup its due.

"No wonder Montgomery's is a success," Adrianna said when her cup was empty. "You were right to recommend it."

"You were saying…" Chase nudged their conversation back on track as her gaze once again traveled to the marina lit with twinkling lights that lay beyond the window.

"The last couple of months have been rather up and down for me," Adrianna revealed, her face still turned slightly from him. "There was my great-aunt's death, which was followed by some setbacks in Seattle." She turned and faced him. "Now I find myself ensconced in Montgomery House with half a county looking to me for the survival of the world as they know it. On top of that, I feel like the challenge set before me somehow represents my last clear chance to make amends. Does that make any sense to you?"

"Yes, it does." Chase was struck by a sudden urge to take her hand in his and assure her that everything would be all right.

Silently, their waiter removed the remnants of their soup course and placed in front of each of them a small salad composed of frisée sprinkled with currants, pepitas and chopped boiled egg, surrounded by paper-thin slices of Granny Smith apple and red pear before Parmigiano-Reggiano cheese had been shaved lightly over all.

"This salad is almost too pretty to eat," Adrianna declared once they were again left alone, nonetheless picking up her fork.

"I, for one, am glad that we are forced to eat it, since neither of us wish to disappoint John," Chase stated and then gave a good impression of resolutely taking a bite.

"Delicious," Adrianna stated. "I can't wait to see what he sends out next."

"So, did Martha leave you with any instructions in her letter?" Chase once again veered their conversation away from the food, determined to satisfy his curiosity on at least this one matter.

At this, Adrianna's expression again sobered, giving him a pang of guilt for having shortened her pleasure.

"There was only one line of writing on the sheet of paper that was enclosed," she told him. "I had just been wondering about her refusal to help me with my educational expenses after the death of my parents when I opened it."

"So what was Martha's explanation for her actions?" He asked, intrigued, finding it hard to glance away from the large dark eyes before him, filled as they were with such a haunted expression.

"The answer is in the garden," she said.

CHAPTER XXVI

Adrianna became gradually aware of the world around her the next morning, choosing to remain snuggled beneath her covers a few minutes longer in order to review her dinner with Chase. In the end, they had not gone on to Patrick's Pub, but had lingered over Irish coffees instead and enjoyed watching the lighted boats passing by the outskirts of the marina.

"Please attend the early church service in the morning," her attorney had requested as they had sampled portions of various main course offerings in a leisurely fashion. "If you're agreeable, I'll pick you up around eleven, and we'll go boating. From the water, you can get a feel for the lay of the land, so to speak. Afterwards, we'll do a tour of the shops and boathouses, and you'll be able to meet most of the owners."

Childhood memories of boating with her great-aunt had immediately washed over her, and she had readily agreed, eager to see Captain's Point from the sea again. Would it be as it was in her memory? She wondered. So much remained the same, and yet so much had changed since she was a little girl - not the least of which, of course, was herself.

With a start, she realized how much different her view of the world was from a few weeks before. Then Brad and her career had been the co-mingled center of her life, filling her thoughts and her days. Now, she was the owner of a sizeable business venture, her responsibility to others her biggest concern. She hadn't even gotten around to investigating all the nooks and crannies of the house yet.

And Brad... For a moment in her mind, she saw his tanned face and deep blue eyes, laughing as she lifted a hand and brushed back a blond curl from his forehead before he enveloped her in his strong grip and kissed her with a need that had taken her breath away. And yet, if she was truthful with herself, the pain that had rocked her when she had first read his letter had now lessened.

Thank goodness she had taken the time to drive back from Seattle – time in which to sob out her pain and scream out her anger, time in which to take a step back and try to understand what had gone wrong, time to recognize that her desire and friendship for him had seemed like the love that it wasn't and had obscured who Brad really was. How wrong she had been!

And Chase… Yes, she might have been wrong about him, too, although she still found him hard to read.

Over a sampling of desserts, he had shared anecdotes about his childhood, often laughing at himself as she had noted a hint of pain in his eyes. How vulnerable he had seemed! Other times, though, he had lounged in his seat, his face a blank slate, only his eyes showing that she had his full attention, laughter often filling them.

As they had prepared to come home, he had slipped her shawl around her shoulders, and she had felt his fingers linger longer than they had needed to. But then, the moment had passed and they had walked slowly to the car, as he had shared a litany of memorable events that had been held under the Japanese lanterns at the end of the pier. Arriving back at Montgomery House, he had come around the SUV and opened her door, as always the gentleman.

"I'll wait until you've had time to reset the alarm." He had sent her alone to the big double doors, and part of her had wanted him to come with her.

Once inside, she had been greeted by Max, his wagging tail a welcome sight. The alarm set, she had waved from the small oval window and then watched as his SUV had disappeared along the drive. It wasn't until she had made it upstairs that she had realized they hadn't discussed her plans for Montgomery House and its surrounding properties.

Slipping from beneath the covers, she discovered both that Penny must have unlocked the suite and released Max to let him out and that she had slept much later than she usually did, her normally infallible internal alarm having let her down. Not looking forward to the entire congregation of her great-aunt's church watching her walk down the aisle to the enclosed

Montgomery pew like some kind of freak, she realized that she felt less guilt than relief.

Throwing open the drapes, she was greeted by a bright, sunny day, a light breeze tossing the branches of the trees that dotted the lawn. Unlatching two of the smaller panes, she let the fresh air in and breathed deeply as she worked her way through her morning Tai Chi routine.

Finished, she perched for a moment on the window seat, focusing on the gardens below. *The answer is in the garden*, her great-aunt's note to her had said, but so far, she hadn't a clue what the line meant. From her vantage point, she could see only the rose garden completely – some of the formal floral gardens and part of the kitchen garden visible beyond and to her far left.

Sliding into her slippers, she donned her light robe and headed up the small staircase to the sitting room where an additional window gave her a more complete view. Even here, though, the back of the house obscured part of the garden's plan. Was it possible that an unimpeded view from the roof would reveal an oddity that would not immediately be obvious from ground level?

Quickly, she returned to her bedroom where she exchanged her slippers for a pair of trainers before heading back up and past the tower sitting room to the door at the treads' dead end, where she found the key to a serviceable lock suspended from a small hook. Opening the door, she stepped out onto a narrow walkway that sloped down to an even narrower, but level walk that led around the upper reaches of the house within a four foot high false façade that acted as a guardrail.

Recognizing that she was four stories above ground, she approached this façade with some care, but reassured by its width when she reached it, she grasped a drainage pipe conveniently placed to her right and leaned over to take in the gardens below her. Not wanting to lean too far out, she was still able to discern that her efforts had not been in vain.

While most of the rose and kitchen gardens, as well as some of the formal gardens were now too close to the back of the house to be safely seen, it was clear from this height that Jebediah had called upon his love of the sea for his garden's design. Projecting outward towards the ocean from the straight line formed by the vine-covered walkway and the path along the back of the kitchen and rose gardens was the clear outline of half of a ship's steering wheel – the hub being formed by a circular, hedge-rimmed seasonal bed that was laid out as a giant sundial. Was it possible that something was hidden beneath the tall obelisk in the middle?

Excited about her find, but realizing she was running short of time, Adrianna hurried to her room where she quickly showered, applied sunscreen and makeup, and dressed in neatly pressed jeans and a striped top with a nautical flair that would be appropriate for boating with Chase. Dashing downstairs she called over her shoulder to Penny, who was in the kitchen, "I'll be right back."

Hastily rummaging through the tool shed, she chose a small shovel and a pick, carrying both to the sundial garden, where she surveyed the layout. A circular bench surrounded the obelisk from which one could view any of the gardens or the sea, depending on the position of the seat taken. Slowly, she walked completely around, noting nothing out of the ordinary until she reached the ocean side.

Here a large stone had been placed between the bench and the obelisk, the initials MM and DS carved deeply into it. Completely disregarding her appearance, she managed with the help of the pick to shove the stone slightly to one side and then stuck her shovel into the dirt, immediately hearing it clink against metal. A few quick motions released a small box, which she bent and pulled free, her excitement at her find dampened by the hard tone beneath the words uttered by Chase Sheffield behind her.

"Playing in your overgrown sandbox instead of coming to church?" he asked.

CHAPTER XXVII

Startled, Adrianna dropped the box and twirled around, immediately filled with a sense of how ridiculous she had made herself look.

"You scared me half to death!" She turned and retrieved her find, which had struck the large stone with the carved initials and now lay face down in the dirt.

Picking up the box, she discovered a wide-mouthed, rectangular bottle lying beneath it. A small chip had been nicked from the side of the initialed stone, but the initials themselves were undisturbed and she thought the freshly exposed rock would soon weather.

"I'm hoping this may be the clue in the garden that my great-aunt meant in her note," Adrianna explained and took a seat on the stone bench that lay between them, setting the box down and indicating he should take the place on the other side of it.

What in the world was the girl up to now, Chase wondered as he obliged. He couldn't remember ever knowing anyone so contradictory. One minute he was bailing her out of a fix into which she should never have gotten herself, and the next minute she was sitting next to him at Montgomery's - a picture of sophistication, sharing insights that he had admired.

"What is it?" He picked up and examined the box that looked like it might have at one time been used to hold fishing lures, two tiny faded feathers still adhering to the inside of the lid.

"That's just a metal box," Adrianna said, her attention focused on unscrewing the rusty metal lid from the thick glass of the bottle.

"Looks like either an old medicine or liquor bottle." Chase held out his hand. "Want me to try?"

"Please. There's obviously something inside." She handed her prize over. "I'm sorry about church this morning. I had every intention of being there, but I overslept, which is unusual for me. I'll set an alarm from now on."

"That would be best," her attorney responded, his face impassive as he relaxed his grip on the bottle. "I'm afraid to twist any harder for fear that the glass will break in my hand. Otis probably has something amongst his tools that would let us cut the glass and then crack it off cleanly."

"Do we have time now?" Adrianna held his gaze for a moment before he glanced at his watch.

"If we hurry, because you're going to have to change out of those before we meet the others at the boat." He indicated her jeans that were now sprinkled here and there below the knee with bits of wet dirt.

"I didn't realize it was a party," she said as she turned away from him, swung her legs over the bench and stood. "Well, come on! This may be important, but take note of the initials carved on the stone there first." She pointed towards the base of the obelisk and then strode purposefully towards the carriage house, carrying the shovel, pick and box with her, forcing her attorney to jog after her to catch up.

"How did you discover the box?" he asked a moment later.

"It dawned on me this morning that the garden might be laid out in some sort of plan that wasn't obvious at ground level. The tower windows only gave me a partial view, so I went out on the roof…"

"You went out on the roof?" Chase grabbed her arm and brought her to a halt. "By yourself? Are you crazy? That roof is in terrible shape."

"You don't have to shout at me, Mr. Sheffield." Adrianna shook herself loose, anger flashing from her dark eyes. "I'm well aware of that, no thanks to you, and if I had been sliding around on loose slabs of slate, your anger would be at least somewhat understandable. The fact is that the door at the top of the tower opens onto a narrow granite walkway that enabled me to look over the edge of the parapet…"

The attorney found it difficult to keep his voice lowered. "You leaned over a four-story high parapet?"

"I held onto a very stable drainage pipe, stood next to a thick, chest-high granite wall and looked down." Adrianna, in turn, found it hard not to grit her teeth. "I discovered that, projecting outward towards the ocean from this walkway, the gardens are planted within a clear outline of half of a ship's steering wheel – the hub being formed by the sundial bed. This, of course, made me wonder whether or not something might have been buried beneath the obelisk."

"Of course." Chase rolled his eyes, but then held the door to Otis's workroom open for her.

"Grabbing these," she said, indicating the shovel and pick, which she set aside. "I then hurried to the obelisk, where I found the initials carved on the stone. I used the pick to shove the rock to one side, and as soon as I stuck my shovel in the dirt, I hit the box."

"Well, I must say you have a knack for uncovering things," Chase said, thinking to himself that the woman certainly didn't lack for either industry or ingenuity. Then he chose a large three-sided file from several arranged on a pegboard and donned a pair of safety glasses. "Now stand away."

Obediently, Adrianna stepped back and over a few paces, allowing herself a good view of his movements.

A few quick strokes of the file later, Chase wrapped the bottle in a red work rag and then picked up a tack hammer, giving the side of the metal lid a sharp tap. "I think that did it," he said, unwrapping the rag from the bottle that now lay separated from its lid."

"Wonderful!" Adrianna hurried forward. "I knew you could do it!"

"Careful." He held her outstretched hand away, feeling inordinately pleased by her faith in him. "Let's see if I can shake whatever this is out."

"The initials MM and DS," Adrianna said. "Martha Montgomery and...?"

"Probably Daniel Sheffield, my great-uncle." Chase shook a small, oil cloth wrapped packet onto the worktable. "Let's see what all the excitement is about." Pulling out his pocket knife, he carefully slit open the aged fabric, revealing a small leather eyeglass case that opened easily.

A folded scrap of paper fell out, leaving two locks of hair – one dark and one blonde – intertwined against what had once been soft velvet. Gently unfolding the note, Adrianna read, "Placed beneath the sundial obelisk in honor of our betrothal – Martha Montgomery and Daniel Sheffield – May 25, 1952."

Then she looked up, her dark eyes awash with unshed tears. "Why that's sixty years ago today," she said, her voice soft with emotion.

And at that moment, Chase knew he had never seen a face that had looked any lovelier.

CHAPTER XXVIII

Back at the house, Adrianna left Chase to show Penny and Otis their find and hurried upstairs. Here she exchanged her jeans and trainers for navy blue linen pants and espadrilles that she felt would be more appropriate for the type of party he had described as they had walked back. In vain she brushed her dark waves in an attempt to control them, finally threading a thin red scarf through her locks in such a way that would at least keep them from her face in the wind that would almost certainly accompany their expedition.

"Well, what do you think?" She paused before young Jebediah's portrait before allowing Max to escort her downstairs. "Will I do?"

Taking his smile as one of approval, she sent him a quick salute. Voices from below told her that Chase and the Plunks were passing time in the foyer, and she forced herself to move gracefully along the walkway and down the stairs, eager to attend a party and perhaps make some new friends.

"Not too bad." Chase glanced from her to the grandfather clock and back, having noted her presence. "We should make it just fine."

"Have a great time!" Otis threw open the door, both Plunks waiting to wave them on their way once outside.

As Chase headed his SUV along the drive, though, Adrianna felt a wave of disappointment wash over her. As sweet and romantic as the locks of hair and message had been, they still had brought her no closer to understanding her great-aunt's note.

"Tell me about Daniel," she requested. "What happened to him?"

"He was killed while on a reconnaissance mission near the 38th parallel, shortly before he was due to return home."

"How sad," Adrianna said.

"And senseless." Chase turned the SUV onto the road that would take them to the marina. "According to my grandfather, Daniel was the brains in our family, and there was no reason why he should've gone. The Korean War was already winding down by that point."

"Perhaps he felt it was his duty."

"Perhaps."

"And my great-aunt never married," Adrianna pointed out. "She must have loved him very much."

"Quite possibly." Chase kept his eyes on the road, his face devoid of expression. "She cried when I gave her his Purple Heart after my mother died, which frankly surprised me. Martha was a strong woman and used to hiding her emotions, but tears streamed down her cheeks when she opened the box that contained it. If I had known how upset she was going to be, I probably wouldn't have offered it to her."

"Oh, no!" Adrianna turned in her seat to face him. "You mustn't think that. It was probably better that she let her grief out. Think how long she had held it in."

Their destination in view, Chase slowed their vehicle for the turn into the marina lot, this time driving towards the opposite end of the boardwalk from where they had parked the previous evening.

"You should have Daniel's medal back now." Adrianna noted how full the lot had already become. "I'll see if Penny knows where it is. After all, it's a family piece."

Merely shaking his head in acceptance, Chase swung the SUV into yet another prime spot that was again clearly marked as reserved for the Montgomery family.

"So what type of boat do you have?" she asked once they had disembarked.

"I own a sailboat, but we're taking your boat out today."

"Not *Martha's Joy*?" Adrianna asked as they strolled towards one of the larger boathouses, her heart quickening.

"In person," Chase acknowledged. "One of Martha's final acts was to take a last boat ride."

"I can believe it. I remember how much she enjoyed taking a party out in it when I used to visit."

"It's been overhauled a few times over the years," Chase acknowledged, "but I think you'll find the interior as beautiful as you probably remember it."

Approaching the boathouse that carried a plaque stating it belonged to the Montgomery family, Adrianna quickly became aware of the hustle and bustle of activity as a bevy of waiters worked to load food and liquor onto the yacht.

"Did we get a bit carried away?" she asked, raising an eyebrow in her attorney's direction.

"Sometimes, it's worth making a statement." His face remained passive, even as a flicker of amusement passed through his blue eyes. "Believe me, Martha would've agreed. Everyone invited today will be looking you over, wanting to see for themselves how things are going to be going forward."

"Well, then, let's try not to disappoint them." Adrianna followed him up the gangplank, onto the main deck and into the lounge of the cabin in which trays of hors d'oeuvres were being passed amongst a small group of guests by waiters wearing standard Montgomery's attire and Mimosas and Bloody Mary's stood arranged at a small bar.

"Adrianna!" Larry Chesterton stepped forward. "Which will it be – yellow or red?"

"Yellow," Jim Laidlaw answered for her. "It'll set off the primary colors in her outfit."

"A Mimosa would be lovely," Adrianna accepted graciously.

"I'd like you to meet my new law partner." Chase introduced her to the woman with whom she had seen him entering a restaurant in Captain's Point. "Adrianna, this is Susan Chesterton."

"She's my cousin, but don't let that set you against her." Larry held out the requested Mimosa.

"It's nice to meet you," Susan sent her a dazzling smile.

"You, too." Adrianna took a sip of her drink, giving herself a chance to appreciate Susan's well-cut pants and blouse outfit, delicate gold dangle earrings and thick blonde hair swept into an almost, but not quite severe French twist. A woman to be reckoned with, she thought. "Am I to understand that you are now filling the vacancy left by the passing of Augustus Chesterton?"

Everyone expected now being on board, the Captain chose this moment to start the engines, which Susan took as a signal, slipping her arm through Adrianna's.

"Let's go out onto the front deck, shall we?" The graceful attorney drew her firm's most important client along, even as she let out a chuckle. "As for my filling my great-uncle's shoes, I'm not sure that's even possible."

Preferring to be in the open air as well, Adrianna allowed herself to be commandeered, noting that most of the other guests remained below. Once on deck, the sea-scented breeze lifted her dark hair from her neck, filling her with a sense of anticipation and freedom.

"When I was a little girl, I used to love coming out with Great-aunt Martha on this boat," she shared, as she joined Susan and leaned against the railing along the bow, glad she had remembered at the last moment to bring a pair of sunglasses.

"I've always been drawn to the sea, too." Susan's focus remained on the view ahead. "It's one of the reasons I accepted Chase's offer and brought my son, Daniel, back here after my divorce."

"So you grew up here as well?" Adrianna turned and studied the attorney's classic profile, noting the same control of emotions she was used to with Chase Sheffield and wondering if it was no more than a mask they had both been taught to assume in law school or if it reflected deeper reserves.

"Yes." Susan laughed. "I used to drive Chase, Larry and Jim Laidlaw crazy, following them around and generally getting in their way, and then, of course, Chase and I dated on and off during high school."

Once again, Adrianna was surprised by a sharp pang of jealousy. What had caused Chase to relinquish his childhood sweetheart, or had it been the other way around?

"So what about you?" Susan turned slightly, the boat now having reached the open water. "How do you like Captain's Point?"

"Very much!" Adrianna was glad she could say so with enthusiasm. "I have wonderful childhood memories of visits here, although there's been a lot of growth in the intervening years. And, of course, my great-aunt has left me quite a challenge."

"So I understand." Susan's eyes narrowed behind her sunglasses. "What are your plans, or have you had time to give them much thought?"

"I haven't had much time to do anything else." Adrianna sent the attorney a wry smile. "I can't tell you how many hours I've spent with your cousin and Otis Plunk going over facts and figures. As far as I can tell, there's no alternative but for Montgomery House and the surrounding properties to become as self-sufficient as the farm's always been."

"From what I know of the situation, I would agree." Susan indicated they should both take a seat on the benches that lined the sides of the boat. "How do you intend to achieve your goal?"

"Very differently from anything my great-aunt would've envisioned." Adrianna took another sip of her drink, as she considered how drawn she was to the graceful attorney despite her initial reaction. "I've established a master plan that Larry, Otis and I all agree is viable. Now, it's a matter of implementation." Adrianna proceeded to present an overview of her plans, gratified by Susan's intent interest.

"Ah, there you are!" A shadow fell over them as Chase approached. A middle-aged man, whose broad chest had long ago sunk to his middle, followed a close second. "Adrianna, let me introduce Captain Reb to you."

"It's so nice to meet you!" Adrianna sent the skipper a smile as she stood. "Was it you who did such a great job of steering us beyond the marina?"

"It's easy to steer a lovely old lady like this one," the captain said. "But still, it's nice that you noticed."

"So what have you two ladies been talking about?" Chase shifted his gaze from Adrianna to his partner.

"We've been discussing the future of Montgomery properties." Adrianna drew his attention back to her, suddenly feeling very uncomfortable.

"Indeed." Chase's eyes narrowed. "I, too, am anxious to hear your plans."

CHAPTER XXIX

"She's planning to do what?" Chase rose from the bench where he had been sitting next to his law partner and began pacing the deck back and forth in front of her. "Martha Montgomery is turning over in her grave."

Captain Reb had stolen Adrianna from them to be introduced to the marina shop owners who were still grazing through the hors d'oeuvres in the cabin, and Susan had felt it in her best interest to share his client's plans with Chase before he heard them from elsewhere. Judging from his initial reaction, she now deemed herself to have made the right decision.

"Okay." He dropped down beside her again on the bench. "What are your thoughts about it?"

"Frankly, I think her ideas run along similar lines to what I would do, if the opportunity presented itself." She glanced anxiously at his profile, afraid she might have overstepped her bounds. "And I'll say this for her, Adrianna exhibits the same guts the Montgomery family have always had."

With a brief motion of his hand, Chase waved his partner's recommendation away, his face once again a blank slate. "Guts are fine when they're coupled with good sense."

"The girl's done her homework," Susan pointed out. "She's spent hours with both Larry and Otis – drawing up plans, getting estimates and developing cost analyses. The cash to complete the first priority work is already available, and she has organized a five-tier plan that impressed me."

"You'll soon be President of the Adrianna Montgomery Fan Club." Her law partner rolled his eyes. "Still, it sounds like she hasn't started off half-cocked."

"Far from it. She's approached the whole matter in exactly the same way that I envision you would have."

"I'll take that as a compliment." He sent her a wry smile, and Susan was glad to see a familiar twinkle reside for a moment in his eyes. "I apologize for my outburst, but you know how I feel," he continued. "Martha Montgomery was the firm's client for many years, and my role as her administrator is to make sure that her wishes are met. The fact is I've underestimated my enemy, and that could prove fatal for Martha's intentions."

"The way I see it, Montgomery House and its surrounding properties leaving the family would have been the last thing Martha would've wanted," Susan stated. "Do you really view her great-niece as your enemy?"

"No, you're right. Enemy is too strong a word. I look upon Adrianna more as an adversary." He relaxed against the railing and took a deep breath of sea air. "I sometimes wonder what Martha really did want. She refused to secure Adrianna's education, then ignored her except for reports from private investigators for several more years. Even at the end, Martha didn't want her called to her bedside, and then she left her great-niece a mess without having given her either the benefit of her considerable experience or any direct instructions. Part of me is glad to learn that Adrianna hasn't put all of her efforts into rescuing abused animals and digging up Montgomery House grounds in search of a clue that is supposedly buried somewhere in the gardens and may or may not explain Martha's strange behavior."

"Has Adrianna dug up anything so far?"

"Oh, several things." Again the twinkle appeared in his eyes. "She's uncovered everything from a 1957 Mickey Mantle baseball card to intertwined locks of hair clipped from the heads of Martha Montgomery and Daniel Sheffield on the occasion of their betrothal. The Smithsonian should be contacting her shortly."

"Keep in mind that Adrianna could've refused to come here at all," Susan reminded him.

"She would've been a fool if she had," Chase made his position clear. "At the very least, she'll come out of this with a year's worth of high-level salary, an expansion of her resume and a quarter of a million dollars – not a bad haul for taking up residence in a grand old home that's fully staffed and having the funds available with which to purchase all the clothes and jewelry that she wants."

"Jealous?"

"You bet I am!" He threw back his head and laughed. "But thanks for putting me in my place, and don't get me wrong." His expression sobered. "I would like to see Adrianna succeed as much as anyone. There have been Montgomerys at Montgomery House for as long as there have been Sheffields at Sheffield Place and Chestertons at Chesterton Cove, and I'm not desperate for that to change."

"So you're okay with her plans?"

"Let's say I'm resigned to them." Chase stood and looked down at her. "As long as the estate's funds are being put into improving the property as administrator I can't complain. The jury is still out, though, on whether Adrianna's plans or any plans for that matter will work sufficiently well to keep Montgomery House off the auction block."

"Let's go see what your problem child is up to." Susan rose and met his gaze, a twinkle now visible in her own eyes.

With the ease of long acquaintance, Chase threw an arm around her and gave her a squeeze. "I'm glad you agreed to come back and keep me on the straight and narrow." He laughed, failing to see the blush that had entered her cheeks.

"That's easy enough to do," she pointed out, adroitly removing herself from his hold. "Don't forget, I've had plenty of experience." Slipping her hand through the crook of his arm, she guided him towards the cabin's door. "You know, it wouldn't hurt for you to do what you can to assist Adrianna," she suggested as they made their way across the deck.

"You're probably right again," he agreed, holding the cabin door open for her.

"There you are!" John Thornburg hurried forward as the two of them reentered the main room. "I was just going to suggest that everyone take a seat. Chase, I've planned on your being at the head and, Susan, you're at the foot." The chef indicated the dining table that ran along the port side windows. "We'll be looking out to sea through most of the main course, and then the shoreline will come into view once the second mate has made the big turn."

"Sounds lovely," Adrianna approved as she joined them. "Where would you like me to be, or are there name cards?"

"Why don't you sit on Chase's right?" Susan suggested. "That way you'll have a great view, and you can ask him to name or explain anything you don't remember from your previous boating excursions."

"Everyone!" John lifted his voice to be heard over the roomful of conversation and raised his right hand to further command the room's attention. "If you all will be seated, my staff will begin serving. The main entrée is Surf and Turf, but if you would prefer vegetarian or Turf only, your waiter can arrange it."

Chase held out her chair, and Adrianna took her recommended seat, glad for at least a brief respite from meeting new people. The good news was that everyone seemed pleased to meet her – welcoming and pleasant. The bad news was that it might only be in deference to either her great-aunt's memory or the fact that she held their shops' leases.

Mentally, she made a note to ask Edwina to join her for lunch at Montgomery's as soon as possible. A little light shopping afterwards would allow a good opportunity for some more casual conversation on an individual basis with the owners along the boardwalk.

"Penny for your thoughts." Chase's words brought her back to the present. "You look a bit worried."

"Not worried, really." Adrianna forced a small smile in his direction, glad for the moment to have him beside her. "Just wondering how I'll ever keep the names and businesses of everyone that I've met today straight, that's all." She paused and allowed the waiter to place a cup of John Thornburg's signature cream of crab soup in front of each of them, then continued. "Somehow it seems very important that I should."

CHAPTER XXX

Despite its failing her on Sunday, Adrianna's internal alarm returned to normal on Monday, and she awakened to a bright sunny day. Opting for a quick shower, she paused afterwards only long enough to apply sunscreen and the bare minimum of makeup. Slipping into a pair of white shorts, a T-shirt and her trainers, she decided that a colorful tennis visor, sunglasses and her seemingly ever present notebook would complete what she felt to be an appropriate outfit for fulfilling her role as co-general contractor.

"What do you think?" she asked Jebediah's portrait as she snapped on Max's leash. "Will I embarrass Otis?"

Once again accepting her forebearer's smile as approval, she hurried downstairs, locating Penny in the kitchen.

"Let me take Max out, while you eat your breakfast." The housekeeper took his leash from her employer's hand. "I'm so excited I can hardly stand it, and I might as well warn you that Otis is even worse. I thought he would never go to sleep last night."

"He isn't worried about what we've lined up is he?" Adrianna felt a stab of anxiety.

"Not at all," her housekeeper assured her. "It's that he's been waiting to do so much of it for so long. He kept going over and over all of the arrangements you've made, until I finally told him that if he didn't roll over and be quiet, I'd make him sleep on the sofa."

"I had trouble going to sleep myself," Adrianna admitted. "Between thinking of stuff I should've said during dinner on the boat and wondering if we're doing the right thing, my mind wouldn't settle."

"I'm sure everyone enjoyed the party," Penny stated. "After all, who wouldn't have? And as for your plans for Montgomery

House and the property, somewhere Martha is quite proud of you."

"Do you really think so?" Adrianna heard an eager tone running beneath her words.

"Very sure." Her housekeeper gave her a quick hug. "Martha would've appreciated the courage it's taken for you to take such a big step. The fact is she let the side down at the end - no surprise given her age. Still, she left Otis and you a mess. Now, enjoy your breakfast and get out there. Otis and Jeff have already disconnected the washer and dryer."

Obediently, Adrianna headed into the breakfast room where she found a small yogurt, a croissant and a carafe of coffee, cream and sugar on a tray waiting for her, along with a copy of the local newspaper. Ignoring the paper, she made quick work of the yogurt, but then took time to enjoy the croissant and coffee as she centered her thoughts on the day ahead.

"The roofers are here," Penny announced from the doorway, Max having preceded her into the room, panting excitedly. "Do you think he would settle down if I closed him in the tower suite?" She nodded towards the dog.

"It would probably be best all around." Adrianna gathered her dishes and carried them to the sink, followed by her housekeeper with the tray. "Wish me luck!" She tried not to think about how nervous she felt as she took a deep breath.

"I'm going to say it again." Penny met her gaze. "Martha would've been real proud of you."

Feeling the prick of tears in her eyes, Adrianna turned and hurried outside where she strode quickly to the carriage house. Here she discovered the roofers, already unloading supplies into one of the unfinished bays under the close supervision of Nip.

"Glad to see that you're getting an early start," she greeted a heavyset man named Norman, with whom she had dealt during the planning stages. "The weather has blessed us."

"Not too bad," the roofer agreed. "We've got a good many days of hard work ahead of us, though."

"Let Otis or me know if you need anything." She turned and headed towards the parked truck beside which Jeff and her property manager were watching as still-boxed appliances were being unloaded.

"That one's for the main house." Otis pointed towards the new stove that was first to make an appearance. "The higher end models all go there."

"I see things have gotten off to a good start." Adrianna joined them, then addressed Jeff. "We'll count on you to keep an eye on the heating and air folks as well as the plumbers. If they have any real questions, beyond where a junction box is or how to find a restroom, direct them to one of us."

"Looks like the plumber's arriving now." Jeff nodded in the direction of the main gates. "It's going to be a fun day."

"It's going to be a fun summer," Otis corrected him with a grin, while at the same time directing that a new dishwasher was also to be installed in the main house.

"That's the key," Adrianna pointed out. "Problems are sure to come up, and things are bound to go wrong. Let's just take them one at a time, and in the end, we'll be okay."

"Heating and air are here," Jeff announced as the plumber's van came to a halt at the entrance to the second unfinished bay.

"Things are rolling now." Otis rubbed his hands together as he rocked back and forth on his heels.

"Someone else just came through the gates." Jeff's eyes narrowed.

"Who else are we expecting this morning?" Adrianna thumbed rapidly to the day's page in her notebook. "Oh, the electrician."

Otis shaded his eyes from the sun. "That's only Chase Sheffield." He slapped Jeff on the back. "Don't get us all in a stew."

Adrianna glanced up. "Already? I was hoping he would give us a couple of days in which to make headway."

"I'd better see if I can help those guys get started." Jeff took off towards the third unfinished bay where the heating and air crew had begun to unload an overstuffed van.

"Don't worry about Chase," Otis said under his breath, once he and Adrianna were alone. "He isn't likely to interfere, and he'll probably only stay a minute or two anyway."

But as the attorney disembarked, dressed in jeans and a golf shirt, they both realized that the property manager might well have been wrong.

"Good morning," Adrianna greeted the newcomer with a smile. "Have you already come to check on us?"

"On the contrary," Chase corrected, his blue eyes twinkling. "I've come to lend any assistance that I can."

And that, Adrianna thought, might be the first problem they would face in their day.

CHAPTER XXXI

Chase surprised Adrianna, though, by turning to Otis and volunteering his services in an unexpected area.

"I thought I could oversee the roof repairs today," he addressed her property manager. "After all, you're the one who taught me the ins and outs of slate roofing when I had to deal with them unexpectedly at Sheffield Place the year my mother was so ill. I've been hoping for an opportunity ever since to return the favor."

"I'm not going to say that won't be a welcome relief," Otis accepted his offer. "Adrianna can sort this lot out." He nodded at the appliance truck. "And that will allow me to keep an eye on the electricians and plumbers who will be concentrated at the dependency and the cottage with Jeff lending a hand wherever he's needed."

Everyone satisfied with this arrangement, the two men left to join the roofing crew and show them the best ways to reach the various areas that needed attention. A few minutes later, though, Adrianna glanced from her notebook and saw that they were returning, Penny now added to their number.

"Chase has had a wonderful idea!" The housekeeper was unable to control her excitement, and Adrianna was surprised to see a shy smile on her attorney's face. "He thinks we should install a skylight over the island in the kitchen."

"If we're ever going to consider such an improvement, now is the time," Otis put in his two cents worth.

"We found that it really brightened the kitchen at Sheffield Place when we installed one," Chase spoke up. "And since you were scheduled to have work done in that area anyway, Norman says you may experience a small cost savings. He can have a remote controlled skylight delivered within an hour."

"Penny's right then," Adrianna agreed as she sent her attorney a smile. "You've had a wonderful idea. Let's do it."

"I was looking forward to all the new appliances, but this is the icing on the cake." Her housekeeper gave her a hug and then hurried off to clear the island so the workmen could cover it with plywood as protection below.

The men dispersed to their respective areas of responsibility, and Adrianna soon had the appliances sorted out – those for the main house now being installed under Penny's competent supervision, while the rest had been stored. As she was wondering what she should check on next, her phone vibrated with a text message from Otis in which he asked if she could please come to the dependency.

Hurrying to join him, she found him deep in discussion with Chuck Rolfe, the plumber.

"I'm afraid we have some bad news," Otis greeted her. "Apparently, the stack isn't in the best of conditions."

"What are we looking at?" Adrianna asked.

"It would be my recommendation that we replace it and all the pipes coming off it." Chuck repositioned the red baseball cap he was wearing. "It'll cost you a pretty penny, though."

Adrianna was aware of activity behind her as others joined them.

"Frankly, ma'am, I think you'd be better served if you let me completely rewire the place while we're about it as well," the soft-spoken electrician stepped forward. "It would be a shame to do all this work and then have to come behind a couple of years later and redo it."

"I agree." Chase's voice surprised her, and Adrianna whirled around. "In the long run, the estate will save money if you do everything right the first time. Treat it as a complete gut, and secure your rental income for as long as you can without worrying about repairs."

Suddenly, it seemed to her that there was no one in the room, but the two of them. "You understand that this is a five-tier plan?" she asked.

"Yes, but you can demand a slightly higher rent for a completely refurbished domicile with touches here and there of high cost finishes," he explained his position. "I say go for it. In for a penny, in for a pound as Martha always said, and it will draw a higher class of tenant as well. It's worth the risk."

"Thank you." She sent him a shy smile. "It's what Otis and I had wanted to do all along, but we weren't sure you would agree. We should've asked you."

"Yes, you should have," he said, a kind look in his eyes.

"Jeff, you and I will finish off the rest of the demolition needed here in the dependency first," Otis said. "And then, we'll move on to the cottage. Thank goodness, we ordered the largest trash container."

"My crew can get started on the stack right away," Chuck stated. "I'll have you an updated estimate in a few minutes."

"Same here." The electrician headed for the back steps with his tablet as Otis and Jeff began work on removing some more of the plaster walls.

"I came to let you know that things are going well on the roof." Chase guided her onto the dependency's front walk, where they could converse in reasonable quiet as they sauntered slowly towards the main house. "I'm afraid I may have given you a wrong impression," he said as they entered the cool shadows of the vine-covered walk, accompanied by Nip.

"In what way?" Adrianna asked, surprised by the gentleness of his tone.

"I didn't know what to expect when you first returned to Captain's Point." He paused and took her hand, pulling her gently back into the end of the shaded tunnel. "You've put a lot of time and effort into your plans for making Montgomery House and its surrounding properties self-sufficient, but for some reason, you didn't feel comfortable advising me of them."

"I..." She fumbled for a reasonable explanation.

"That was my fault," he interrupted her. "I now see that I overstressed my powers under Martha's will, while at the same time failing to advise you that as our firm's new client, we would always be there to help you in any way possible. I'm walking a fine line, but it isn't for the first time, I can assure you. Besides, I think you're on the right track. In fact, Susan and I are both impressed with the way you've approached the situation in which you now find yourself."

At the sound of Susan's name, Adrianna felt a sharp pang of unwanted jealousy, for a moment not noticing that her attorney had stopped talking, even as she became aware of the scent of his aftershave blending with that of the roses. Suddenly recognizing his intent silence, she raised her face towards his.

"I will keep you informed from now on," she promised, and his gaze softened.

"There you are!" Norman hurried up to them as Chase released his hold on her hand, and they stepped into the sunlight. "I need you to look at a situation with one of the gutters that we've uncovered."

CHAPTER XXXII

As the next morning had progressed, it had become apparent that her attorney would not be joining them again, and Adrianna had been surprised by the strength of her disappointment. Gone had been his haughty gaze the day before, and she now realized that she had in him an ally, if not a friend.

A small problem here, a decision to be made there, had soon won her attention, and the days had passed quickly, until she had realized that Wednesday evening was upon her. Remembering she had intended to lunch with Edwina at Montgomery's, she had immediately arranged to meet her friend there at noon on Friday.

This day now arrived, she again walked along the vine-covered path towards the dependency - Nip walking beside her - eager to review with Otis the week's progress before dressing for lunch.

Finding her property manager for once in his office, she plopped into his visitor's chair. "I thought we'd pause for a moment and review our progress," she said.

"Things have gone well, I think." Otis relaxed in his chair. "You're bound to have unexpected surprises when you're working with older buildings, but you had budgeted for those. The appliances have all been installed in the main house as well as the skylight, and the roof and gutter repairs are well under way."

"Chase was right about that skylight," Adrianna pointed out. "It's made a huge difference in the kitchen."

"Penny's in Hog Heaven, that's for sure," her property manager agreed, "and I had no idea someone could have that much fun working around a hot stove."

"We're down to one more area of slate and the rest of the copper work on the roof, right?" Adrianna flipped to another page in her notebook and checked off an item.

"That's right," Otis agreed. "They should be finished by the end of next week, even with this being Memorial Day weekend."

"You've done wonders with the dependency and the cottage." She sent him a smile. "I can't believe how quickly the drywall went in."

"We'll install the kitchen and bathroom cabinets today," her property manager filled her in. "Both of them should be ready to show and rent no later than mid-June, which is a lot accomplished in a very short time."

"Speaking of rent, I talked with another realtor, and she thought the first one had underestimated what we could charge." Adrianna named new numbers that she had found hard to believe. "These figures are comparable to what I would've expected in Seattle. Do you think they're in line? They seem high to me."

"I think we should at least try for them." Otis rested his arms on his desk. "Both buildings have top of the line finishes, and we've maintained a number of historic touches. Besides, there aren't that many high-end properties available in Captain's Point. Why not go for the gold?"

"I suppose we can always drop the price, if we don't garner the interest we expect," she agreed. "I'll be at the main house writing up sample ads if you need me. We can decide this afternoon, which one we'll use."

"Sounds like a plan," Otis said as both of them stood and walked into the sunlight. "You did a great job of organizing it all," he continued as they paused where their paths diverged. "Martha would be proud of you."

"Thanks, that means a lot to me." Impulsively, Adrianna kissed her property manager's cheek. "We make a great team, don't we? And we've had a lot of fun doing it."

"As well as having worked our tails off." Otis threw back his head and laughed.

"That's for sure." She grinned, massaging her sore right shoulder, a victim of all the painting she had accomplished during the past couple of days. "Remember now, I'm meeting

Edwina for lunch at Montgomery's, but you can reach me on my cell if you need me," she reminded him and then headed back to the main house.

A few hours later found her transformed. Wearing a light summer dress in shades of pale rose and green that set off her dark waves, she disembarked from her car that she had parked in the reserved spot as expected, only to hear her name called.

"Adrianna!" Susan joined her as they walked around the building that housed Montgomery's. "What brings you out? According to my law partner, you should be knee deep in paint right about now."

"No, that was yesterday and the day before." Adrianna laughed as they entered the restaurant, where she was surprised to see Jim Laidlaw, dressed in a suit coat, open-necked shirt and creased jeans."

"Not too late for a lady," he addressed Susan, but sent Adrianna a wink, before he and the attorney were led away to a reserved table.

"Right this way, Miss Montgomery," the maitre d' directed her towards the elevator that led to the upper floor and the family table Penny had advised the restaurant staff would be needed.

Emerging from the elevator onto the second floor, Adrianna immediately glimpsed Larry Chesterton with a party of similarly suited men at a table for six that was placed by one of the large paned windows. Catching sight of her, the investment broker excused himself and came to her table, once again reminding her of Brad as he approached.

"I understand you're making great progress with your renovations," he greeted her.

"Otis and I were just reviewing the week, and things appear to be pretty much on schedule," she agreed. "I haven't worked physically this hard in years, and we've had some ups and downs. Still, overall, it's been fun."

"Keep me posted. We'll do lunch one day so you can bring me up to speed." He patted her shoulder and returned to his group.

Everyone, it seemed, had determined to lunch at Montgomery's this day – everyone, that was, except Chase, and again she felt disappointed. Below her on the boardwalk, pedestrians sauntered, obviously enjoying the lovely day and the sea breeze - some licking ice cream cones, others carrying shopping bags. Three sailing ships provided a pleasant view beyond the marina.

Adrianna sipped her water, taking advantage of the quiet moment to take stock. Otis had been right. Things weren't going half badly. Montgomery House was beginning to feel more and more like her home. Penny and Otis, Max and Nip provided welcomed companionship. Her renovation project was going well.

For a moment, Brad's face loomed in her mind, but she quickly pushed it aside, determined to enjoy her lunch and, indeed, her day.

"I'm sorry I'm late." Edwina's soft voice interrupted her thoughts as her friend was seated by the maitre d'.

"Enjoy your luncheon ladies." He offered a second menu to the older woman and left them to their meal.

"I've only been here a moment myself." Adrianna assured her guest. "Have you been to Montgomery's before?"

"No, but Ginny says it's 'The' place to go for a good meal in Captain's Point," Edwina stated, her blue eyes twinkling. "I'm to try the cream of crab soup."

"Definitely, I'll be joining you in a cup of that. How are Ginny and the baby?"

"The baby is already smiling," Edwina replied and then dropped her voice, "but it's probably only gas. Ginny is a wonderful mother." Then her face sobered. "Frankly, my dear, I was glad that you called."

"Is something wrong?" Adrianna asked, concerned.

"Not wrong exactly." Worry filled her friend's face. "The fact is I want your advice, and I may need your help."

CHAPTER XXXIII

Their waiter choosing the precise moment of Edwina's surprise announcement to arrive at their table for their drink order and to advise them of the day's specials, it was not until cups of cream of crab soup had been placed in front of them that Adrianna could relieve her curiosity.

"So what's troubling you?" she asked her guest.

"It's a compliment really to have been asked." Edwina dipped her spoon into her soup. "This is really delicious, you know."

"Yes," Adrianna agreed. "I'll never tire of it, but tell me, what have you been asked?"

"To move to Captain's Point." Edwina placed her spoon alongside her now empty cup. "Ginny and Jason have asked me if I would move here to be closer to them."

"That is a big decision." Adrianna felt unsure about her willingness or even her ability to advise the older woman.

"Ginny only asked me this morning," her luncheon guest explained as seafood salads were set in front of them and a basket of warm breads was added to the table setting. "In some ways, it makes perfect sense. I've been a widow for years now, and my friends seem to either be dying off or moving away. Jason's father is in the diplomatic corps, so they are often stationed overseas, while Jason can work from anywhere."

"This may be impertinent, but can you afford to do so?" Adrianna asked. "Long-distance moves are expensive." She took in the lovely diamond wedding set on her friend's left hand, her well-styled hair, her stylish dress and pearls.

"The simple answer is 'yes.'" Edwina sent her a shy smile. "My husband was a corporate attorney and left me well provided for. I sold our house two years ago, downsized and bought a condo, so that's already behind me. The question is should I subject Jason and Ginny to taking care of me in my later years."

"I see." Adrianna chose a cornbread stick from the bread basket and spread it with butter, allowing herself a moment to think. "It strikes me that you may be putting the cart before the horse, so to speak."

"In what way?" The older woman looked up from her salad, surprised.

"Driving back here from Seattle provided me with lots of thinking time," Adrianna explained. "One of the things I realized was that, for me, life is a series of chapters. Chapter One was my early years, then came the chapter that was filled by my parents, followed by my years at Stanford and UW. This year's chapter will be titled Captain's Point."

"I think I see where you're heading." Edwina pierced a large chunk of lobster with her fork. "Right now I'm able to move, and the children want me here with them. In the future, when my son and his wife have retired and settled, I may want to reevaluate."

"Exactly."

"My dear, I can't tell you how much you have helped." Edwina patted Adrianna's hand. "It's so easy at my age to start believing that one's life is over, and it's been wonderful to feel needed by Jason and Ginny."

"Then don't deny yourself," Adrianna counseled. "You appear to be in good health, you're financially independent, and they need you. It sounds to me like you're moving here right now would be win/win for everyone."

"I'm going to do it!" Edwina's blue eyes twinkled. "I feel twenty year's younger just thinking about it. Now the only problem will be for me to find somewhere to live. Jason and Ginny have a lovely guest room, but long term I would want my own things around me."

"What kind of space do you need?"

"I would still want two bedrooms and a nice sized kitchen," the older woman stated. "That way, my son and his wife would always have somewhere to stay, if Jason and Ginny were to have another child."

"Are you thinking of buying or renting?" Adrianna asked. "I haven't noticed any condos since I've arrived, but that doesn't mean that there aren't any."

Edwina took a moment to consider, before answering. "I think I would rent first. From what the kids have told me, Captain's Point is growing, and if I'm going to move, I want to do so quickly. Once I'm settled in, I could get to know the area a little better, and perhaps purchase something later. Would you have time to look at some places with me?"

"Sure, but would you include the dependency at Montgomery House as a property you would consider?"

"Now why didn't I think of that?" The older woman's face lit up. "Living there would solve everything. I would feel safe, it's convenient, and needless to say, the neighbors and the grounds are both lovely! There wouldn't even be any stairs, which is something to consider at my age. When would it be ready for me to move in?"

"Otis was saying this morning that both the dependency and the cottage should be ready by mid-June," Adrianna said. "Right now, the walls have been primed, but not painted in the dependency. If you have time, we could run by there after lunch, and you could see if you think it will suit you. If so, once we've signed a lease, you could pick out your own paint colors."

"Now I am getting excited!" Edwina absentmindedly accepted a dessert menu from their waiter and then laughed, as she realized that her words could have been misconstrued. "I meant about my moving to Captain's Point," she explained to the puzzled waiter, who had been about to describe the homemade banana pudding that was the day's special.

"I'll have the crème brûlée." Adrianna handed back her menu. "And a cappuccino to celebrate."

"Make that two," Edwina agreed, wearing a bright smile as she turned towards her hostess. "Who knew when I woke up this morning that this would be such a lovely day?"

CHAPTER XXXIV

The two ladies having lingered over their cappuccinos, while Edwina shared a bevy of photos of the blossoming Lucy and described in detail her great-granddaughter's many virtues, it was mid-afternoon by the time they picked their way through the construction debris littering the large, airy main room of the dependency and entered the bright kitchen. Here they discovered the crew screwing on the last cabinet door.

Edwina clapped her hands with delight. "You've chosen cherry, and I love their clean, simple lines! I have oak in my condo, and every time I watch a design show on TV, I covet ones like these."

"The countertops will be dark granite," Adrianna advised, pleased with her friend's initial reaction to the two main rooms. "We're carrying the hardwood floors throughout, except for in the bathrooms. The powder room is here." She opened a door. "And the washer and dryer will be installed in here." She revealed a small laundry room. "I think this was the cold storage area when the dependency filled the role of the house's main kitchen, because of the perceived fire hazard."

"I've never lived in an historic property before." Excitement shone from Edwina's face. "You know, many years ago now, I was a history teacher. Is this the guest room?"

"Yes, and this is the master suite that includes an ensuite four-piece bathroom and a walk-in closet," Adrianna pointed out, thinking that if nothing else, she was practicing what she would say to prospective renters in the future.

"I can't imagine anything more to my liking." Edwina led them back to the main room. "The ambience, the convenience and the room sizes are all better than I had expected, and the price you quoted me earlier seems right in line. Would I be able to move in July 1st?"

"Certainly," Adrianna agreed. "I'll make an appointment for us to meet at Chase Sheffield's office and sign a lease early next week." She escorted the older woman back to her car, before returning to the main house by way of the vine-covered path.

"Hold on, please," Penny said into the wall phone as she entered the kitchen, then placed her hand over the receiver. "It's Larry Chesterton for you."

"I'll take it in the Captain's study." Adrianna hurried to the phone. "Hello," she said into the desk phone's receiver, noting the click as Penny hung up the extension.

"Larry Chesterton here. Glad I caught you. I meant what I said earlier today about wanting to hear what all you've accomplished. Chase says you've really been busy."

"Me and several crews of construction specialists." Adrianna laughed. "I can hardly take all the credit, but we're making good progress." She filled him in. "In fact, I've just rented the dependency beginning July 1st to the elderly woman I met on the plane when I flew here back in April."

"That's wonderful," Larry responded to her news. "I'm really proud of the way you've taken the bull by the horns. Keep me posted on how things are going, and by all means, let me know if there's anything I can do for you. No one understands more than Chase and I do the scope of the challenge that you're facing."

"Thanks, I'll remember that."

"Actually, I called to ask if you would be free to join us at Chesterton Cove for a clambake on Memorial Day, say around two o'clock. Nothing formal, you understand. Wear jeans and casual clothes."

"I'd love to come," Adrianna accepted the invitation with pleasure. "How nice of you to invite me! Can I bring anything?"

"Only yourself. Susan has everything well under control. Penny or Otis can give you directions, but you shouldn't have any trouble finding us. We're just the other side of Sheffield Place."

"I'll see you at two o'clock on Memorial Day then," Adrianna said her goodbyes and hung up the phone, which immediately rang again. "Hello?" she answered.

"Adrianna, is that you? Jim Laidlaw here."

"Hi, Jim. Are you calling to check up on Max?" She looked down at the rescue who was sitting by her chair, his face wearing an expression of interest at the sound of his name. "He's doing fine."

"He should be." The veterinarian laughed. "Penny and you are probably spoiling him rotten."

"Not rotten exactly, although he's leading a soft life," Adrianna acknowledged, wondering exactly why the vet had called if it wasn't about Max.

"I apologize for not honoring my promise to show you around sooner," Jim answered her unspoken question. "Things have been crazy around here, but I'm now in a position to get back into your good graces. Do you have any plans for next Saturday, because the annual sailboat regatta is scheduled that day, and I wondered if I could take you out on my boat to watch at least some of the races?"

"As a matter of fact, I'm free as a bird," Adrianna accepted her second invitation, "and a regatta sounds like fun. What time should I be ready?"

"Why don't I pick you up around eleven, and we'll have lunch at Chester's before we go out on the boat?" her date suggested.

"I haven't eaten at Chester's yet. You really will be fulfilling your promise by introducing me to what I understand is the best crab shack in the area."

"So I'm forgiven?"

"Absolutely!" She made a note of the date and time on a convenient pad. "I'll see you at eleven o'clock next Saturday then. I'll look forward to it."

Her goodbyes said, Adrianna hung up the phone and headed upstairs to change clothes with Max at her heels, her steps light on the treads. A clambake at Chesterton Cove and a regatta with Jim Laidlaw, and both of them sounded like fun!

Slipping out of her dress, she donned more comfortable jeans and a Stanford T-shirt, before plopping onto the window seat where Max joined her. Absentmindedly, she stroked his back, watching for a moment as two sailboats tacked a course northward.

How far away her condo in Seattle seemed! Edwina's freedom to pick up and move at the drop of a hat had made her realize how tied down she now was. Still, she thought with a pang, at the moment that might be a good thing.

True, she was feeling more and more at home here at Montgomery House, and things were certainly going forward with the property renovations as planned. She had even made some treasured discoveries in the gardens. Life, though, held no guarantees as her sudden layoff from work and breakup with Brad had clearly shown her. It was possible that she would give her great-aunt's challenge her best and still fail.

As her fingers stilled on Max's back, she let out a small sigh, no longer focused on the scene before her. There was no getting around it, her future ultimately lay in Chase Sheffield's hands.

CHAPTER XXXV

Adrianna had jumped out of bed each morning to help oversee the renovations and would have preferred a nice lazy lie-in on Sunday, but instead she tossed back the covers, unwittingly burying Max who promptly exchanged her bed for his own in front of the fireplace. There was no way she could miss services again at her great-aunt's church.

Throwing open the drapes, she discovered a gray, dismal day - whitecaps on the ocean beyond the grounds signifying the presence of wind. Clipping on Max's leash, she hurried him downstairs and out the back door where, feeling a fine mist, her spirits sank at the thought that it might be a bad hair day. Hopefully, she thought, the front that had brought with it the dark, hanging clouds would clear through before the clambake tomorrow. Max signaling he was done and ready to go in, she held the door open for him.

Even with the new skylight, the kitchen seemed dark as she prepared an espresso, relishing the aroma of coffee that soon filled the room. Balancing her mug and a muffin on a plate, she headed for the morning room, where she started an Enya CD, sat on the couch with her feet pulled beneath her and prepared to flip through a copy of *Forbes*.

Max immediately joined her, obviously interested in both conversation and a bite of her muffin – not necessarily in that order.

"You just ate your breakfast," Adrianna scolded, even as he curled into a ball between her knees and the back of the couch. "You'll be here alone for a while this morning while I go to church. I'm counting on you to behave."

Looking at her with an expression of reproach, Max responded with a sigh and closed his eyes.

"Attending the service doesn't bother me," she addressed the dog, the house seeming uncharacteristically large and lonely. "I've been in the habit of going to church all of my life, although sometimes it was a Buddhist temple when my parents and I were on site." She let out a chuckle, at which point Max partially opened one eye but, thinking better of it, soon closed it.

"It's that annoying Montgomery pew," she continued. "Even as a child, I didn't understand why we should be so separated and special, but there we were front and center. At least the Sheffield and Chesterton pews are at the front of the rows on the outsides of the two aisles. I'm glad that Penny and Otis are going with me."

As if in sympathy with her frustration, the storm broke outside and sheets of rain lashed the windows. Reaching over, she turned on the lamp on the side table, sending out a cozy glow that illuminated an oil painting on the wall across from the fireplace. One of several small works arranged in a group, she recognized it as an Impressionist school work done in oils. Depicting a garden scene, complete with a wood nymph fountain and a rose trellis, she was immediately drawn to it, never having been consciously aware of it before.

The answer is in the garden, her great-aunt's note had said.

"Let's see who it's by." She risked disturbing Max by getting up and, having used the opportunity to flip on another lamp, lifted the small painting from the wall.

Unable to make out the artist's signature that read more like a doctor's scrawl, Adrianna turned the painting over, where she discovered a white card taped to the back beneath the gallery's label.

Presented to my beautiful bride Sophia on the occasion of our marriage.

May our lives together be as rich and beautiful as a country garden.

Walter Montgomery

For a moment, Adrianna viewed the room through a watery gaze, but then wiped away her tears, replaced the painting on its hanger and turned, her glance settling on a seated portrait of Jebediah and his family that hung over the fireplace. "They loved each other so much," she said to her most memorable ancestor, his face in this portrait appropriately sober. "Why did they have to die?"

Returning to the sofa, she picked up her plate and mindlessly unwrapped the blueberry muffin before tearing off a bite and popping it into her mouth, not even aware of its homemade flavor as she chewed. Now alert, Max nuzzled her wrist with his cold nose as if to remind her of his willingness to remove the struggle from her of having to eat the muffin.

"Don't be silly." She gently pushed him away with her hand, recognizing she would have to get dressed for church soon.

Slowly, she replayed fond memories of her parents in her mind – a picnic in Provence, an alfresco dinner under the stars in Tuscany, a light meal of grilled fish and salad in a Greek isle town composed of buildings so white that the sun had almost blinded her. But mostly, she remembered the laughter – her father's, her mother's and all of them laughing together.

"Their lives may have been short, but they had been lived to the full." She stroked the dog beside her. "I don't know about Great-aunt Martha, but I'm sure they would be proud of me."

Her muffin and coffee gone, she rose from the couch and turned off the two lamps. Outside, the rain had subsided, and for a moment, a shaft of sunlight sprung through a rift in the clouds and shone onto the painting, causing it to take on a three-dimensional quality. In her mind, Adrianna heard her mother's tinkling laugh, followed by an exclamation. "Oh, look, the pink rose is in bloom!"

"Why now, isn't that nice!" She could almost feel her father as he crushed her to him in a bear hug. "But it's not as beautiful as either of my girls."

"I love you," she whispered to the empty room, her eyes on the painting. "I miss you both."

And then she picked up her plate and mug and headed to the kitchen, knowing that it was time to get ready for church where she would face the Montgomery pew with her chin up.

CHAPTER XXXVI

Adrianna was pleased to see the sun peeking from behind the clouds as she backed the Elantra from the carriage house and headed along the drive to pick up Penny and Otis. She had chosen a simple, but well-cut navy blue business suit and matching pumps to wear for the occasion, and her dark waves were pulled from her face. Overall, she didn't believe she would give the church matrons too much to talk about.

"My, don't you look nice!" Penny's words upon entering the back seat were encouraging.

"Nervous?" Otis asked.

"Just a little." Adrianna turned the car onto the main highway. "I appreciate your willingness to come with me. Walking down one of those long aisles and taking a seat in that pew by myself would've been hard to do this first time. As it is, I'll still feel on display."

"It's a friendly church," Penny pointed out, "and we have a new Associate Minister, Paul Lynch, who is only a year or two older than you."

"A lot of the artists are younger, too," Otis added.

"We should stay for the reception afterwards, so you can meet some of the members who are your age," Penny suggested.

Adrianna slowed the car, preparatory to turning into the parking lot. "Sounds like a good idea," she agreed, pleased to see that, at least here, there was no reserved parking spot for the Montgomery family.

Disembarking from the car, she was struck by the similarity in materials and construction that the building bore to her home, the granite exterior and slate roof giving the impression that God's house would stand firm against the elements.

"There you are!" Larry Chesterton separated himself from a small group visiting on the front lawn and hurried to join the threesome as they approached the steps leading to the church's front entrance. "I was hoping you would be here today."

As the two men dropped back, Penny took Adrianna's hand and gave it a gentle squeeze before releasing it as they reached the double oak doors – now wide open to accommodate the large congregation as they flowed in and out.

"Good morning." A tall, slim, white-haired gentleman in a gray suit greeted the ladies and handed each of them a program.

"Good morning," Adrianna and Penny answered in unison.

"That was Arthur Stern," the housekeeper whispered as they crossed the lobby and entered the sanctuary. "He's a dear man, local, and a fine artist. Otis and he have been friends for years, and I have one of his smaller seascapes hanging in the living room at the gatehouse."

"You'll have to point it out to me the next time I'm there," Adrianna said, thankful that this small bit of conversation had carried them halfway to their destination.

From a pew on her right, Maggie Daniels, the occasional helper, smiled and waved discreetly as they passed. Up ahead on the left, a plump, middle-aged woman smiled, and Adrianna recognized from the luncheon on *Martha's Joy* the owner of the candy store at Montgomery's Marina.

Ahead of her, Penny paused and gestured for her to enter the gated pew first, which would allow Otis to slide in next to his wife when he finally caught up with them.

"See?" The housekeeper whispered as she passed Adrianna a hymnal. "That wasn't too bad."

Nodding her agreement, Adrianna marked the first hymn with her program, then glanced to her right where Larry was joining Susan and her parents in the Chesterton pew, pleased when Susan leaned forward and sent her a smile. In the Sheffield pew to her left, Chase sat alone and apparently lost in thought, his profile turned to them.

A lanky young man approached the pulpit and the choir filed in, resplendent in their wine-colored robes. The deep tones of the pipe organ filled the air, and Adrianna took a moment to review the order of service.

"That's Paul Lynch." Penny leaned over and whispered. "Father Thompson and his family are on vacation."

Adrianna relaxed as the familiar words and hymns of the service washed over her, pleased when she realized that Paul Lynch had chosen the story of Ruth as the subject of his sermon. After all, here was another young woman who had successfully left familiar surroundings to make a new home amongst strangers. Perhaps, Adrianna hoped, she could take this as a sign.

The new Associate Minister gave the final blessing, and the organist began playing with a flourish the strong chords that signified the end of the service.

"Adrianna, this is Joan Palmer and her brother Charles," Penny stood and introduced an elderly man and woman who had been seated behind them.

"Nice to meet you." Adrianna shook the man's cool, blue-veined hand.

His sister leaned forward, and she noted the unmistakable scent of English Lavender. "Your great-aunt and I were lifelong friends," the older woman whispered. "We must call on you."

Slowly, the Plunks and Adrianna made their way through the crowd to the reception room where a small sign proclaimed that the altar society was responsible for this week's offering of refreshments. Dutifully, Adrianna took a cup of punch and looked around her, receiving a smile here and a nod there, dismayed as she realized she had already forgotten most of the names of the people to whom Otis and Penny had faithfully introduced her since leaving the Montgomery pew.

"Is the church the same as you remember?" Chase's suave voice sounded in Adrianna's ear, and she turned.

"It seemed even larger, when I was smaller." She laughed. "I enjoyed the sermon."

"Lynch is new, but the Search Committee spent time finding him." He took Adrianna's elbow and pulled her to a quieter spot away from the refreshment table. "How are things going at the house?"

"Everything's going well." Adrianna was pleased to be able to pass on her news. "Edwina is renting the dependency effective July 1. I told her that I would arrange an appointment for us to drop by and sign a lease one day next week. I'll call Bridgette first thing on Tuesday."

"Be sure and give her Edwina's social security number for the credit check," Chase reminded her.

"A credit check? For Edwina? You've got to be kidding." Adrianna fought to keep her voice down.

"I agree that she seems nice." Chase's jaw set. "Keep in mind, though, that you just met her."

"The two people I wanted to see." The new Associate Minister chose this moment to join them.

"Adrianna, this is Paul Lynch," the attorney handled the appropriate introductions.

"I was glad to hear you go into the bigger message of Ruth's story in your sermon," Adrianna said.

"I appreciate the positive feedback." The minister brushed a lock of brown hair off his forehead. "I'm new to the church, which is why I wanted to speak with you. Larry Chesterton tells me you'll soon have a cottage for lease, and I was wondering if I could stop by Tuesday morning and take a look at it."

"That will be fine," Adrianna agreed. "Would ten o'clock be okay?"

"Ten would be great," Paul confirmed. "I'll see you then. Now, if you'll excuse me, the altar society appears to have a question for me."

"So…" Adrianna turned her back on the crowded room. "It appears that I may be needing the minister's social security number as well. After all, he's new to the area, too."

"No, that won't be necessary." Chase held her gaze. "The Search Committee that I chaired has already seen to that for you."

"At first, I found you aloof, but then everyone told me you were shy." Adrianna's eyes flashed. "Now, I know you're just plain heartless."

And with that, she turned her back on her attorney and went in search of the Plunks, certain that it was time to go home.

CHAPTER XXXVII

Adrianna treated the Plunks to a leisurely Sunday dinner at Montgomery's, left them at the gatehouse and returned home alone, grateful for the happy greeting that Max had given her. As the weather had continued along on a fickle course of intermittent rain and partially cloudy, she had busied herself for the rest of the day with her furry companion's walks, emails to distant friends, two old movies and her Jane Austen reread.

Finally, she had taken a long bubble bath in the master suite's mahogany-surround tub, content for the warm water to soothe her as she had cleared her mind, pushing any troubling concerns about either Brad Williams or Chase Sheffield resolutely aside. Hopefully, she thought as she turned back the rose-colored duvet, the weather would be better for the clambake.

Awakened by the shrill chirps of a family of birds who had chosen the deep indentation of the front bedroom window as the place for their home, Adrianna allowed herself to float in and out of sleep, recognizing that there was no need for her to hurry and get up, it being a holiday. Behind her on the duvet, Max let out a muffled bark as he dreamed, perhaps chasing a squirrel. The baby birds now fed, they soon settled down, and once again the old house fell silent.

Gradually, Adrianna drifted deeper into sleep until she felt the warmth of a sunny beach and recognized that her head had been resting in the lap of her mother. Pushing her short curls from her eyes, she watched as her father pulled a one-man sailboat from the surf and walked towards them - a broad grin on his face. Leaping up, she ran and threw her short, childish arms around one of his knees, only to be picked up and tossed in the air for her efforts.

"Put me down! Put me down!" She screamed as she laughed, and he did – into the back of a sports utility vehicle that was taking a series of mountain curves much too fast.

"Slow down! Slow down!" Adrianna attempted to shout, but no sound would come out as her mother and father talked gaily in the front seat, apparently oblivious to the danger.

Then their vehicle swerved from the road, where for a moment it remained suspended in the air before it plunged towards the fields far below. Just before impact, she let out a scream and awakened herself, opening her eyes to find Max standing over her, a concerned expression on his face.

"It's okay." She hugged him to her as tears streamed down her cheeks.

It had been a long time since she had suffered that particular dream, and she had hoped its appearances were behind her. Perhaps, she told herself, finding the painting of the garden the day before had brought on a repeat. If so, it had been worth it.

As they moved from one archeological dig to another most of their adult lives, her parents had relied on furnished rental housing when not living in tents at a site. Even their clothes had been donated by an overly helpful colleague after their deaths before Adrianna could object, leaving her with only a precious few of their belongings. Her father's time capsule and his gift to his new bride had been exposed to her by the house, and she viewed them as treasures.

Drying her tears, she tossed back the duvet and threw open the drapes, revealing a clear blue sky and a light breeze that tossed the newly opened blossoms in the rose garden below – a perfect day for the Chesterton's clambake.

Dressed in a pair of shorts, a T-shirt and her trainers, she snapped on Max's leash, saluted to Jebediah as he smiled from his portrait and headed downstairs. Once in the floral gardens, she strolled along at a sedate pace, allowing Max to sniff here and there beside the paving stone paths at his leisure.

Her nightmare had disturbed her, and while the breeze lifting her waves did its best to raise her spirits, her mind seemed unable to push aside darker thoughts. What was she doing rattling around in this huge old house by herself? How had she ended up so alone?

As if sensing her need for him, Max turned and glanced up, a questioning expression on his face.

"I told Chase Sheffield yesterday that he was minus a heart," she shared with the dog as they headed back towards the kitchen garden. "Now, part of me wonders if I'm not in the same boat. Perhaps I show the world the same sort of reserve, having been damaged by the death of my parents. Great-aunt Martha certainly turned a cold shoulder to me. Maybe it runs in the family."

Max, who had wandered a few paces ahead, chose this moment to pause and exhibit a considering expression before he released a sneeze that presented him in the same way as if he had been shaking his head in disagreement.

In spite of her gloomy mood, Adrianna laughed and, sitting on her heels, drew him to her. "You, at least, love me, don't you?" she asked as she held him close. "And I think Otis and Penny appreciate having me around."

Realizing it was time to get dressed for the party, she stood and led their way back to the house through the kitchen garden.

An hour later, having donned jeans and a bright top, she grabbed a chartreuse tennis visor she knew would set off her dark hair and her sun glasses, before heading downstairs.

The breeze would be welcome, she realized as she approached the Elantra, the sun now bringing its full force to bear. Turning right, she drove the short distance to the Chesterton Cove property's entrance, realizing for the first time that the point and the shoreline probably lended themselves to the formation of pie-shaped properties.

Following a series of homemade signs, Adrianna turned off the paved drive onto a gravel roadway that led to a parking area at the edge of the Chesterton's private beach upon which a large pavilion had been constructed. Even from this distance, she could see that it housed a fair number of people, and a wave of shyness washed over her.

Disembarking, she was greeted by the scents of pine from the woods behind her, smoke from a seaweed covered clam pit on the beach and shouts from her host and hostess.

"Over here," they both cried out in unison.

Waving her understanding, she weaved through the other parked cars and made her way up a short flight of stairs, her eyes focused on the sailboats that abounded on the open water. Reaching the top of the steps, she turned her attention towards the other guests, surprised to find her way barred by Chase Sheffield.

"May I get you something to drink, Miss Montgomery?" he asked. "A lemonade, a beer or a soft drink? You see, I'm determined to show you one way or another today that I do, after all, have a heart."

CHAPTER XXXVIII

Chase's words spoken so softly, for a moment Adrianna remained speechless, unsure if he had meant what he said or was teasing her.

"Don't hog the woman!" Larry Chesterton slapped his friend's shoulder. "Get her something to drink."

"I'll have a lemonade, thank you." Adrianna found her voice again, grateful for the interruption.

"Let me introduce you to some of these folks." Larry took her elbow and guided her towards a group of chatting women seated on the wooden bench that lined the perimeter of the deck. "Everyone's dying to meet you."

"I hope not." Adrianna laughed. "So many corpses would certainly limit the success of your party."

"Checkmate!" Her host sent her a grin as they paused before the now attentive group of women. "Adrianna, let me introduce you to…" He waved his hand from left to right including all the ladies in his gesture as he glanced towards the beach. "Just give her your names, girls. Susan appears to need me," he finished and then abandoned his newly arrived guest to her fate.

By unspoken agreement, the group separated in the middle and made room for her to be seated. "I'm Jill," a pleasant looking, thirty-something woman introduced herself and then looked to the gal on her right.

Trying hard to keep their names straight, Adrianna focused on their faces until another young woman joined the group and handed her a lemonade. "Chase asked me to bring you this," she explained. "He's helping to uncover the fire pit."

"Have you ever been to a clambake?" Jill asked.

"Years ago, when I visited my great-aunt," Adrianna replied. "My strongest memory is that I burnt my tongue while biting into some corn on the cob and Penny Plunk cut the rest of the corn off for me. Are they a regular event around here?"

"I wouldn't say regular," the brunette on her left picked up the conversational thread. "A lot of work goes into a real one done in these conditions. You have to hunt for the clams, gather the seaweed, dig a pit if you don't already have one like the Chestertons, not to mention bringing in the firewood and stones that are needed."

"Goodness, I had no idea all that was required."

"It isn't." The blonde next to Jill leaned forward to be better heard. "You can do a much smaller version in a large steamer on your stove or even on an outdoor barbecue, although the food always tastes better done this way with the salt air and the gulls flying overhead."

"A nice set-up like this doesn't hurt either." Jill indicated the granite-topped bar and built-in kitchen that Adrianna now realized filled the center of the pavilion.

"So how do you like Captain's Point?" the brunette asked. "Are you settling in?"

"It's starting to feel like home." Adrianna sent her a smile and then relaxed as conversation flowed around her, beginning to distinguish her new acquaintances from each other.

Someone dragged a bench over from one of the picnic tables that dotted the pavilion, and the group grew around her as more introductions were made and remembrances of Adrianna's great-aunt were shared with her.

A tall, willowy woman paused before Adrianna. "Chase asked me to check and see if you needed anything," she said. "He's still tied up at the fire pit."

"No, I'm fine," Adrianna answered, feeling several of the other women's eyes on her.

"I'll never forget the time I had to do a report on an area garden, and I drew the one at Montgomery House," Jill continued the previous conversation. "I was a senior in high school, and I was still scared of her."

"Scared of her?" Adrianna asked, surprised.

"Well, she was the great Martha Montgomery," Jill explained. "I had heard her spoken of with reverence and respect all of my life, and I didn't know what to expect. As it turned out, she spent over an hour with me, made sure that I had collected all the samples and photos I needed, and then took me inside for tea and scones in what she referred to as the morning room. I felt like a princess sitting there in my jeans and tennis shoes."

"You wouldn't have been so worried if you had been a Girl Scout instead of a Blue Bird," a newcomer entered the conversation. "Martha was always dropping into our meetings and offering the use of the farm or gardens at Montgomery House, if we needed them to complete our badges."

So her great-aunt hadn't been down on teenage girls in general, Adrianna thought as the women chatted around her, only her in particular, and not until after her parents' deaths. Of course, traveling from dig to dig with her parents, she hadn't had the opportunity to be a Girl Scout.

"Looks like dinner is ready to be served." Jill stood along with the other women and indicated Adrianna should take a seat at one of the picnic tables, each of which had been covered with a bright red and white checked tablecloth held down by condiments, place settings and crab mallets.

Teenagers wearing Chester's T-Shirts carried pitchers of lemonade and trays of soft drinks from table to table as the ladies all took seats and the men began carrying large paella pans filled with steamed lobsters split in two, crabs and quahogs to the various tables. Platters of baked potatoes, corn on the cob, grilled onions and tomatoes were set beside bowls of potato salad, and individual containers of drawn butter were passed out.

"Who's going to eat all of this?" A redhead, who Adrianna now knew as Patsy, looked around the table.

"I am, if you're not," a pleasingly plump blonde named Margaret answered.

Even though some of the women wore wedding rings, Adrianna noticed that none of them had gone to the trouble of reserving a place for their spouse, the tables appearing to have divided for the most part into those for the boys and those for the girls like an overgrown kindergarten, probably the result of the manual labor required to maintain, uncover and serve from the fire pit.

Having skipped breakfast, Adrianna took a sampling of everything, prepared to enjoy a real treat, and soon learned that she was not to be disappointed. "This is delicious," she said to Jill at her side. "I'm so glad that Larry and Susan invited me."

"The Chestertons have always entertained lavishly." Jill pulled another bite of lobster from a reddened claw. "Probably because of the businesses they're in."

"That and the fact that they're genuinely nice people," Patsy added.

"It's a shame about Susan's divorce." Margaret scooped another bite from her baked potato.

"Her parents are thrilled to have their daughter and grandson back at Chesterton Cove, though," Patsy pointed out.

"Maybe Chase and she will get back together," Jill suggested. "After all, they were a couple through most of high school, and he didn't waste any time bringing her into his firm after Augustus died."

Everyone else focused on their plates, Adrianna paused for a moment and looked around, catching sight of Larry, Susan, Chase and Jim Laidlaw seated together at another table. A bored expression on his face, Chase turned towards his hostess and muttered something, to which she nodded and laughed, her eyes sparkling as she looked up at him.

So the two of them had been more than a casual couple in high school, Adrianna mulled over this new bit of information, glad she had learned it in time. She had been right to push aside thoughts of her attorney. The last thing she needed right now was any more hurt in her life.

And with that, she turned her attention to the bowls filled with homemade vanilla ice cream drenched in hot fudge sauce that the Chester's waiters and waitresses were now passing around.

CHAPTER XXXIX

"Well, ladies, it was great, but I'm going to see if they're putting together a game of volleyball anytime this afternoon," Jill excused herself from the table, just as everyone finished their sundaes.

"Wish I had that kind of energy." Margaret laughed and patted her stomach. "All I want right now is a nap."

"Is everyone enjoying themselves?" Susan asked, having appeared at their table.

"We're having a wonderful time," they all assured her.

"Why don't you come and let me introduce you to some of the others?" Her hostess suggested and placed her hand lightly on Adrianna's shoulder.

"I'll look forward to seeing you gals and Jill on Wednesday at noon," Adrianna told the others as she rose. "I've invited the girls to lunch at Montgomery House," she explained to Susan as the two women walked towards a standing group of laughing guests. "Would you be able to join us?"

Her hostess's face lit up with pleasure. "Let me check my calendar, and I'll let you know," she said. "Off of the top of my head, I think I can make it, although I'll probably feel sinful being away from the office in the middle of the day for a strictly social event."

"Is Chase such a hard taskmaster?" Adrianna asked and then wished she could withdraw her question.

"Not at all." Susan laughed, apparently unaware of her discomfort. "Quite the contrary, but then he knows better than to try."

The next several hours flew by as Adrianna's hostess made it a point to introduce her to everyone possible, steering her from one group to another.

"I really have had a wonderful time." She gave Susan a quick hug when it was time to go. "Please thank Larry for me." She glanced over the pavilion's railing to where a mixed group, including Jill and Chase Sheffield, was indeed playing a game of beach volleyball organized by their host.

"Hopefully, between church yesterday and this today, you're beginning to feel more part of a community." Susan's face sobered. "Captain's Point needs a Montgomery in residence at Montgomery House."

"And a Chesterton at Chesterton Cove." Adrianna met her gaze. "Is that why you returned?"

"Not really," Susan answered. "Larry was already here, and even though he's a cousin, he filled the need. Providing the best possible home for my son was the main reason, although my parents are now spoiling him rotten." She chuckled and lightened the moment. "I'll let you know about lunch on Wednesday no later than tomorrow morning."

"If you can't make it, we'll have to plan something else." Adrianna sent her a smile, then headed to her car where a tap on her passenger window surprised her as she started to back from her parking place.

"Hold on a minute," Chase shouted through the glass and rounded the front of her vehicle as she lowered her window. "Things didn't pan out anything like I'd planned today," he apologized as the scent of wood smoke from the fire pit and sweat from his having played volleyball wafted her way.

"I'm sorry to hear that," she replied, putting her car back into reverse. "I had a wonderful time. Now, if you'll excuse me, I need to get home and let Max out." She released her foot from the brake, leaving him no alternative but to remove his hands from the driver's door.

Concentrating on negotiating her way through the parking area that was now filled with departing guests, she tried not to notice the lost little boy look on his face as she slowly left him behind.

Believing Chase wouldn't leave things alone, she prepared to face him the next morning as work on the renovations continued, but when he hadn't shown up by mid-afternoon, she began to relax, only to be surprised when he appeared promptly at nine on Wednesday morning.

"Just the man I need!" Otis greeted the attorney with enthusiasm. "I'm tied up with the heating and air crew at the cottage, and the roofing crew has run into some snags on the west end. Hurry up there, and see what you can do for me!"

"I'll be getting ready for my ladies' luncheon," Adrianna reminded her property manager, after Chase had left them. "Let me know if you need me." She allowed Max a few more moments in the fresh air before heading back into the house.

Two hours later, she and her housekeeper surveyed the dining room table complete with its place settings of china, crystal and sterling silver, along with two round floral presentations arranged low enough to allow for conversation.

"Thank you so much! Everything is perfect!" Adrianna said.

"It's easy to set a nice table when you have such pretty things." Penny made no attempt to hide her pleasure. "You go and get dressed now, while I pop the hot chicken salad and rolls in the oven."

Once in her tower bedroom, Adrianna took time over her choice of a lightweight, powder blue dress trimmed in white and open-toed white shoes with a low heel, hoping to strike a middle chord between those who might arrive overdressed to Montgomery House and those who might feel they were dressed too casually.

Exiting the room, she bumped into Chase as he was returning from the roof.

"Excuse me." She suddenly felt shy in the close quarters of the tower suite's foyer.

"That's a good color for you," Chase gave his approval. "It brings out your eyes. Adrianna, I…"

But his words were interrupted by the chimes of the doorbell, and Max barking a greeting as he ran around in tight circles in the main foyer at the base of the stairs.

"I'm sorry, my luncheon guests are arriving," she excused herself and brushed past her attorney without looking back, thankful when she reached the door to find that Edwina and Ginny, with whom she was more comfortable than her new acquaintances, were the first to arrive.

"Enjoy your lunch, ladies." Chase smiled as he passed them and headed along the hallway to the kitchen.

"He's been overseeing the roofers," Adrianna sought to remove the questioning look from Edwina's face. "As the estate's administrator, he's taking a personal interest in the renovations."

"A very personal interest," Edwina said, her blue eyes twinkling as she exchanged a meaningful look with Ginny and the doorbell rang again.

"Please take a seat in the parlor until everyone has arrived." Adrianna indicated the second parlor that she had once again chosen as her party's gathering place. "I'll introduce you as the others arrive."

Opening the door to Jill, she had only a minute to direct her new acquaintance's steps, before the doorbell rang again, her guests dribbling in until a slightly flustered Penny finally relieved her.

"The girl I hired to help with the serving just arrived," her housekeeper whispered an apology.

"I'm expecting two more," Adrianna let her know and then headed into the parlor to join her guests, hoping that their presence around her would be enough to get her mind off the feelings that had been aroused by her close proximity to Chase Sheffield in the tower's tiny foyer.

CHAPTER XL

The ladies enjoyed their meal and then remained seated at the mahogany table, chatting pleasantly over their coffee.

"I really should return to the office," Susan commented, belying her words by pouring herself a second cup.

"I'm glad you were able to join us," Adrianna replied. "Looking back on my work in Seattle, I can see now that I would have been better served by allowing myself a few similar treats here and there. After all, we only live once."

"It won't be long before Edwina and you will be neighbors," Ginny stated.

This comment resulted in a bevy of questions from her guests, and Adrianna explained her plans for the property and then offered a tour to anyone who was interested. Susan excusing herself at this point, the rest of the ladies willingly viewed the much heard of rooms of Montgomery House and then made their way through the vine-covered tunnel towards the dependency.

"I can't wait to see it all finished," the older woman smiled. "I'm beginning an exciting new adventure. Remember, I fly home tomorrow and won't be back until the 30th."

"Send me an email so I'll have your address, and I'll keep you posted on the progress," Adrianna promised as they cleared the obstruction of the main house just in time for her to glimpse Chase's SUV driving away.

"Have you rented the cottage yet?" Jill asked and then appeared disappointed when Adrianna explained that Paul Lynch, the new minister, had already claimed it as his.

For her own part, Adrianna felt somewhat relieved, there being something about Jill that made her feel the other woman might have been more prone to invade her landlady's own life.

The tour now being over, her guests headed in a group towards their cars, thanking their hostess profusely for a wonderful outing.

"Have a safe trip." Adrianna opened the passenger door of Ginny's car for Edwina. "Everything will be ready when you get back."

"That reminds me, mark the first Sunday afternoon in July on your calendar," the older woman said as she slid onto the seat. "There's a gallery opening in Captain's Point, and Jason has gotten us four tickets. We want you to be our fourth."

"I'll look forward to it," Adrianna accepted and then closed the car door, standing back and waving to her visitors as they departed.

"They seemed to have had a good time." Otis chose this moment to join her.

"Well, they could have hardly done otherwise." Adrianna laughed. "They're all nice women, Penny's food was as always delicious, and they received a free tour of the legendary Montgomery House."

"Did I detect a note of sarcasm in the latter?" Her property manager searched her face.

"Perhaps, just a little," she acknowledged and walked beside him through the vine-covered tunnel back towards the kitchen garden. "I'm still not used to the aura that surrounds the Montgomery, Chesterton and Sheffield names."

"A triumph!" Penny exclaimed as they entered the kitchen. "They all cleaned their plates, and they were chattering like magpies." She turned to her husband. "Did you mention it to her?"

"Nope, I forgot." Otis turned to Adrianna. "There's a town meeting tomorrow night, and they'll be discussing Captain's Point's expansion. Would you want to join us?"

"Absolutely," she answered and watched as relief filled both of the Plunks' faces. "I definitely need to stay on top of that issue, don't you think?"

"That and your presence could make a real difference," Penny stated in her outspoken way. "We probably should get there by seven-thirty."

"I'll put it in my daybook then," Adrianna promised.

A few minutes later, having donned her jeans and a T-shirt, she scooped Max up from his bed on the hearth and carried him to the window seat. "I'm beginning to make friends," she shared as she stroked his back. "And now I've been invited to a gallery opening by Edwina."

As if acknowledging the importance of this event, he reached up and licked her chin before settling into a ball on her lap.

Taking in the long view through the multi-paned window, she noted that the sea was minus its customary whitecaps and hoped there would be a bit more wind for the regatta on Saturday.

Movement below attracted her attention, and she lazily watched for a moment as Jeff Stuart weeded a small bed, his movements practiced and efficient.

The answer is in the garden...

What had her great-aunt meant?

The mantel clock chose this moment to chime the hour, and she automatically glanced its way, taking in the intricately carved wooden mantel surround as she did so. Here roses vied with peonies that, in turn, pushed aside gardenias - a sweet smelling garden indeed.

"Max..." She set the dog on the floor and stood. "Do you see what I see?"

Above the mantel, the young Jebediah watched from his portrait. Was it possible there was a hidden panel in the mantel? She eyed it carefully, before approaching and systematically attempting to twist, turn or push each raised detail in the carved wood.

"This may be one of the dumbest things I've ever done," she commented to Max who waited patiently at attention beside her, affected by her excitement.

And then her hand settled on the round center of a large peony that at first glance seemed no different from the rest. When she twisted it counter-clockwise, though, she heard a distinct click as a portion of the panel that ran along the top of the frieze slid open before her. Reaching inside, she removed a long slim wooden box.

Taking a seat in the nearest Queen Anne chair, she flipped open a brass clasp and revealed all the correspondence she had sent to her great-aunt. Tied into bundles by year with strips of narrow satin ribbon, they told the story of her life, from crayon scribbles on a postcard sporting a view of Thebes to a long handwritten letter sent from the Swiss finishing school she had been attending when her parents had died. Creased and recreased, they showed the wear and tear of having been read through repeatedly.

"She kept them all," Adrianna addressed Jebediah's portrait through tear-filled eyes. "No matter what happened in the past, regardless of the future, despite our disagreement at the end, this proves that she loved me."

CHAPTER XLI

Despite their good intentions, Adrianna and the Plunks arrived at the Captain's Point High School cafeteria for the town meeting a few minutes later than they had planned, only to find limited seating still available. Otis located two seats together near the front and motioned for the ladies to take them, but Adrianna noted Susan waving to her from the front row and moved forward to join her.

"Chase made me promise to save you a seat in case you came with Otis and Penny," Susan stated as she indicated with a nod where her law partner was seated with the town councilors at a long table stretched across the front of the room.

"Thanks. I had no idea there would be such a crush. Are all Captain's Point town meetings like this?"

"A good many of them." Susan chuckled. "Those around election time are packed as are any that have a tax increase on the agenda. Growth and expansion draw a fair crowd as well."

"As I understand it, no one has a vote except for the mayor and the councilors, is that correct?" Adrianna asked.

"That's right, but that doesn't keep every Tom, Dick and Harry from having an opinion."

"Or every Tammy, Donna and Harriet from the look of things," Adrianna pointed out and then changed the subject. "How old is the high school? It seems fairly modern."

"Construction was completed the summer before Chase's and my junior year." Susan's eyes took on a faraway look. "Those were the magic times. Would you believe that Chase and I were crowned Prom King and Queen just about where the councilors are sitting now?"

"That's the sort of thing I missed out on moving around the world with my parents, but I imagine you made a handsome couple."

"We did," Susan acknowledged. "His dark looks and my blonde ones – everyone thought we were made for each other. We dated pretty steadily those last two years, you know. Everyone was sure we would end up married once we both finished college."

"That must have put a fair amount of pressure on your relationship," Adrianna said, surprised by the sharp glance she received in return.

"You've hit the nail on the head." Susan attempted a laugh that fell a bit short. "Also, it was a bit like dating my brother. Then, of course, Chase's father embroiled the Sheffield's in the world's greatest scandal. His mother went into hysterics that lasted for the better part of five years, and my fun loving high school dreamboat withdrew into a hard shell comprised primarily of hurt pride and overwork."

"Surely, now that his parents are both deceased and he's established in his own firm, Chase has returned to being his old self." Adrianna hoped the emotions that were vying for position in her thoughts were not reflected on her face.

"Not completely." Susan shrugged. "He's shoved most of the hurt deep down inside, and the Sheffields have always been known for their pride. Every now and then, though, I see a glimmer of the old humor peeking through."

"Ladies and Gentlemen, if I could have your attention!" The mayor stood and pounded a gavel. "We're going to terminate our meeting promptly at ten, so we want plenty of time for everyone to be heard."

Except for an occasional cough, a chair scraping here and there, and a small child crying in the back of the room, silence descended on the audience. Referring to his notes, the mayor brought the meeting to order and quickly disposed of the acceptance of the last minutes.

"The purpose of this meeting is to provide for open discussion of various items related to the ongoing growth and development of Captain's Point," he now stated. "In the interest of fairness, each participant will be allowed five minutes in which to make their point. Any of you who have a comment to make please raise your hands."

From the sounds behind her, Adrianna felt sure half the room's occupants now had their hands in the air. "Is there a lot of dissension surrounding the issues?" She whispered her question into Susan's ear.

"Definitely."

"I want to go on record as having said that we're in danger of turning our town into an interstate highway the way things are going," a burly man dressed in a dingy T-shirt and a pair of stained overalls commented, having been the first participant to be recognized. "All we need is another wide highway running through the county's best farmland."

A murmur of agreement met his comment, and Adrianna prepared to learn more about both sides of the issues.

"What about those of us who want to see more consumers brought in?" A thirty-something man wearing a white shirt and a tie asked. "Prime Development wants to build high rise condos south of Captain's Point on the beach. If we want to attract big city professionals, we have to provide them the means to get here quickly."

"As a mother, my first concern is our children," a young woman juggling a hefty toddler on her jean-clad hip commented next. "I say our interests would be better served by further developing our park system and schools, while maintaining the small town quality of life that has always been the way in Captain's Point."

One by one a wide variety of participants took advantage of their five minute opportunity, and Adrianna was impressed by the orderly way in which the time passed, recognizing good points made on both sides.

"We're coming into the last half hour now," the mayor drew everyone's attention to the large clock hanging on the wall behind them. "Would any of you council members want to state a position?" He looked along the table to his right and left for a raised hand. "Yes, Chase?"

"It strikes me that we have a newcomer in our midst." The attorney stood and directed his hand to where his partner and Adrianna sat. "Someone who now has a vested interest in the future of Captain's Point, but who can also offer us the value of her wider perspective. Miss Montgomery, would you share an opinion with us?"

Aware of the whispers now filling the room and recognizing that she was required to stand and present a reasonable argument on a subject she was just beginning to understand to a group of virtual strangers, Adrianna could have willingly wrung her attorney's neck. Plastering a smile on her face, she stood and turned to address the greater group.

"I can't begin to claim a complete understanding of the issues facing Captain's Point," she began, "although I intend to study them further in the future. I've heard good points on all sides, and two things strike me. What we already have here in Captain's Point is precious and deserves protecting by taking care to thoroughly research and review prospective changes as they come up."

A murmur of agreement passed around the room, joined by a mild attempt to begin a round of supportive applause.

"Having recently moved here from Seattle, I would point out that both my former city and neighboring Portland have experienced tremendous growth during the past several years. In both cases, the city fathers worked hard to expand public transportation, the parks system including bike trails, and various wildlife sanctuaries, while keeping a strong focus on environmental issues. These cities are now frequently cited as best places to live for their size and appeal to both new businesses and the young professionals employed by them. Given the fact that Captain's Point is a coastal community, we might do well to follow their examples wherever possible."

Concerned that she might have overstepped her five minute limit, Adrianna quickly sat down, surprised by a burst of real applause from behind her as she sought Chase Sheffield's face, from which only his smiling eyes reflected his approval.

CHAPTER XLII

Chase Sheffield turned off the treadmill in what had once been a guest bedroom of Sheffield Place but now served as his gym, mopped his face and neck with a small towel, and took a long swig of water from the bottle that had waited in its holder. Glancing out the window, he was pleased with the whitecaps that danced on the waves beyond the lawn, thinking they couldn't have asked for a better day for a regatta.

Leaving the swank bathroom showered and shaved a few minutes later, he entered the overly organized walk-in closet his mother had thought the perfect high school graduation gift and donned his lucky racing clothes – white shorts, blue golf shirt and deck shoes, which he had set out beforehand. Ready for his day, he strode into his boyhood bedroom where he paused for a moment and took stock, thinking how little he had changed it over the years.

Sure, he had long since relegated his high school track and wrestling trophies into a barrister's bookcase under one of the large windows, but the same shabby armchair and floor lamp waited for him where he could read or daydream with an ocean view. His childhood bunk bed had been replaced by a king, leaving enough room for a small skating rink. The same scarred oak desk on which he had done his grade school homework now held his laptop and served for paying personal bills.

A small framed photo of a young man wearing a navy dress uniform caught his eye, and he picked it up, dusting it lightly with the palm of his hand. "I still miss you, Cuz," he whispered in the room that was empty save for himself. "Sometimes I think Aunt Ruth and you were the only ones who cared. Certainly, Augustus and you two were the only ones who ever took much notice."

Recognizing it was still too early to leave for the marina, he replaced the photo and plopped into the shabby chair, swinging a long leg over one of its upholstered arms as he gazed at the sea spread out beyond the window, his mind traveling back to a summer day on Cape Cod.

"Hurry up!" his cousin Jack had urged. "If we get stuck running errands for my mom, I won't have a chance to teach you!"

A still sleepy twelve year old, he had thrown back the sheets and shrugged on a pair of swim trunks and a T-shirt, not wanting to miss an opportunity to learn how to sail. Fifteen minutes later, Jack and he had left the shore behind them, and his first lesson had begun. Never had he known such freedom, he had thought as the wind lifted his hair and caught the small craft's single sail. Each subsequent summer, he had begged his mother to allow him to spend at least a few weeks at the Cape with Jack and his Aunt Ruth, grateful she cared too little to be jealous.

Then his cousin had graduated from the Naval Academy full of promise and hope only to be killed on a rescue mission a few short months later, mirroring the death of his father in Vietnam. Aunt Ruth had sold the cottage on the Cape, but she had given him Jack's more recent and much larger boat, and he had raced it in memory of his cousin in the regatta every year since. With a sigh, he shoved maudlin thoughts aside and rose, his glance taking in the row of regatta trophies he had won over the last eight years.

"Well, Cuz..." He saluted the photo. "It's time for me to give Larry Chesterton and his scruffy old boat another run for their money. Wish me luck!"

And with that he left his room and strode through the house that he couldn't really afford to maintain, but couldn't quite bring himself to sell, where he lived with so many bad memories and one treasured photo.

Unaware of her attorney's preparations, Adrianna was at this moment controlling her dark waves with a brightly colored scarf in hopes that it might keep her hair out of her eyes as she watched the regatta. Jim Laidlaw had said he would pick her up at eleven, and she was looking forward to lunch at Chester's.

Her dinner with Chase Sheffield had been more of a business meeting, and now she found that it felt strange and uncomfortable to be going out on a real date with anyone other than Brad. At least, she thought, Jim was light-hearted, informal and full of fun.

Glancing at the small crystal clock on the vanity, she realized she had finished with time to spare and headed to a window seat in her bedroom where she plopped down and patted the spot beside her, indicating for Max to join her. Beyond the open lawn, the sea stretched before her, decorated by a myriad of whitecaps.

"From the looks of it, the regatta organizers should be pleased." She stroked Max's back.

Near the horizon a large yacht made its way northward, while closer to shore several smaller boats were in evidence as well as one large sailboat, its sails unfurled, and in her mind, she traveled back to a summer spent cruising the Greek isles with her parents.

"It'll be us and a small crew," her father had promised as he had hugged his 'girls' to him. "We'll take in all the sights and eat like a king, his queen and their princess."

And so they had journeyed from one fishing village to another, sometimes leaving the boat for a meal at a local café, where they made friends with the residents and danced holding hands into the night.

Then her memories shifted, and she was sitting in the stern of Brad's boat on Puget Sound, the wind lifting her hair as they made their way towards Port Townsend – a picnic lunch of flaky smoked salmon, cream cheese, crackers and a chilled bottle of wine awaiting them in the two berth cabin.

"Where are you now?" she asked the image of her ex-fiancé that floated in her mind, only to have Max nuzzle her hand in response to the words she had not realized she had spoken aloud. "I still miss him, you know." She hugged the dog close. "Brad was my best friend, but enough of that."

She stood and indicated for the dog to follow her. "Let's take you for a quick walk. I want to be ready when Jim arrives, so we get off to a good start."

Oblivious to his date's concerns, Jim Laidlaw paused by the master bedroom's large window in the ranch house he had bought from his parents when they had retired to Florida. A quick look showed him that the weatherman had been kind as the wind tossed the pine trees' branches at the back of the yard.

Satisfied, he turned to the dresser where he filled his pockets with his wallet and some change, before checking his appearance in the large mirror. Who would've thought as he was growing up in this house that he, a mere Laidlaw, would one day be taking the Montgomery heiress to lunch at her own marina? Certainly none of the guys in that crowd, although they had treated him with respect after his pivotal lap in the high school track team's all-state relay win.

Of course, it had been Chase Sheffield to whom he had handed the baton, Chase who had run the last lap and broken ahead of the competition by the length of his patrician nose, and Chase who had been handed the trophy, his arm held high by their track coach.

Still, he had to admit that both Chase and Larry Chesterton had welcomed him home after vet school, each offering to sponsor him for membership in the yacht club. He grabbed his keys and sunglasses, mentally running through a checklist of supplies already stored in his car.

"Your guy's doing okay," he addressed an ancient gray cat engrossed in grooming herself on his bed. "I'll be receiving a few jealous glances myself during the next couple of hours."

And then, having blown the disinterested animal a kiss, he left the middle class home of his boyhood whistling a jaunty tune as he headed into uncharted upper class waters.

CHAPTER XLIII

As they turned onto the road leading to the marina, Adrianna wondered why she had been nervous about spending a chunk of time with Jim Laidlaw. Talk about a man with a sense of humor, most of it self-deprecating. She didn't think she had stopped laughing since she had locked the front door of Montgomery House.

"Is it always like this?" she asked as they neared their destination, and the first rows of cars parked alongside the already narrow road came into view.

"Sometimes it's worse." Jim sent her a grin, then focused on securing them a makeshift slot of their own.

"Use the Montgomery space in back of Chester's," Adrianna suggested and then wished that she could call back the words, sensing from his expression that she had somehow offended him.

"Might as well." He signaled a turn into the full parking lot, where it required his complete attention to successfully dodge the constant flow of pedestrians until he brought his car to a stop. "Could I ask you to grab the duffle bag off the back seat?" he asked as he opened his door.

"Sure." She disembarked to be immediately greeted by the aromas of grilled sausage and onions.

"Let's stow the cooler and then head to Chester's." The vet slung a backpack over one shoulder and hoisted a large cooler from the car's trunk.

As they walked alongside the crab shack, Adrianna was surprised by the number of impromptu street vendors that had set up shop, the most prominent being a series of large grills manned by members of the Captain's Point Volunteer Fire Department. Their main offering appeared to be kielbasa sausages served on sub rolls with a healthy covering of grilled onion and green pepper drizzled with mustard, although tubs of bratwurst simmering in beer laced with more onions were also in evidence.

For a moment, she considered suggesting to Jim that they forego Chester's in favor of sampling the vendors' wares, but then she remembered how she had inadvertently upset him earlier and reconsidered. "What kind of a boat do you have?" she asked as they reached the main boardwalk and turned right towards the boathouses.

"Pops sold me his motorboat when my folks retired to Florida." Jim indicated for her to enter one of the smaller boathouses. "Once we're anchored in the observers' area, I'll set up a canvas cover over the seats that will allow us to take in the action without your pretty face getting all sunburnt." He set the cooler on the dock, dropped into the boat and then disappeared into the small cabin, returning a few seconds later for the cooler.

"Sounds like you've taken care of everything." She ignored the compliment and handed him the duffle bag and her beach bag to put away as well. "When did your folks move to Florida?"

"Right after I set up my practice." He rejoined her on the dock and led the way back to the boardwalk. "I bought the family home, relieving them of the mortgage they had taken out so I could go to vet school, and that freed them to retire."

"Sounds like a win/win." She hoped she had said the right thing and was pleased when he seemed pleasantly surprised by her response.

"Get ready for a feast." Jim held open the door to Chester's with a flourish.

Adrianna had not been prepared for the noise and activity that greeted her. Several long tables dissected the main floor of the restaurant that made no apologies for serving family style. Thick brown paper covered the tables, and crab mallets ranged haphazardly along their surfaces at the ready. Several high chair attachments indicated that the table along the back wall was reserved for families with small children.

"I see you've selected a two washbowl establishment." She indicated two stainless steel sinks that had been provided for the use of diners who had finished their meals. "I feel honored."

"Nothing but the best for Jim Laidlaw," he teased.

"And here I was thinking you had chosen such a fine place with me in mind," she flirted back, caught up in the moment, but then felt suddenly embarrassed by her actions.

"Hey, Doc!" Captain Reb waved from the table running along the boardwalk windows. "Over here!"

"Guess we'll have to join them." Jim escorted her to the seats that had been cleared by other diners scooting their chairs this way or that. "Captain." He held out his hand to the older man, who made a show of using a lemon-scented towelette before taking it. "Adrianna, this is Gloria Graham, owner of the candy store along the strip here, who has apparently lowered herself to join the up-to-no-good skipper for lunch." He introduced her to the pleasingly plump woman whose name she couldn't remember, for which she was grateful.

"Gloria and I met during the luncheon on the yacht." Adrianna sent the older woman a smile. "I'm surprised you could take time for lunch on a day like this. Your candy store must be booming."

"My grandchildren are taking care of all that." The store's owner dimpled. "Under the watchful eyes, I might add, of their parents who are keeping up with the demand for funnel cakes we offer out front on regatta days. Otherwise, we run out of gelato before noon, and everyone gets in a tizzy."

"Nothing like a good regatta." The captain pushed his chair back from the table and proceeded to open three more towelettes. "Gets the summer season off to a good start."

"Christmas in June." Jim turned to Adrianna. "The standard fare here consists of steamed crabs, fried corn, French fries, hush puppies and iced tea. It's a little heavy on the carbs, but you won't regret it. Is that okay?"

"Sounds great," she agreed as he held up two fingers and signaled their order. "Max and I will have to fit in an extra jog."

"How's the little guy doing?" the vet asked. "Is he giving you any trouble?"

"Only when one of us is eating." Adrianna laughed. "He simply won't buy into the fact that the Plunks and I aren't willing to share."

"Well, stick to your guns," Jim said as their food arrived.

"Time to get back to the store." Gloria stood. "You two enjoy your food."

"Think I'll tag along and grab one of those funnel cakes." Captain Reb followed after his luncheon partner.

"Funnel cakes on top of French fries, fried corn and hush puppies." Adrianna sent her date a knowing look as she reached for a steamed crab. "How does he do it?"

"One bite at a time, I would imagine." Jim laughed. "The same as I plan to."

Two hours later - their lunch consumed and a funnel cake shared much to Adrianna's chagrin – the two of them strolled back along the boardwalk, each licking on a cone of chocolate gelato.

"I'm never going to eat again," she announced to which her date rolled his eyes.

But then she noticed a couple up ahead – the young man blonde and well-built, the woman's dark curls tied with a bright ribbon to keep the hair from her eyes in the wind blowing off the sea. It was as if she was looking at Brad and herself from behind at a distance, and her mood fell.

Would she ever stop missing him?

CHAPTER XLIV

"So what exactly am I watching?" Adrianna asked once Jim had found them a slot in the area marked off by buoys that was reserved for spectator boats.

"Basically, two things." He handed her a chilled can of lemonade and popped one open for himself. "Farther out, you have the larger sailboats that are manned by two person teams. In the lanes closer to shore, the single person boats are racing against each other. If all goes well, the larger boats racing will finish first, according to what I saw on the notice board outside of Chester's."

"Do I know any of the competitors?" She adjusted her grandfather's binoculars that she had found in the Captain's study and placed into her beach bag at the last minute.

"Take a look." Her date pulled a printed list of registered entrants for each event from his back pocket and handed it to her.

Quickly running her finger down the first page, she let out a laugh. "I wish I had seen that one!" She pointed to where Jill had been entered into a paddle boat competition that had been held earlier in the morning. "I had no idea they had all of these events."

"The inner tube races the kids compete in can be fun." He sent her a grin. "You're looking at the winner of the 10-12 year old boys' race a few years back."

"I didn't realize I was in the presence of a celebrity," she teased, flipping to the next page. "Oh, my goodness, they have beach volleyball and rowing competitions, too."

"Yes, but the two that we're watching now are the main events."

Having come to the last page, Adrianna took her time reviewing the lists. "I don't recognize anyone in the two person team event, but of course, I know Larry and Chase." She glanced up. "So who are you betting on to win the singles event?"

"Easy money would be on Chase." Jim relaxed against the back of the bench seat. "He's won against Chesterton for the past seven or eight years, but I might be tempted to lay a fiver down on Larry to win, if for no other reason than that he's due. Both of them have sailed since they were kids, and Larry's boat is newer and possibly lighter."

"Might be tempted, or already have a bet placed?" she asked. "Because if there's money involved, I would feel duty bound to cheer for Larry on your behalf."

"Actually, I have a ten-dollar wager with my office manager." Her date presented a passable imitation of a man who was deeply shamed. "She's a die-hard Chase Sheffield fan, ever since he handled her grandmother's estate."

"Then I'll support you by all means. Cheers for Larry it is."

"How do you like living in Captain's Point?" Jim changed the subject, surprised when Adrianna considered a few moments before responding.

"Overall, I'm enjoying myself much more than I expected," she answered finally. "I've lived in big cities for the past ten years and thought of myself as being quite urban. Now that I'm here, though, I've realized that I always gravitated to neighborhoods where everything was contained within a small area – shops, cafes, dry cleaners – and you recognized almost everyone that you passed on the sidewalk."

"Basically, you found what had the benefits of a small town in the big city."

"Exactly," she agreed, "and thinking back on it, my parents and I mainly lived in small towns or even tent encampments near digs. The biggest difference between Captain's Point and Seattle is the limited local access to cultural activities, but Baltimore and D.C. are both just a short drive away."

"How does it feel to live in Montgomery House, or is that too personal?"

Again, Adrianna took a few moments before answering. "If I didn't have Max, there would be times when I would be lonely."

She paused, and then decided to make a clean breast of things. "My great-aunt and I had a difference of opinion after my parents' funeral, and I hadn't been back since, although I have many happy memories of being here when I was a child. The house has given up several treasures since I've arrived – small things like a time capsule that my father buried in the kitchen garden and a painting he had given to my mother. I'm hoping it will somehow explain to me why my great-aunt treated me the way she did at the end, because I have also found certain proof that she loved me."

She glanced up and was surprised by the understanding and something else – sympathy perhaps – that she found in her date's eyes. "What was that?" she asked as a horn blew three strident tones.

Jim immediately straightened. "You might want to aim your binoculars over there." He pointed to their starboard side. "I think it signifies that the team leads have made their final turns. They should be heading this way at a fairly fast clip in this wind."

"And I think that's Chase and Larry tacking in the opposite direction in the lane one row in." She passed the binoculars to him as a larger than normal wave tossed the boat, and she grabbed the front of the bench seat with her other hand.

"You're right." He handed them back and reached for an oar, adjusting their position in regards to the incoming tides. "Looks like we may have a storm brewing, too." He glanced towards the horizon. "Hopefully, the singles' race will be over before it reaches here."

"Where's the finish line for the team competition?" Adrianna asked. "No, wait! I see it. Chase just passed it. The boat with the blue stripe along its side looks like it's going to win."

"Wait a minute," Jim said, his tone reflecting alarm. "That's not right."

Adrianna watched helplessly as the man steering the sailboat with the blue stripe suddenly sagged to the deck, and the larger craft turned sharply to port. His teammate, a woman, rushed to him, but then, apparently realizing she needed to regain control of the boat, stood and began frantically lowering the larger sail.

"What is Chase doing now?" she asked as his boat turned slightly towards the larger one.

"I'm not sure," Jim answered. "Probably trying to get close enough to help if he can. I'm sure motorized assistance is already on the way."

An even larger wave chose this moment to hit their own small craft, and Adrianna let out a gasp as Jim once again dipped a oar into the water and made a correction.

"We may need to start back to shore soon," he pointed out.

"Larry has turned his boat, too," Adrianna said. "Can we wait here another minute or two?"

"Only a couple more." Jim nodded towards the sky, where a bank of dark clouds was fast approaching.

All around them, other boats were turning on their engines and raising their anchors, preparing to head back to shore.

"Oh, no!" A cry came from a small yacht off to their port side as the wind caught the blue-striped sailboat and it slowly rolled over.

Taken unawares, the woman aboard the capsized craft slid down the now uprighted deck until she managed to catch her foot on a raised storage box, just above the level of the waves, while the body of the man now hung bent over the column of the steering wheel, his suspended legs waving back and forth as the boat lifted and fell.

"Chase and Larry are both trying to reach her!" Adrianna shouted, as a siren sounded from a motorized boat that was making its way rapidly towards the capsized craft through the stream of returning spectators.

"I've got to get us back in," Jim shouted above the noise and began raising the anchor. "Can you keep us pointed into the waves until I get this up?"

"Sure." Adrianna jumped to assist him, grateful for all the time she had spent on various types of boats over the years. Even so, she kept one eye on the drama in front of them.

"Here we go!" Jim turned the key, and his boat's engine roared to life at the same moment in which the woman on the capsized boat lost her hold and slid into the waves.

Adrianna watched in horror as Chase nudged his own boat a few feet closer and then reached over the side, grabbing hold of the woman's hand and pulling her from the water just as the wind changed direction, his own sail swinging sharply until its boom appeared to strike him a glancing blow on the head.

"Help him!" she shouted as Jim steered them slowly towards the shore.

"It's best if we stay out of the way," he called back.

"I meant the woman. Look at her! She's amazing! I think she has the boat under control, and the rescue boat is there, too."

"Larry's pointing at the man," Jim commented over his shoulder, having taken a quick look.

"An EMT is bent over Chase, and they're trying to throw a rope over…" Adrianna watched in amazement as a crewmember from the rescue boat shimmied up the rope that had been lassoed onto the steering wheel, secured the man's body to his and then lowered himself onto the rescue craft, grateful that she had thought to bring the binoculars with her. "It looks like they're strapping Chase onto a stretcher," she kept Jim informed.

"They'll take him to the hospital," he pointed out as they reached the boathouse. "Let's head over there once we get the boat docked."

"Please!" Adrianna fought to keep the hysteria she felt from her voice.

"Can you hook us onto the dock?" Jim asked, and she grabbed for the closest nylon loop, grateful for something to do as he cut the engine.

Quickly, he secured the boat and removed the canvas cover from over the seats as Adrianna gathered up their portable belongings. He handed her a golf umbrella he had retrieved from the tiny cabin, then he hoisted the cooler onto the dock and took the smaller bags from her, before giving her a quick hug at precisely the moment that the first sheet of rain struck the roof of the boathouse.

"I promised you an exciting time." He smiled down at her. "But I would never have wanted anything like this to happen. Please don't worry too much. Chase proved long ago that he has nine lives, and I think he's only on number four. I'm sure he's going to be okay."

CHAPTER XLV

Utilizing the Montgomery parking place had seemed a good idea at the time, but it now proved to be a detriment as Jim and Adrianna found themselves at the end of a long slow line of fellow spectators, all trying to make their way home. Finally reaching the hospital's entrance, they turned in as two of three ambulances passed them going out and the third pulled away from the curb.

"I'll drop you off and then find a parking place," Jim announced.

"In case things get crazy in there, I want you to know I had a lovely afternoon before all of this happened," she thanked him, and then disembarked as the car came to a stop.

Once through the automatic doors, she was immediately greeted by Susan who was seated in one of the blue chairs that lined the walls, and Adrianna hurried forward to join her.

"Chase and Tiny Slocum are both being checked out now," her friend told her. "Buzz Slocum is dead. Apparently, he suffered a massive heart attack. My high school BFF Bev Lockhart is on duty this evening, and she's keeping us posted."

"Another advantage to living in a small town." Adrianna took the seat beside her. "Did you get a glimpse of Chase as they wheeled him in?"

"No, I was parking my car, but Bev said he's unconscious."

"Chase?" Jim asked as he hurried towards them.

"Yes," Susan said. "He has a lump on the top of his head, a cut on his left cheek almost at the temple, and they think he may have a broken right wrist. They're taking x-rays now."

"And the woman – Tiny you said her name was – what about her?" Adrianna set the beach bag Jim had thought to bring her on the seat beside her.

"She swallowed some water and appears to have sprained her ankle when she caught herself on the storage box, but other than that, they think she's okay," Susan filled them in. "They'll x-ray her ankle as soon as they're done with Chase."

"Is there anyone we should call for her?" Adrianna asked, recognizing that the waiting room was empty except for the three of them.

"I can't think of anyone, can you?" Susan addressed Jim.

"No, as far as I know, it's only been the two of them since her mom died several years back," he replied. "Tiny and her dad own and run or rather ran a small store and bait shop south of the marina, closer to the main harbor," he explained their background to Adrianna. "I ran into Vern Whistler in the parking lot as he was leaving work, and he told me about Buzz. Tiny's going to be devastated."

"Ah…" Susan's attention focused on the nurse that had entered the waiting room and was coming towards them. "Bev, this is Adrianna Montgomery," she introduced the two women. "How are they?"

"Chase is still unconscious," the attractive brunette filled them in. "Pug stitched up the cut on his cheek, and he's back having an MRI. The good news is there doesn't seem to be any type of neck or spinal injury, but Pug's making very sure."

"Pug?" Adrianna asked.

"Pug Brownley," Jim explained. "So named by Larry in the third grade because of Pug's unfortunate resemblance at the time to Larry's mother's new puppy."

"He's since morphed into someone quite normal and is now a very competent ER doctor," Bev stood up for the absent physician. "For better or worse, though, the nickname stuck."

"One of the downsides of small town living." Jim grinned.

"What about Tiny?" Susan brought the conversation back to their reason for being there. "How is she doing, and can you think of anyone we could call for her? Jim and I drew a blank."

"We're moving her to an observation room for tonight, because of the sea water she swallowed," Bev said, "but other than her ankle and the shock of having lost her father, she's physically okay."

"Would it be possible for me to see her?" Adrianna asked, surprising even herself with the question. "The thing is I know what it's like to suddenly lose a parent, and I hate to think of her being alone."

"I'll ask her for you." Bev's face brightened. "It might be good for her to have some company, and we're pretty tied up with Chase, which reminds me that I need to get back there. I'll let Pug know you're here," she promised and left.

"Incidentally, I called Otis on my way in from the car," Jim addressed Adrianna. "He'll see to Max, so you don't have to worry about getting back to Montgomery House."

"Thanks, I was concerned about your patient." Adrianna sent the vet a smile. "I've never left him alone in the house for this long."

"From what I know of him, he probably hasn't minded." Jim laughed. "Although, he would get hungry after a while."

"Adrianna," Bev called to her from the doorway leading into the emergency room proper. "Tiny said she would like to see you."

"I'll watch your bag," Susan promised.

Adrianna had hoped to catch a glimpse of Chase as she passed through the treatment area in Bev's wake, but all of the draped examination areas appeared to be empty.

"She's in the first room on the right." The nurse held open one of a set of double doors that were clearly marked as the entrance to the observation rooms. "I'll come back and check on you in a few minutes."

"Tiny?" Adrianna tapped lightly on the doorframe of the patient's room a few seconds later.

"Miss Montgomery?" The injured woman asked and indicated for her to take a seat in a visitor's chair that was drawn up to the bed.

"Adrianna Montgomery, yes." She approached and took a seat. "I'm sorry that we're meeting under such sad circumstances."

"It hasn't hit me that he's gone." Tiny pushed a button on the other side of the bed that raised her to a sitting position.

A quick examination of her new acquaintance had shown Adrianna that the other woman's name was a misnomer. Big boned, she appeared to be close to six feet tall, her heels resting against the bottom of the bed, and her deeply tanned, well-lined face indicated that she had attained middle age.

"You lost both of your parents at the same time," Tiny continued. "I attended their funeral. Miss Martha was devastated."

"I'm afraid I don't remember you," Adrianna replied, "but then the funeral remains almost a blur."

"Both Dad and I went," the older woman said. "Martha had been wonderful to my father when my mother was dying, and he wanted to be there for her. Your great-aunt was my Sunday school teacher you know."

"I believe she taught Sunday school for many years."

"At least twenty of them," Tiny stated with certainty. "Martha was a force to be reckoned with, and woe to anyone who didn't have their lesson prepared come Sunday morning. I will say this for her, though, you knew she would stand strong in a storm. You could count on her to come through in powerful winds or high waves, and a lot of folks in Captain's Point did. She was a real role model to me."

"Susan Chesterton and Jim Laidlaw are in the waiting room," Adrianna mentioned. "We wondered if there was anyone we could call."

"Not really." Tiny shrugged. "I'll let them know at the store in the morning that I won't be in, but it was just Dad and me at home. It may sound awful for me to say it, but he would've been glad to have known that he would go this way, suddenly on his boat in full sail."

"I think most men would prefer to go in harness," Adrianna agreed.

"He'd been diagnosed with pancreatic cancer just last week," Tiny shared, "and his heart had given him problems for some time. He knew this would be his last regatta, possibly his last time on the boat."

And at this, the older woman's shoulders began to shake as large tears rolled down her cheeks. Adrianna moved the small box of tissues from the metal bedside cabinet to within Tiny's reach and then, impulsively, took the older woman's hand in hers.

"It's best to let it out as much as you can," she counseled quietly as the other woman pulled a couple of tissues from the box. "I still tear up from time to time when I think of my parents."

"I'm not normally one to cry." Tiny wiped her cheeks and then blew her nose with her free hand before dropping the soggy tissues into the wastebasket on the other side of the bed. "You're very understanding."

"Well, I think you're amazing," Adrianna said. "I was impressed with your quick thinking on Chase's boat. Is there anything you can tell me about what happened that wouldn't have been obvious to me watching through my binoculars?"

"Dad just collapsed as you probably saw," the older woman began. "He was already gone when I reached him, so I don't think he suffered. Then the boat capsized, and I managed to catch myself against the storage box until that big wave hit and I landed in the water. Chase shouldn't have come in that close, but he's always been one to rush in and help. Did you know he saved a little girl from drowning when he was a teenager?"

"No, I didn't."

"It was right there on the beach below Montgomery House, although she had no business being there in the first place."

Adrianna thought back to the day she had found Max and felt she had a better understanding of Chase's reaction to her predicament.

"I swallowed a bit of sea water, and then Chase reached over the side of his boat," Tiny continued. "I didn't see how he was going to get me aboard for a moment. I caught my good foot on the boat's side just as he tugged me out of the water, and between us we managed it. Then the boom headed our way, and I shouted at him to look out as I fell backwards onto my fanny, which was lucky for him because I pulled him forward just enough that the boom missed him."

"What a relief!" Adrianna exclaimed. "From where I sat, it looked like it had hit him."

"No, but he fell forward and hit the deck pretty hard before he slid into the side of the boat. That's when he hit his head."

"How are you two doing?" Bev interrupted from the doorway.

"Fine," Adrianna replied, "but I imagine it would be best now if Tiny got some rest. Let me know tomorrow if you need any help getting home." She squeezed the older woman's hand and then released it.

"I'm going to miss Dad, but he's in a better place now," Tiny said. "You've been very kind, just like Martha always was. She'd be proud of you."

"You take care now." Adrianna smiled, thinking as she followed Bev back through the emergency room to rejoin her friends that she certainly hoped, somewhere in Heaven, her great-aunt was indeed proud of her, just as Tiny had suggested.

CHAPTER XLVI

Larry Chesterton waited patiently at the foot of Chase Sheffield's ICU bed while Dr. 'Pug' glanced at his patient's chart.

"Who would've thought that someday we would all be here in this scenario?" he asked when the doctor finished.

"Not me." Pug grinned. "I wanted to be a fireman, remember?"

"Well, I'm glad you changed your mind," Larry stated. "If I were lying there instead of Chase, there's no one in whose hands I'd rather be, and I'm sure he feels the same way."

"You understand what I want you to do now, don't you?" the doctor asked, ignoring the compliment. "Just talk to him in your normal voice, using a conversational tone. Reference good times you've had together. Retell some of your old fishing lies, and make sure, every once in a while, you mention his name and identify yourself."

"Got it." The broker's normally laughter-filled countenance was now one hundred percent serious.

"Sit here." Pug pulled a visitor's chair over to the side of the bed, and then circled around to the other side, where he leaned close to his patient's ear. "Chase, it's me, Pug, and Larry Chesterton is here, too. If you've got time, would you wake up and talk to us?" He waited a minute. "Okay, it looks like you're busy, so I'm going to check on some sick folks, but Larry is going to stay here and chat with you in that nonsensical way of his."

Both men remained silent as they watched their friend for any sign of a response, but they were soon disappointed.

"You're on," Pug said. "I'll bring Jim up to relieve you if he's still here."

Left alone with his injured friend, Larry fought the urge to reach out and take his hand, instead resting his forearm on the edge of the hospital bed's mattress as he leaned closer.

"Chase, it's me, Larry," he began. "Pug's left us alone, so if you want to wake up and tell me something private you go right ahead." He paused for a few moments, but reaping no response continued, "Jim and Susan and Adrianna are all down in the waiting room. Tiny is doing just great and said to thank you for pulling her out of the drink. I, on the other hand, think that was a crazy stunt to pull, just so you wouldn't have to lose the race to me in the last lap. Frankly, old fellow, I feel cheated."

Again, he remained quiet for a few moments, willing Chase to blink an eye or move a finger. How could Chase – track star, wrestling trophy winner and all around great guy – be lying in this bed completely unresponsive? It wasn't right, and more to the point, it wasn't fair. Hadn't the poor guy gone through enough to last a lifetime?

"Chase, it's me, Larry," he continued. "There's something you ought to know. Remember that time in Miss Sutherland's fourth grade class when someone put a frog in Bitsy Long's desk drawer, and you took the blame because no one else came forward? It was me, Chase, and I'm glad you now know, 'cause I've always felt bad about that."

A gray-haired ICU nurse approached, checked one of the IV bags suspended from the stainless steel tree by her patient's bed and then withdrew.

"Chase, it's me, Larry. So tell me, what do you think about Adrianna? She's a pretty neat gal with those big dark eyes a fellow could get lost in and her shy smile, isn't she? And she's got a head on her shoulders, too, make no mistake about that."

Without having elicited a response, but liking his subject, he continued, "You see, Chase, the fact is, if you're not going to pursue her, I thought I might give it a spin. There's something about her that's head and shoulders above the rest. Aw, heck, I can't explain it, but you must know what I mean. It's not the sophistication or her sense of style or even her looks, although they certainly don't hurt. Maybe it's the way she gives you her full attention as if you're the only guy in her world. The thing is, though, I'd feel more comfortable going for it if I knew you weren't interested."

Hearing firm footsteps approaching, Larry glanced over and stood as Pug walked towards him, Jim following close behind.

"Any response?" the doctor asked.

"None that I could tell."

"Well, I want as many of you as are willing to do so to keep at it for as long as you can," Pug stated. "Studies have shown that patients in this condition are aware of what's being said to them." He turned and addressed the vet. "You understand what you're supposed to do?"

"Yes, I'm to act as the cavalry, replace Larry and make contact where he hasn't managed to do so. Basically, I introduce myself every now and then, mention Chase's name and then make conversation."

"Okay, we'll leave you to it." Pug indicated for Larry to follow him.

"Chase, it's Jim Laidlaw here, veterinarian extraordinaire. How are you doing, old buddy? That was pretty fancy sailing out there today. I think you would've beaten Larry again, if you hadn't decided to play Sir Galahad when Tiny plunged into the water. Adrianna was glued to her binoculars watching the whole thing, although she probably thought you were crazy to take such a risk. The rescue boat would've been there in a couple of minutes. Still, who knows if Tiny could've held on long enough? And, of course, Larry was right behind you trying to save her dad."

As his friend had done before, he paused for a moment, only to be met by the beeping of the machine to his left.

"Chase, this is Jim," he continued. "I don't think I've seen anything so full of wires and IVs since I had to remove a rubber duck from Tammy Sue's Rottweiler's stomach last year. I know you've always worked hard to be the best and brightest, but don't you think you may have gone a bit overboard? I mean really. Now, the stitches near your temple, I can see those. Susan and Adrianna will have fits over them. You know how ladies are about scars, always wanting to touch them and ask you for the story behind them. I can't tell you how many times I've had to explain to some half-crazed female about how that squirrel left those gouged out pockets on the front of my right calf when it climbed up my leg trying to get at my egg salad sandwich. You remember. It happened when we were hiking with the scouts along the Appalachian Trail."

He paused and ran a practiced eye over the machines surrounding the bed that were so similar and, in some cases, identical to those he used in his own practice, taking a few minutes to study the readings for himself.

"Chase, this is Jim." He leaned forward a little. "Speaking of Adrianna, I've been meaning to ask you. How interested in her are you? You see, I think she's the neatest thing since cream cheese, and I don't just mean that she's good looking, although she is. Anyone can see that. You know what I mean, though, I'm sure. Anyone who has spent time with her would be bound to pick up on it. Take for instance earlier today, when we were on my boat waiting for Larry and you to get your acts together and I asked her if she liked living in Captain's Point. She didn't just give me some sort of flip answer. She took her time about it and considered my question seriously, and then she shared with me how she really felt about moving here. There's a whole deeper layer to being with her than I've ever experienced with another woman, and I'd like to pursue that further, if I wouldn't be stepping on your toes."

The ICU elevator choosing this moment to announce other visitors, Jim stopped talking and watched for any change in Chase as footsteps approached.

"Anything yet?" Pug asked.

"Nope."

"Then make way for Susan, you old clodhopper."

Jim stood and held the visitor's chair for his replacement. "Maybe this sort of thing needs a woman's touch," he suggested and patted her shoulder.

"Wish me luck." She waved them both on their way.

"Chase, it's me Susan." She took stock of his injuries – the stitches just short of his left temple, the splint on his right wrist, a bruise here and there. "I'm sorry this had to happen to you," she began, "but I've got to say that I'm proud of you for assisting Tiny. It was the right thing to do, and it took courage. You're a great guy, Chase Sheffield, but you know I think that."

For a few moments, she concentrated on looking for any change in his appearance, but was disappointed.

"Chase, it's Susan. I want to say how grateful I am to you for offering me a partnership in the firm, giving my little guy and me a fresh start. Did I hurt you when I ran off with Bill all those years ago? I didn't think so at the time, you were already so withdrawn from me, but as I've gotten older, I've begun to wonder. I didn't do it to hurt you. I want you to know that. Stupid me, I really loved the guy. Unfortunately, he didn't know how to love anyone back. Talk about a bad apple."

She let out a sigh and waited quietly for a couple of minutes, again watching for any sign of a change.

"Adrianna's down in the waiting room, Chase. Pug's bringing her up in a few moments, and I'll head home to tuck Pipsqueak into bed before coming back for my next shift, if you haven't returned to us. Have you admitted to yourself yet that you love her, Chase? You do, you know. I'm sure of it. I know that look in your eyes, or at least, what a fraction of it meant when we were teenagers and thought we knew all about love, but were clueless.

"Please don't hold back, Chase. Don't let her slip through your fingers. Adrianna's perfect for you. She's smart and funny and beautiful, and you two share so much in common. Everyone that has met her just loves her. The gals she sat with during dinner at the clambake couldn't stop talking about her after she left. I wish you could've heard them, and you've got to admit there aren't many women out there like her."

She paused and stroked his hand for a moment as she blinked back a few tears, then pulled herself together as she heard Pug and Adrianna approach.

"Nothing yet." Susan gave up her seat to her replacement. "I'll be back in time for my next shift."

"Any questions?" Pug addressed Adrianna.

"No, I've done this before when one of my college friends was injured in an auto accident," she answered.

"We'll leave you to it then." The physician took Susan's arm and steered her towards the elevator.

For a few minutes, Adrianna sat quietly, fighting back tears that she hadn't expected as she took in the tubing and IVs that surrounded her attorney. Examining the black stitches that stood out starkly against his bruised flesh, she tasted bile and swallowed quickly.

Don't be silly, she chided herself. Pull yourself together, and help him. This is Chase, and he needs you, even if he does look green in these ICU lights and is lying still as opposed to sitting up, healthy and strong.

Leaning forward, she cradled his hand in her own and took a deep breath. "Chase, it's Adrianna," she began. "You're going to be okay. I'm here now. I'm right beside you. I'm holding your hand."

And then she watched amazed as his eyelids fluttered and she felt his grip tighten, at first weakly and then stronger. "Adrianna," he whispered and then left her again.

CHAPTER XLVII

At first Adrianna wasn't quite sure what she should do or even if what she had perceived had been real. Perhaps his eyelids fluttering had merely been a reflexive reaction to dreamlike activity that he was experiencing in his current state, and maybe his hand had just twitched.

"Chase, it's me, Adrianna." She brought her other hand up, so that she was now holding his limp one in both of hers. "Remember how you saved Max and me on the beach, and then you came to our aid when Ginny went into labor? Well, now it's your turn to be rescued." She held his hand in a slightly firmer grip. "I'm here to help you. If you can just hold onto my hand, I think I can do it. Can you wake up and assist me?"

Behind her, Adrianna heard the squeak of the ICU nurse's rubber sole against the tile floor as she approached.

"Chase, it's me, Adrianna. I think we can get you out of this, if you'll just hold on."

"Adrianna…" Again his eyelids fluttered as she felt his grip tighten. "Tired…"

The second word had been whispered so softly that she wasn't sure she had heard it correctly.

"What did he say?" the nurse asked, pulling his chart from the end of the bed so she could make a note.

"That was the second time he's said my name in response to something I've said, and I think the other word this time was 'tired.' He's also tightening his grip slightly on my hand."

"That's a good sign." The nurse placed her fingertips on his wrist. "Just keep talking to him."

"Are we getting a response?" Pug rejoined them.

"Seems so." The nurse passed him the chart that he glanced over and then returned.

Adrianna watched quietly as the physician bent near to his patient's ear. "Chase, this is Pug, and Adrianna is still here. Think you could open your eyes for us, buddy?"

"Pug..." This time Chase's eyelids opened almost completely. "Adrianna here."

"He's holding onto my hand," Adrianna whispered. "No, he's let go again."

"Why don't you stay with him a bit longer?" Pug patted her shoulder. "Just let him rest for now, though. I'll come back for you in a few minutes. Thank goodness everyone is too tired from the regatta to get into trouble and end up here in the ER this evening. So far, the PA has been able to take care of almost everything."

Pug and the nurse having left her alone with their patient, Adrianna did as she was told and remained quiet, still holding Chase's hand in hers even as she wondered what he would think if he regained consciousness. Would he care, be appalled, or be embarrassed for himself or her?

For a moment, she wished she had followed Pug from the room, but then realized just as quickly that she much preferred to be where she was, not that she had much faith in her ability to do anything for her attorney.

Her attorney... The words remained in her thoughts. Yes, Chase was that, but if she was honest with herself he was also a friend – someone who had told her that he was there for her and would continue to be so should she need him, someone she could trust.

One of the machines to her left let out a pronounced beep, and she patted Chase's hand. "Don't pay any attention to that noisy thing," she reassured him. "I'm here, and it won't hurt you."

Again, she thought she felt a slight tightening of his fingers, but then admitted to herself that it could have been nothing more than her imagination.

Relaxing, she examined what she could see of the man before her. Tall, tanned and strong with a jaw that often reflected determination, but could just as easily relax into a smile – how different her perception was of him now than it had been when she had first met him!

She had found him so cold and distant that day in his office, but he had been right when he had spoken to her since of having to walk a fine line between meeting her needs as a new client and fulfilling her great-aunt's wishes. Penny and Susan had both spoken to her of Chase's reserve, but there were times when she had received the impression of a shy little boy.

Was it possible that he had to work hard to produce his public personae? If so, he had done a wonderful job of it – serving as a councilman, volunteering for committees at his church, appearing on the Chamber of Commerce's annual calendar year after year – a man of whom you could be proud. And no one could say that he didn't have friends. According to Susan's high school BFF, the hospital's switchboard had been swamped by calls from well-wishers.

And then there had been the times when his eyes had twinkled with laughter or his expression had softened - the times when she had felt something electric passing between them.

"How are we doing?" the ICU nurse asked as she checked one of the IV bags and made another note on her patient's chart.

"Nothing since Pug left," Adrianna said.

"Sometimes a body needs to rest," the nurse assured her, "and I can believe Chase's does. I've never known anyone who works harder at whatever they're doing, and he just spent a number of hours in the sun on the water."

"That's true," Adrianna agreed quietly.

A man of whom you could be proud… She returned to the words once she was alone again. Well, she had once thought the same about Brad, for all the good it had done her. He, too, had worked hard, earning money throughout his years as an undergrad so he could attend med school. He, too, had had lots of friends. He, too, had said that she could trust him. And yet, in the end, he had abandoned her for another.

Thinking that it had been a long day in the sun for her as well, she closed her eyes against the glare of the ICU lights and let out a small sigh.

"Tired?" Chase asked, his voice clear as once again he tightened his grip on her hand.

CHAPTER XLVIII

Adrianna's dark eyes flew open to be greeted by the steady gaze of Chase's deep blue ones. "Just a little," she admitted. "It's been a long day. How are you feeling? You've given us all quite a scare."

"My head hurts." He attempted to shift his weight and grimaced. "How bad is my face?"

She laughed, hoping to assuage his fears. "And you men say we women are vain. You have a small cut near your left temple that Pug has stitched closed, a really lovely shiner around your left eye from when you hit the deck, and a badly strained right wrist that's in a splint."

"Tiny?"

"She has a sprained ankle, and they're keeping her overnight for observation," she told him, relieved that he remembered the events leading up to his accident.

"Buzz?"

"It was a heart attack."

"Dead?"

She glanced up at the ICU nurse, who had hurried over when she had noted the change in her patient and now nodded her approval. "Yes," Adrianna confirmed.

"Better this way." He closed his eyes for a moment, but then reopened them.

"Tiny told me about the cancer," Adrianna said.

"Here comes the quack." Chase's gaze traveled over her left shoulder.

"I'll have you know that I graduated at the top of my med school class, despite the fact that you beat me out for valedictorian at Captain's Point High," Pug shot back as he joined them. "How are you feeling?"

"Like I've been hit by a truck." His patient moved slightly and again grimaced.

"Nope, a sailboat," the physician corrected him. "From what I hear, you were lucky not to have been killed by the boom."

"I don't remember the boom." A crease formed between Chase's brows.

"You wouldn't have seen it coming," Adrianna told him, wondering what Pug thought of the fact that Chase was still holding her hand.

"I think we'll keep you here in the ICU through the night." Pug made a note on the chart the nurse had handed him. "We'll want to wake you up every so often." Then he turned and addressed Adrianna. "Will you let the rest of them know when you go back to the ER waiting room?"

"Sure."

"Only a couple of more minutes." The physician patted her shoulder. "He'll want to sleep, and we'll want to awaken him. Good job." Then he left with the nurse to check on a patient who was being shifted from a gurney onto a bed placed at the other end of the unit.

"Who are the rest of them?" Chase asked once Adrianna and he were alone.

"Pug had asked Larry, Jim, Susan and me to take turns talking to you to see if you would respond to our voices," she told him.

"Jim's scars…" He suddenly looked very tired.

"I think I should go." She attempted to withdraw her hand as she stood, but he tightened his grip.

"Thank you for sitting with me." His gaze softened.

"It was my turn." She smiled. "Now, though, you need to rest, and I ought to let everyone downstairs know you're okay. I'll come back in the morning."

"Okay." His eyelids sagged. "In the morning…, but it was you…who stayed…with me."

And then, his eyes closed, and his grip on her hand slowly relaxed. She waited a moment, but he slept on. Raising the fingers of her right hand to her lips, she kissed them and then touched his cheek gently, before heading back to the ER waiting room where she discovered Jim had left a few minutes earlier, since Otis and Penny had arrived with sandwiches and a promise to wait for her.

"He's sleeping normally," she told the small group that greeted her. "Pug said they'll keep him in ICU overnight."

"What a relief!" Larry reached his arm around Susan's waist and gave her a hug. "I told you he's a tough cookie."

"Tiny's the real heroine," Adrianna pointed out. "If that boom had hit him…"

"Well, it didn't." Otis stood and collected a small insulated bag. "Penny kept an egg salad sandwich for you. Why don't you eat it in the car on the way home?"

"I wasn't sure I'd ever be hungry again after the huge meal I enjoyed at Chester's, but now I'm famished." Adrianna sent Larry a thumbs-up, dropping behind to walk beside Susan as they all headed to the parking lot.

"Did he really seem alright?" Susan asked.

"He said his head and face hurt," Adrianna said, "but he remembered pulling Tiny out of the water and Buzz having collapsed."

"Then he should be okay." The relief Adrianna had felt earlier filled Susan's face. "We have a key to Sheffield Place back at the house. Larry or I can run by in the morning and bring him some pajamas."

"Here you go." Otis held open the Lincoln's back door.

Adrianna slid in and then accepted the insulated bag from him, unzipping it and pulling out her sandwich. As she ate, Otis started the big car, and Penny chatted quietly with him in the front seat about some friends who had brought in a sick child while they had been waiting.

As the darkened world passed by the Lincoln's windows, her sandwich now finished, Adrianna's mind traveled back to the soft look in Chase's eyes as he had thanked her and the feel of her hand as it had rested so comfortably in his.

CHAPTER XLIX

Despite having fallen into her half tester bed utterly exhausted, Adrianna awoke with the sunrise the next morning. Snapping on Max's leash, she took him for a good run both to stretch her own muscles from sitting so much the previous day and to insure he received the exercise that he needed. She then heated a blueberry muffin in the kitchen's new microwave and prepared an espresso that she carried back to her tower suite, where Max had already fallen asleep in his bed in front of the hearth.

For a moment, as she lounged on the window seat and munched on her muffin, she toyed with calling the hospital to check on Chase's condition, but then nixed the idea. Instead she would shower, dress and go see him herself before heading to church.

But when she carried her mug into her dressing room to set out her church clothes, she reconsidered. Hospitals, she determined, could be downers, and she would do what she could to bring a bit of cheer into Chase's presence. Resolved, she rummaged through the drawers and cupboards that held her more casual clothes, carefully selecting a pair of jeans and a bright top to wear with comfortable, flower-print espadrilles along with a pair of fun dangle earrings.

Her shower behind her and light makeup applied, she reviewed and approved her choices in the long dressing room mirror.

Thirty minutes later, she disembarked from the Elantra, just in time to catch Pug as he was leaving the hospital.

"You're an early bird," he greeted her, "but you're not the first. Larry's already popped in and left. They're moving Chase into room 326 right now."

"How is he doing?" Adrianna asked.

"Great!" The doctor's face sobered. "He was lucky, though. We were worried at first that there might be some swelling around his brain, but the specialist at Johns Hopkins agreed with me when he reviewed the test results. Your great-aunt did this county a real service when she negotiated the connection and purchased the equipment for Captain's Point General that allows for inter-hospital collaboration, and of course, it didn't hurt yesterday that Chase has always been so hard headed."

"I know my great-aunt would be pleased that her efforts on the hospital's behalf are being put to good use," Adrianna replied, "and I'm glad that you were on duty when Chase was brought in."

"Wait until he starts complaining about the size of my bill," Pug said with a grin. "Now you hurry in and make sure that he doesn't start browbeating the nurses."

Adrianna took his advice and hurried through the sliding doors of the main entrance, pausing at the reception desk to secure a visitor's pass before heading to the third floor. Here she followed the signs to room 326, where an orderly was wheeling away an empty gurney.

"Is it okay if I go in, or should I wait?" she asked.

"Knock on the door first, but I think it's okay," he advised and then left her to it.

"Come in," Chase's strong voice responded to her hesitant taps.

Adrianna took a quick glance around the room as she entered, pleased that it resembled more of a hotel room in style than rooms she was used to seeing in larger facilities.

"Don't you look pretty!" Chase beamed at her as she approached. "And I bet you don't plan on sticking a needle into me either."

"Maybe just a small one," she teased, glad to see that he was lounging in a more normal upright position. "How are you feeling?"

"Much better, although Pug plans on keeping me here for another night."

"Better safe than sorry." Adrianna slid her eyes from his face to his toes and back. "I must say, though, that you haven't quite mastered the Hollywood look."

"You mean the stubble?" He rubbed his chin with his good hand. "Larry dropped by this pair of exercise pants and a T-shirt this morning, but forgot a razor. He's promised to bring an electric one by after church."

"So where's the T-shirt?" she asked, eyeing the blue and white striped hospital gown that he still wore over the pants.

"In the drawer." He nodded at the bedside table. "It was too much trouble to get it on over the splint and IV tube, so I decided to go mix and match."

"I do plan to attend the late church service," Adrianna assured him, not wanting him to think ill of her.

"Don't." Chase reached out and took her hand. "I'd rather you stay."

"Here we go, sir," an aide announced as she brought in his breakfast tray.

"Thank goodness!" He released his hold on Adrianna and struggled to sit up straighter. "I'm famished, and they've promised to remove the IV once I start eating."

The aide placed his meal on the movable bed tray and then slid the latter into position, before raising the top of the hospital bed a bit further. "Are you okay on your own?" she asked.

"I'll help him," Adrianna promised and began removing the paper covers from his orange juice and coffee as the aide left them, shutting the door partially behind her.

"One sugar and two creams," Chase responded to Adrianna's questioning look as she held up two sugar packets, "but I didn't mean for you to remain here so you could wait on me."

"And just how do you intend to manage on your own with your right hand in that condition?" She nodded toward his bruised and swollen fingers, where they protruded from the splint. "Frankly, I'm looking forward to watching the suave and debonair Chase Sheffield eating left-handed. It'll be a treat."

"It is a bummer that my right hand was injured," he agreed, "and according to Pug, my having broken this wrist when I was twelve probably strengthened the bone, so that this time I only strained it, which is worse. A bone would have healed in about six weeks, but a strain can take as many months."

"That is bad." Adrianna removed an insulated cover from his breakfast plate to reveal scrambled eggs, bacon, a sausage patty, hashed browns and a toasted English muffin. "These look like grits, she uncovered a small bowl. Pug must have ordered you one of everything."

"Maybe he still sees me as a growing boy." Chase reached for his orange juice, while she buttered the muffin and spread it with jelly.

Picking up the fork, he stabbed at the scrambled eggs, managing to secure a mouthful as Adrianna proceeded to cut up his sausage.

"Just take your time, and use your fingers as much as you can," she suggested as she ignored the comfortable lounge chair and instead pulled a more utilitarian upright visitors' chair close to his bed, where she could assist him as needed.

"Girl, you have no idea how hungry I am." He gnawed on a piece of bacon. "Even marginally warm, this is some of the best food I've ever eaten."

Adrianna laughed, relieved to see that he had such a good appetite. A little while later, Chase had consumed every scrap of food as well as having drunk his juice, a container of milk and his coffee, so she rolled aside the bed tray, returned to her seat and met his gaze with concern.

"How are you going to manage on your own?" She returned to her earlier question.

"To tell you the truth, I'm not sure," he admitted. "I'll be fine once I get to the office. Bridgette already waits on me hand and foot when I'm there, and I can drive one-handed if necessary as long as I proceed slowly. I suppose Susan could knot my tie for me, and I can eat out if I have to. Hopefully, I'll be able to take the splint off some of the time before long."

"I guess it's a good thing you enjoy a challenge," Adrianna teased him.

"How did you like your first regatta?" He changed the subject.

And so, the morning progressed pleasantly as she shared with him her impressions from the previous day and he passed on memories of former regattas until Larry and Susan joined them, fresh from the early service at church.

"Paul Lynch offered to take up residence in one of your spare bedrooms if he could be of any use," Larry announced as he pulled Chase's electric razor from a small paper bag.

"There's no need for that." Susan seated herself on the lounge chair. "Mom is insisting that he'll stay at The Cove until he can fend for himself. There's plenty of room, and she's always wanted to get her hands on him."

"That settles it then." Larry rolled his eyes. "Once Aunt Elizabeth has spoken, there's no sense in arguing, and it solves a lot of problems. I can pop up, grab a free breakfast and make sure you're presentable for work in the mornings."

"Love the shiner!" Jim chose this moment to make an entrance.

"So how are your squirrel scars?" Chase shot back.

"Still there." The casual tone in the veterinarian's voice belied the concerned look on his face. "Just out of curiosity, since you obviously remember what I was saying to you yesterday, do you also remember that cemetery incident when we were kids?"

"Cemetery incident." Chase gave a mock impression of having to search through his memory. "Can't say that I do."

"Then I guess both of our memories can be accused of having failed just a little bit."

"What cemetery incident?" Susan demanded, sensing a good laugh on someone that wasn't being shared with the rest of them.

"Trust me." Chase sent Jim a meaningful look. "We're not going there."

As the relaxed conversation swirled around her, Adrianna sat quietly in her chair, wondering if she would ever feel truly part of the group. And then she realized that Chase's gaze was concentrated on her, the soft look once again filling his eyes, and her heart glowed.

CHAPTER L

Awakened by a loud clap of thunder on Monday morning, Adrianna seriously considered pulling the covers back over her head and remaining in bed, since the roofers would not be able to finish the cottage's repairs in weather like this. Still, there were items she wanted to discuss with Otis about the second stage of the renovation, and such weather would provide a good opportunity, she told herself firmly as she threw her feet over the side of the bed.

"Your breakfast is on the table," Penny greeted her a little while later as she entered the kitchen, and then nodded towards Max who was waiting hopefully by his water bowl. "He's already had his, so don't let him fool you."

"Is Otis in his office?"

"I think so, but he'll probably drop in here for his second cup of coffee in a few minutes." Penny bent and removed a pan of brownies from the oven.

"Why don't you two both join me then," Adrianna suggested. She took a step towards the breakfast room, but then paused. "As long as it's going to be a bad hair day anyway, can you recommend somewhere I can get a quick trim?"

"You should ask Susan who does her hair," Penny chuckled. "The woman I go to does it out of her home and specializes in old women and blue rinses, but she's a good friend of mine so I stick with her."

"Susan it is then," Adrianna agreed. "I can ask her how Chase is doing at the same time. They're supposed to take him to The Cove when he's released from the hospital this morning."

"I wondered how he would manage with his right hand in a splint, but Elizabeth will take good care of him."

Adrianna had consumed a pain au chocolate and was sipping espresso and reading the local newspaper, when the Plunks joined her a few minutes later.

"I see the Council has set aside more acreage along the beach south of here as a wildlife sanctuary." She looked up as they both took seats at the table.

"The storm seems to be blowing on past us." Penny nodded towards the large window, beyond which the sun was attempting to peek through the dark clouds.

"It's about time," Otis stated and chose a lemon poppy seed muffin from the basket that had been left for Adrianna's breakfast.

"Help yourself." His wife slapped his wrist with the tips of her fingers.

"I already have." He grinned back.

"If you two children will settle down now, I'll call this meeting to order." Adrianna looked severely down her nose at them both, but a twitch at the corner of her mouth gave her away.

"Actually, I've wanted to talk to you about the caretaker's cottage and Paul Lynch." Otis chomped another bite from his muffin.

"You don't want him as a tenant?" Surprise filled his wife's face.

"I'm thrilled he's renting it," Otis cleared the air. "It's providing him with parking that concerns me. We reserved a slot in the new garage for the dependency, which Edwina will now be using, but except for parking in front of the cottage or our providing some sort of pad alongside it, there really is no designated spot for Paul unless we give him a slot in the carriage house."

"Which would mean we would lose rent from one of the retail spaces," Adrianna picked up where he had left off.

"Exactly," her property manager agreed, "which I don't think we should do, but neither do I wish to see Paul forced to park his car out in the salt-filled rain that comes off the ocean."

"No, you don't want to do that." Penny tore a bite from a pumpkin scone she had lifted surreptitiously from Adrianna's breakfast basket a moment before. "So what are your options?"

"I suppose there are two of them," her husband continued. "We could build a one-car garage with a covered walkway to the cottage, which would enable Paul and future tenants to still have the windows for light, or we could build on a carport, which would also allow for the windows to take in light." He met his employer's thoughtful gaze.

"So which one are you favoring?" Adrianna asked, having realized that her mind was more consumed by thoughts of Chase taking up residence at Chesterton Cove than by concerns with Montgomery property renovations.

"There are good and bad points with both," he replied. "The carport is cheaper, but I think it will show its age quicker. Also, I'm concerned that a carport would withstand the winds in a Nor'easter. On the other hand, a garage and a short covered walkway will look better and last longer, but it will cost more."

"Right on both counts." Adrianna refolded the newspaper she had been reading out of habit, then addressed Otis. "How soon can you work up a cost estimate, and when do you think we could start on construction?"

"By the end of today, and the middle of next week, with some wiggle room on the latter."

"Will you have to charge Paul more rent to cover it?" Penny asked.

"The property is worth more with a garage, but I've already quoted Paul a figure," Adrianna answered. "Right now, that sum is written in stone, but the next tenant could definitely be asked to pay more."

"That's the ticket." Otis beamed at her. "I think even Martha would agree."

"I keep remembering what Chase said that day about in for a penny, in for a pound," Adrianna said, "so I'm leaning towards the garage option. Let's get the figures together, and then I'd like to run it by him before making a firm decision." She concentrated on refilling her mug from the carafe as the Plunks exchanged surprised glances.

But then, Penny's face filled with understanding as she sent her husband a knowing smile while drawing the outline of a heart over her own before she rose and returned to her kitchen.

"Guess it's time to get back to work." Otis stood and replaced his chair.

"I'll join you in your office in a few minutes," Adrianna said, her gaze directed at the garden beyond the window.

Left alone, Paul's parking concerns and her desire for time alone with Chase merged. Would this need for Chase's opinion provide sufficient reason for her to storm the battlements of Chesterton Cove, and if so, when should she go there?

CHAPTER LI

The next morning found Adrianna still uncomfortable about making an uninvited personal visit to Chesterton Cove. Determined to clear her mind by taking Max for another long run, she was lacing her first trainer when she was interrupted by a tap on her bedroom's doorframe. Glancing up, she was surprised to find Susan standing there, dressed in a navy blue suit comprised of a scallop-necked short jacket and a white silk blouse, worn over a skirt that ended just at the wearer's knees.

"If the jury is stocked with men, you'll definitely win your case in an outfit like that," she greeted her friend.

"Think so?" Susan struck a pose and then crossed to the bay window nearest the bed. "I had forgotten how lovely the view is from this room."

"I'm sure yours at The Cove are just as nice." Adrianna wondered, as she slipped her left foot into the other trainer, why she was receiving this particular visit.

"No, yours are framed by the points of land on both sides." Susan bent her head to take in the gardens. "And I certainly don't see such a profusion of beautiful roses each morning." She returned to the doorway. "Chase asked me to stop by on my way to the coffee shop and bring you a message."

Wondering why he had chosen not to phone her himself, Adrianna stood and indicated they should both head downstairs. "Why don't you have a mug of coffee here with me?" she suggested. "I wanted to ask you for the name of your hairdresser anyway. Mine needs a trim."

"Sure. I go to Bitsy Long – Bitsy Wilder now. She owns Long and Short."

"Cute name." Adrianna made a note on the kitchen phone tablet a minute later. "Do you think she'll fit me in?"

"I'm sure she will if you can be flexible about the time." Susan accepted a mug and plate from Penny, who was unloading the dishwasher, and followed Adrianna into the breakfast room. "Tell Bitsy that I gave you the recommendation."

"Name dropping is such a small price to pay for a good haircut," Adrianna joked as she filled their mugs from the carafe and then indicated for Susan to help herself to sugar, cream or a pastry. "Now what was Chase's message?"

Her guest took a sip of her coffee. "Has Chase ever mentioned his Aunt Ruth or his cousin Jack?"

"No." Adrianna wondered where this could possibly be going.

"His Aunt Ruth lives in Boston," her visitor explained, "and she is Chase's mother's only sister. Jack was her son, and he was killed. He was a few years older than Chase, but they were both only children. Chase spent serious time with them on Cape Cod every summer, and it's Jack's boat that he sails."

"Sounds like they were close," Adrianna said.

"They were." Susan tore a bite from the scone she had chosen from the basket of pastries and played with it on her plate. "Jack was Chase's mentor and role model, during a time when his parents were completely letting him down."

"His death must have devastated Aunt Ruth as well."

"It did," Susan acknowledged. "My mother and she were both undergrads at Vassar, and Mom says she aged overnight. She's lived in her big old house with her memories and two retainers like a recluse ever since. Chase has visited her once or twice every year, but there have been times when he's felt his presence caused her pain, because he's alive and Jack isn't."

"How awful for both of them."

"We were working on a puzzle last evening, when Chase's phone rang," Susan continued. "It was Aunt Ruth's attorney, who told us Ruth had been admitted to Massachusetts General and isn't expected to last long. There Chase sat, his right hand in a splint and his face stitched and bruised. Then Larry offered to drive him to Boston."

"Thank goodness for Larry!" Adrianna made no effort to hide her relief. "Have they already left?"

"By the time Larry had packed a suitcase, and we had managed to pull Chase's things together at Sheffield Place, it was past nine." Susan glanced at the china mantel clock. "They should be in Boston by now, but whether or not they've made it to the hospital, I don't know. They were stopping by the house first."

"Will you keep me posted?"

"Sure." Susan snapped open her purse and withdrew a small piece of paper. "This is Chase's personal email. He has his laptop with him if you should want to contact him for any reason, but there's another complication. Apparently, his Aunt Ruth's Boston attorney and he are co-administrators of the will she had drawn up after Jack's death."

"Is her estate large?" Adrianna asked, but then quickly continued. "I'm sorry. I shouldn't have asked you that. What I really want to know is how long it might require Chase to remain in Boston."

"He has no idea how long he'll be gone. His aunt and uncle were wealthy at one time, but for all he knows, she's been living off her capital for years. The two things he knows for sure are that she sold the Cape Cod house and gave him her son's boat after his death, although she always said when he asked that she didn't need anything."

"That's going to put a big strain on you at the firm, isn't it?" Adrianna refilled her friend's mug.

"I'm going to be busy, that's for sure," Susan acknowledged. "Chase felt that you had everything well in hand here, but if you need anything, let me know. Bridgette will always put you through. I have access to everything, but Chase's personal opinion, and you can email him for that."

"Don't worry about us." Adrianna sent her a smile. "The renovations are running smoothly, we have plenty of cash available, and Otis can tap into all sorts of resources. It's Chase and you I feel sorry for."

"Actually, work right now is a release for me." Susan sent her a wry smile. "It's Chase you should be concerned about. He's been hurt so much over the years, and this will bring up memories." She paused and considered for a moment, before continuing. "Maybe I shouldn't say this, but he cares for you,

Adrianna. I can see it, even if he may not have acknowledged it to himself yet. He's a good man, and he deserves better treatment than he's received for a long time."

"If what you say is true, I hope I never hurt him." Adrianna patted her friend's hand where it rested on the table, even as she fought the image of Chase, injured and soon to be alone with his memories.

CHAPTER LII

Chase gradually awoke to the slow stop and go motion of Larry's Mercedes, realizing that they must now be stuck in a mass of commuters heading into Boston. It had been a nightmare of a journey.

First had come the call from Aunt Ruth's attorney, George Mason, followed by his friend's welcomed offer to drive him northward and the subsequent scramble to pack what it was thought they would each need for an undetermined time period. It had not escaped his notice either that Larry had added a dark suit to his carryon or that, after a whispered comment from her mother, Susan had selected his own black suit and added it to a growing stack of items Elizabeth had been folding into a suitcase on his bed at Sheffield Place.

He had planned to stay awake and keep Larry company on the long drive up I-95, but his injured body had obviously felt otherwise, his head beginning to nod shortly after they left Captain's Point. Somewhere short of Baltimore, his friend had pulled into a gas station, reclined his seat and thrown a blanket over him, before continuing.

Later, he had roused himself only to find the car parked at the far end of a rest stop and Larry snoring quietly, slumped against the side window. In the pre-dawn hours, his friend had awakened him yet again with orders to rise and shine, and they had both stretched their legs, consumed large breakfasts and drunk horrible coffee at a franchise restaurant.

Once they regained the highway, he had expected the caffeine to kick in, but it couldn't have been long before the rhythm of the wheels on the road had sent him to sleep again – this time his rest disturbed by dreams of his Aunt Ruth and Jack as they had been during simpler, happier times on the shores of Cape Cod, followed by a replay of his watching Adrianna drive away from the clambake, beyond his reach.

The sharp blast of a horn and the sudden braking of the car sent him forward, and he opened his eyes to the glint of bright sunshine hitting the chrome on the sea of vehicles around them.

"About time you woke up," Larry greeted him as he fumbled to find with his left hand the control button that would raise his seat to a more upright position.

"You need a shave," he shot back once he had settled himself.

"So do you, and you've got a great case of bedhead besides," Larry replied as he punched a button on the GPS that activated its voice component. "We're still set to go to the house first. Is that what you want?"

"I think so," Chase acknowledged. "Aunt Ruth won't want to see me like this if she is conscious, and there's no telling how long I'll want to stay at the hospital. You, though, should go to bed once I'm presentable. I'll take a cab to Mass General."

"I'm not going to argue that one." Larry sent him a wry smile. "Frankly, I'm bushed, but let me know when you're either ready for me to join you or pick you up. And don't bother to say all of that again." He held off further comment by raising his right hand, palm towards his passenger. "I know that I'm free to head on home as soon as I'm rested, but I'd rather stay here until I know for sure that you can handle things on your own. The ladies at The Cove would never forgive me if I left you too soon."

"Now I won't hear a word spoken against either Susan or your aunt," Chase objected. "They had us both organized and out of there in no time at all."

"They were pretty great, weren't they?" Larry switched on his blinker and began shifting lanes in response to a command from the GPS. "Any idea who will be at the house?"

"None at all. Normally, Edmund and Marissa, my aunt's live-in couple, would both be there, but either one or both of them may be at the hospital." He tried unsuccessfully to stretch out a kink or two. "George also mentioned that one of his associates would be placed at our disposal." He reached over and switched off the GPS. "Turn right at the second light, and then it's two blocks along on the left."

A few minutes later, the car parked, the two men disembarked in front of a Beacon Hill mansion, its red brick exterior warmed by the morning sun.

"Let's not worry about the luggage until we know whose here," Larry suggested and headed up the front walk, Chase close behind.

The doorbell's chimes had barely ceased ringing when the shiny black door was opened by a spry man in his late sixties, who was dressed in dark pants, a white shirt and tie, a pair of gold-rimmed glasses adding a touch of sophistication to his sober face. "Mr. Chase." He opened the door wider. "Whatever happened to you?"

"Had a bit of a sailing accident on Saturday." Chase nodded towards his friend. "Edmund, this is Larry Chesterton, who was kind enough to drive me up here."

"Nice to meet you," the older man shut the front door behind them. "Mr. Mason's associate is waiting for you in the library." He led them to a door on the right of the main staircase. "Mr. Sheffield and Mr. Chesterton have arrived, sir," he announced and then left them.

A man of their own age, dressed in a navy blue business suit, looked up from a laptop opened on a dark oak table. "John Mason," he introduced himself. "George's youngest."

"Chase Sheffield and this is my friend Larry Chesterton." He held out his hand. "I appreciate your taking the time to assist us. Has there been any news since I spoke with your father last night?"

"Not really." John's face sobered. "As Dad probably told you, Mrs. Stanford has suffered a stroke, which has left her paralyzed on the left side, and at last report, she has not yet regained consciousness. Her condition is considered to be guarded, but the doctors will fill you in much better than I can."

"Then it would be best if we brought in the luggage, so I can shower and shave before heading to Mass General," Chase stated.

"I'll be glad to drop you off, once you're ready," John followed them towards the front door. "Please consider me to be at your disposal as long as you're here."

Comfortably attired in khakis and a golf shirt that allowed for the splint and Larry settled in his room, Chase announced himself ready to leave an hour later.

"How familiar are you with my aunt's household?" he asked as John steered them towards the hospital.

"Very familiar," the other man answered. "Her affairs have been my number one priority since I passed the bar."

"Does she have any staff besides Edmund and Marissa?" Chase asked.

"There's a maid that comes in three days a week and a landscape service that also handles snow removal in the winter. A professional chef is under contract, and she prepares meals on site once a month."

"That's what I thought from my visits over the years, but you don't always see all the staff in a large house."

John brought the car to a stop in front of the hospital's main entrance, and then withdrew a slim card case from the inside breast pocket of his suit. "I left both my father's and my business cards on the table in the library, but here's another set for you to keep on hand. You can reach me on my cell anytime, day or night. Please don't hesitate to call."

"I appreciate your help this morning." Chase accepted the offered cards. "I'll get back in touch, just as soon as I know what I'm dealing with."

He disembarked and walked through the sliding glass doors, secured a visitor's card and headed for the critical care unit where his aunt lay, wishing with all of his heart that he was back in Captain's Point.

CHAPTER LIII

Chase had spoken with the doctor and sat with his aunt's tube and IV riddled body for the five minutes he had been allowed, finally purchasing two paperbacks and a newspaper from the gift shop off the main lobby. In between similar short visits, he had proceeded to read his way through the day, breaking only for a quick lunch in the cafeteria. It was with relief then that he glanced up to see Larry approaching.

"How's it going?" His friend remained standing.

"I went in a few minutes ago," Chase filled him in. "She suffered a massive stroke. The doctor said there's a chance, but they always say that. It's my impression that we're waiting for a second stroke to end it for her."

"Let's get out of here for a few minutes." Larry placed his hand on his friend's shoulder. "The gal at the visitor's desk said there's a good neighborhood restaurant within walking distance. It'll do you good to get some fresh air and stretch your legs."

"Sounds like a plan," Chase agreed, "but I'd like to come back once we're finished."

The restaurant proved to be cozy, but comfortable, and both men ordered the oversized cheeseburger platter that was featured on the menu and slices of cherry pie, warmed and served with a scoop of vanilla ice cream.

"This is on me," Chase insisted once they were finished and settled the bill, adding in a large gourmet coffee to go for each of them.

It was a pleasant evening, and the wide sidewalk along which they returned was busy with couples strolling to area pubs, restaurants and parks - a sharp contrast to the sterile environment they entered when they passed through the hospital's double doors.

"You're welcome to this one if you haven't already read it." Chase handed his friend a paperback once they reached the waiting area, and then left him for yet another five minute visit.

"I'm here, Aunt Ruth," he told her as he held her free hand, "and I'll take care of everything, including Edmund and Marissa, no matter what happens." He paused a moment. "If you should see Jack anytime soon, tell him I miss him and give him my best."

Returning to the waiting area, he plopped into a chair and turned to his friend. "No change."

Larry nodded, flipped to the next page in his book and kept reading.

Chase leaned his head against the wall and closed his eyes against the scene around him, forcing himself to remain seated and stay the course. Free to wander, his mind traveled from the wrench it would be for Edmund and Marissa if he sold his aunt's house to a review of all the work that he had dumped onto Susan's shoulders, before ending on the renovation plans at Montgomery House for the current week.

For a moment, he smiled as he remembered Adrianna, dressed in a pair of white short shorts and a bright top, a chartreuse tennis visor holding back her dark waves, giving orders to two burly construction guys on the day he had first shown up to help. Hearing a soft tread on the linoleum tile, he opened his eyes to see the doctor approaching and sat up straighter.

"There's been a slight change for the worse," the physician filled them in. "It's possible that it won't be much longer. I'll keep you posted."

"I know it sounds trite, but it would be for the best," Chase said once he and Larry were alone. "She hasn't been happy since Jack died, and she wouldn't want to be paralyzed."

Six hours later, Chase's aunt had joined her husband and son without ever regaining consciousness, and Larry had driven them back to her house, where the two men now faced one another from opposite chairs set in front of the library's fireplace, each nursing a cold beer.

"I'll call John Mason first thing in the morning, advise him of the situation and ask him to stop by," Chase said. "He'll know the name of the funeral home she preferred and how to gain access to the mausoleum."

"Any idea what's ahead of you?" Larry asked.

"Not really." Chase shrugged. "The house seems to be in good condition. My hope is that she's made some sort of provision for Edmund and Marissa that will allow them to enjoy a reasonable retirement. I know it sounds strange, but I didn't know her that well. She was Jack's mom and my aunt, if you know what I mean. I liked her, and she was fun when I stayed with them at Cape Cod. Our visits since Jack's death, though, were formal and short with nothing beyond polite conversation."

"Did you know she had a master's degree in finance?"

"No, I didn't." Chase looked taken aback. "Although that explains why the one thing I do remember her stating on a fairly regular basis was that both my parents were fools when it came to money, as if she would've known and done better."

"Aunt Elizabeth said she was the smartest girl in their class at Vassar and the prettiest."

Chase took a swig of his beer. "I'm not surprised. A portrait of her as a young woman hangs over the mantel in the front parlor if you're interested. From what my mother always said, Uncle Mike was considered a prize, and he adored her."

He didn't mention that what his mother had often said was, "Unlike your father's lack of reasonable feeling for me, your Uncle Mike adored your Aunt Ruth."

"If she has left any investments and you want free advice about what to keep and what might as well be liquidated, give me a call." Larry finished off his beer and then stood. "I'm ready to hit the hay. Need any help?"

"If you don't mind." Chase rose and began switching off the lamps in the room with his good hand. "Which reminds me, I need to ask John for the name of a doctor who can remove these stitches and check on my wrist."

A little while later, alone in his room, he turned on his laptop and prepared to check his email, wondering as he hadn't done on previous visits why his reclusive aunt had felt the need to have Wi-Fi installed. Hopefully, Edmund or John Mason would know any required passwords if she had been in the habit of conducting business online.

Surprised to see that he had several incoming emails awaiting him, he quickly disposed of several. One from Susan requesting his opinion on a client's legal concerns required a few minutes attention, and he took his time, frustrated, as he keyed one-handed a several paragraph reply. Finally, he opened the one from Adrianna, unaware of the previous versions she had deleted and rewritten before this one.

Chase –

We were all sorry to hear about your Aunt Ruth when Susan stopped by this morning, and I'm glad that Larry was able and willing to make the trip with you.

Please don't worry about us. Things are progressing smoothly, and we're moving into the final stages of the first round anyway. Can you believe that in just a few days both Edwina and Paul will be installed as paying tenants?

I can't think of anything, but I hope you know I'm available if there is something I can do to help you, just as you've helped me.

Know that you're in our thoughts.

Adrianna

Hitting Reply, he again began typing one-handed.

Larry's a big help. My aunt passed away a few hours ago.

Keep me posted re reno progress.

For a moment, his hand remained poised over the keys, but then he typed his name and hit Send, thinking as he did so that he should have allowed himself to add the words '*Wish you were here.*'

CHAPTER LIV

Even though she had become a more casual user of the internet since her arrival in Captain's Point than she would have ever thought possible, Adrianna found herself drawn to her laptop the next morning before she had even consumed her espresso. Pleased to have discovered Chase's reply awaiting her, she first read and answered a newsy email from Edwina in which she was told not to forget the gallery opening on the first Saturday in July.

Finally, she opened her attorney's message only to be disappointed by its brevity and saddened by his news. Quickly, she responded that she would advise Otis and Penny of his aunt's death and that he would continue to be in their thoughts, thinking as she did so that she probably wouldn't receive any further communications from him for a while.

A few minutes later, Chase glanced up from reading Adrianna's reply in response to Edmund's having quietly cleared his throat in the dining room's doorway. "Mr. John is here, sir," his aunt's factotum announced. "I've shown him into the library."

"Please tell him I'll be right with him," Chase responded, then addressed Larry who had lowered the newspaper he had been reading upon their having been interrupted. "It's against my religion to keep an attorney waiting."

"They get nasty if you do," his friend acknowledged with a straight face. "I'll be here if you need me."

"Actually, I was wondering if you would join us." Chase stood and awkwardly replaced his chair. "You could take notes as to dates, times and places if nothing else."

"Sure, if you think it would help." Larry put his paper aside and followed his friend to the library, where the two men found Ruth Stanford's attorney removing documents from a slim briefcase, a small laptop turned on beside him in case it were to be needed.

"I'm sorry we're meeting again so soon under such sad circumstances," John Mason said as he stood.

"From what I was able to determine, my aunt would've preferred it this way," Chase replied, indicating for the other lawyer to resume his seat. "I appreciate your making yourself available this morning. I've asked Larry to join us, so that he can take notes on my behalf." He crossed to the large desk that held court at one end of the room, where he located a pad and pen before returning to the table.

At about the same time the three men were beginning their discussion of the funeral arrangements that were now necessary, Susan rose from the table in the cheery breakfast room at The Cove and planted a kiss on her mother's cheek. "I'll get the name of the funeral home from Larry this morning and order flowers," she promised.

"Make sure you pass the information along to Adrianna and the Plunks." Her mother absentmindedly replaced a strand of her auburn streaked-with-gray hair into a loose coil at the back of her head.

"I may just remember to do so," Susan teased, stacking her plate and mug to carry them into the kitchen. "Now that I'm of age."

"Mommy, Grandpa says I can go with him to the store, can I?" A sturdy, blonde-haired, four-year-old ran into the room, a large golden retriever following closely behind.

"Not until I wipe the powdered sugar off your face." Susan laughed, eyeing the telltale remains of a jelly donut. "You look like a clown, and don't let Casey lick it off either." She pushed the willing retriever away.

"I'll take care of him." Elizabeth Chesterton rose from her chair and took her grandson's hand. "You get to the office. Otherwise, you'll return home later than you did last night, and even though you're a grown woman, your father will worry."

"No he won't," her daughter strove to keep the record straight. "You will. My last appointment is at three, so I should make it home for dinner."

"Will you bring me a white tablet with lines on it?" her offspring pleaded.

"I'll bring you two of the little ones for you to practice writing your letters on," Susan promised, but Grandma will put one of them up for later. She bent and kissed the top of his head, wishing that it was she with whom he would be spending his day.

Twenty minutes later, as she had settled at her desk, her phone vibrated with a text message from Larry.

Aunt to be cremated. Private service Thurs at mausoleum. Only two retainers, attorney(s), minister, Chase and myself. In lieu of flowers, contributions to USO.

"It's Susan." Penny handed the cordless receiver to Adrianna a few moments later.

"Hi, have you heard from the guys?" she asked eagerly.

"Only a text from Larry," Susan answered, reading the short message. "I thought I might send a small round floral arrangement to the house from my parents, the Plunks, you and me, if you think that would be appropriate. Nothing big, just something to let Chase and Larry know that we're thinking of them."

"Yes," Adrianna agreed. "Let me know what our share is, and keep me posted."

"That's the funeral arrangements all settled." John Mason returned a few sheets of paper to his briefcase, unaware that Susan and Adrianna had just terminated their call. "Ruth has made all of her wishes very clear as you'll see."

"I must admit that I'm glad," Chase said. "I know she made me co-administrator of her estate in the will that was drawn up at the time of Jack's death, but quite honestly, we never discussed her affairs after that. I'm not even sure that the will I knew about is the one now in force."

"Are you telling me that you have no idea of your aunt's financial situation or the terms of her will?" Her attorney's face reflected his obvious surprise.

"None at all," Chase acknowledged. "I'm not even that familiar with the house beyond the main rooms on this floor, the room I've slept in when I've visited and my cousin's room, which I was in once when I was dropped off here by my parents for an overnight stay before my aunt, Jack and I went to the Cape."

"In that case, gentlemen, I'm going to ask you to accompany me to the third floor." John stood. "The two of you are in for a surprise and a rare opportunity."

CHAPTER LV

Thursday morning found Chase standing under a large black umbrella in front of the Stanford family mausoleum. Ignoring the white cardboard box in the funeral director's hands that he knew contained the bronze urn, he concentrated instead on remembering his Aunt Ruth during happier times – her smile as she had waved at Jack and him from the Cape Cod shore, her glee as she had won a particularly aggressive round of double solitaire, her joy whenever she had played her violin.

And then Jack had been killed, and life for her had become cruel once again. Somehow she had found the strength to persevere, wrapping herself in her memories and, except for a long early morning walk when she was unlikely to meet her neighbors and the occasional concert or charity event, rarely leaving her home. He wished now that he had made more of an effort to bring forth her smile during his occasional visits, even though he had always been a poor substitute for those she had lost. Now, though, she had died and given him the shock of his life.

He shifted his weight to avoid a small stream of water that was dripping from Larry's umbrella onto his own shoulder and glanced at his friend's face – the strong jaw, his eyes focused on the minister as if he had nothing to do but attend someone else's aunt's funeral. What would he have done without the Chestertons and the Plunks all these years?

Gently, he pressed the flesh-colored bandage that covered his itching stitches. Thank goodness Edmund had made him an appointment with his aunt's general practitioner for in the morning to get the obnoxious things out! Hopefully, he would also be told to use his wrist more. The bruising on his fingers was now more green than purple, and the swelling had definitely gone down.

"Ashes to ashes, dust to dust," the minister brought his words to a close, and George Mason moved forward to open the mausoleum's door.

"That went well," Larry said a few minutes later as he steered his Mercedes from the cemetery onto the main road. "The restaurant should be only a few blocks along on the right."

Lunch in a private room at an upscale restaurant had seemed the easiest way at the time to repay those who had assisted with and attended the service, but Chase now found himself wishing that it, too, were over – not that he didn't know how to conduct polite conversation with virtual strangers. It was an integral part of his job.

"There it is," Edmund pointed out from the back seat where he had been sitting, quietly holding Marissa's hand.

Edmund and Marissa... Chase's thoughts continued as he mechanically played host.

Edmund, who had shown up at his aunt's house as a hired musician for a cocktail party forty years ago and had remained to assist an aging butler, provide musical accompaniment to future gatherings and relieve the Stanford family's aged nurse by entertaining his cousin. Marissa, her twinkling dark eyes, red full lips and dancer's body reflecting her Puerto Rican heritage, had been hired to replace the nurse, who had given up and retired two years later. He supposed it had been inevitable that these two total opposites, thrown together as they were in the confines of the tightly knit household, had fallen in love and married.

His aunt had thoughtfully renovated the fourth floor servant's quarters into a spacious bedroom suite and lounge, Marissa had taken over the day-to-day cooking as Jack had no longer needed a nanny, and Edmund had happily filled the hours on the music room's grand piano in between opening the front door to callers and running errands, often providing accompaniment to his aunt as she had played her violin. It had worked out well for all of them, but now it was over.

Hopefully, the plans that had begun to take hold in his mind would meet with their approval. There was no way they could remain in the house on Beacon Hill, and he would appreciate their help.

Two hours later, the luncheon behind them - the funeral director, the minister and his aunt's attorney having been sent on their respective ways - Chase once again joined his friend in the library of the large home.

"Brought you a beer," Larry said as he glanced up from his computer and then made a note on a legal pad that appeared to be covered with figures. "Nice to work by." He nodded towards the doorway onto the main foyer through which pleasant strains of Edmund's playing Chopin merged with the aroma of brownies baking in the oven.

"I hope they'll agree to what we're suggesting." Chase took a swig of the cold beer that Larry had thoughtfully provided. "Aunt Ruth's left them financially independent, so they don't have to."

"This has been their home for forty years." Larry waved his hand to encompass the room around them. "I think they'll be thrilled with your generous offer unless they've already made other plans, which I doubt."

"They haven't said anything to me," Chase agreed, "and Edmund seemed relieved when I told him we would like to meet with them around four to discuss their future."

Larry laid his pen on the tablet and picked up his own beer. "Do you think you can handle all of this and your firm at the same time?" He tapped the edge of his computer screen.

"I'm going to give it the old college try." Chase shot him a grin. "It's been building for a long time, and this has given me the push that I needed. What a mess!"

"It's going to surprise a lot of people." A broad smile spread across his friend's face. "But then, the citizens of Captain's Point can stand a bit of change now and again."

"I'm hoping to take a page out of Adrianna's book," Chase said. "Throughout the renovations at Montgomery House, she has consistently told everyone that they would just take things one step at a time and attempt to have fun while they were doing it."

"Wise woman," Larry acknowledged.

"Great gal." Chase raised his beer bottle in a toast.

"Speaking of the gals, have you emailed Susan and Aunt Elizabeth yet?"

"No, I thought I'd let you type that one for me," Chase filled him in. "It needs to be long, but I sent a brief message to Adrianna before coming downstairs."

"They're going to think we're crazy." Larry's smile widened.

"They already do." Chase's eyes twinkled back, unaware that at this very moment the two younger women included in their conversation had just spotted one another at the downtown drugstore in Captain's Point.

"Have you heard anything from Chase or Larry?" Adrianna asked as she added a bottle of shampoo to her cart.

"Only a brief text that said, and I quote, 'We're fine. Really busy. More later. Larry.'" Susan laughed. "Men!"

"Can't live with them. Can't live without them," Adrianna agreed. "I guess we'll just have to wait."

And on attaining that note of total agreement, the two women parted.

Reaching the end of a chapter in Jane Austen's *Emma* a few hours later, Adrianna closed her novel and let out a small sigh, trying not to disturb Max who was snoring gently, stretched out beside her atop the rose-colored duvet. Having placed the book on the bedside table, she retrieved her laptop from where it, too, had been in sleep mode atop the duvet, lying next to her right ankle.

"I'm beginning to be obsessive," she whispered to Jebediah's portrait over the mantel, then hoped that his twinkling gaze was laughing with her and not at her.

Bringing the computer's screen back to life, she clicked on her email, sent several ads from various retailers to the trash, and then opened the single personal message, disappointed once again by its brevity as she read:

Please do whatever Susan asks of you!

C

CHAPTER LVI

Adrianna strolled slowly along the rose garden's paths, allowing Max to take his time and investigate whatever caught his fancy as she let her mind wander. It had been two weeks since she had received Chase's email asking her to do whatever Susan asked of her.

She had replied that she would follow his wishes and had received an even shorter answer that had read simply:

Stitches out!

Hoping to provide him with a moment of humor, she had written to him about an ongoing war between Max and a large black crow that seemed to have taken up residence on the obelisk, but to date she had received no reply.

At first, she had thought Chase had a specific request, but now she was inclined to think he had been directing her to contact Susan with any needs concerning the renovations. Obviously, his aunt's estate was taking up more of his time than he had anticipated.

Max having glimpsed Otis coming towards them from the dependency, he tugged on his leash, tail wagging, and Adrianna quickened her pace.

"Hope this weather holds out." Her property manager glanced up at the sky as he acknowledged Max's greeting by scratching behind the dog's ears. "The roofers are coming tomorrow."

"I can't believe how quickly you've gotten the garage built," Adrianna paid him the compliment she knew to be due, "and I'm glad you convinced me to enlarge the project to a three-car garage with space for a future studio apartment over it. The cottage is removed enough from the main house that the additional traffic won't affect my privacy. I hope Chase approves when he hears of it."

"Don't see why he won't." Otis led their way into the kitchen garden and closed the door behind them. "Adding a rough second floor was a small portion of the cost, and it should pay for itself fairly quickly, once you've finished the interior during the third round. Have you heard anything from Chase or Larry?"

"No, but I spoke briefly with Elizabeth Chesterton at the office supply store. She hasn't heard from Larry either, beyond a couple of cryptic emails." Adrianna removed Max's leash and placed it on its hook in the mudroom. "Apparently, the two of them are hatching something big, though, because Larry says they'll both be staying in Boston until mid-July."

Max fed and his water bowl refilled, Adrianna adjourned to the Captain's study, planning to transfer her plans for the rest of the renovations into the three-ring notebook she had bought. Checking her email Inbox out of habit, she was pleased to find another message from Chase, thinking it was a sign of life as she clicked it open.

Susan will call soon. Thanks so much!

C

Not sure whether she should be glad that he wanted her help in some way or frustrated by his minimalist style of communicating, she typed a reply stating that she would be expecting Susan's call, then told him the finishing touches had now been completed on the dependency before adding:

I can't wait for you to see how nice it looks. Edwina will be thrilled. Paul Lynch met with Susan and signed his lease for the cottage. Otis and I have taken steps to provide him with better parking and generate additional income.

The Plunks and Max all said to tell you, "Hi!" The latter, of course, in his own way. Elizabeth told me today that she doesn't expect Larry and you to return much before mid-July.

Are you two staying out of trouble or painting the town red?

I hope your wrist is bothering you less.

Not completely satisfied, but thinking it was the best she could do, she hit Send, and then pushed aside all other thoughts but those of the renovation until Penny called her into supper – steaks for the three of them that Otis had cooked on the grill.

"Delicious!" Adrianna commented after her first bite. "I can't remember the last time I had a steak that tasted this good."

"Otis does have a way with them," Penny acknowledged, "and, of course, he won't let me anywhere near that grill."

"Some things are better left to the men," her husband said with a straight face, at which his wife rolled her eyes.

Every morsel of Otis's steaks consumed, they all agreed to enjoy dessert and coffee in the garden. Adrianna carried their plates to the kitchen and loaded the new dishwasher, while Penny cut and served slices of pecan pie, topping each with a dollop of whipped cream.

"What a pleasant evening!" Adrianna said as they settled into their chairs around the outside table. "Look at that sunset!"

"Lovely," Penny acknowledged.

For a moment, silence reigned, but then Adrianna's phone vibrated that she had an incoming call.

"Hello?" she answered, hoping her voice hadn't translated the excitement she had felt when she had seen Susan's number.

"I only have a couple of minutes," her friend sounded stressed. "Has Chase emailed you?"

"Only to say that you would call and I was to do what you asked."

"I don't know what has gotten into those two." Susan didn't hide her exasperation. "I'm run off my feet here at the office. I had no idea how large a workload Chase was carrying, and now Larry and he are playing cloak and daggers."

"Is it possible to enter your second childhood in your early thirties?" Adrianna asked, a grin spreading over her face.

"Apparently, it is, if you're a man." Susan laughed. "Anyway, please tell me that you have no plans for Saturday."

"I'm completely free, much to my chagrin."

"Excellent!" Susan now sounded relieved. "Can you be at The Cove as early as eight in the morning? Come in something comfortable – jeans or shorts – you won't believe what Mom, you and I have been asked to do. Hold on a minute!"

Adrianna heard her friend respond to someone that she would be right with them.

"Sorry." Susan returned to their call. "I've got to run. Daniel will probably be in bed by the time I get home again. Saturday at eight, okay?"

"I'll be there," Adrianna assured her.

"You're an angel. See you then."

And with that, Susan terminated the call, leaving Adrianna no more knowledgeable about what Chase wanted her to do for him than she had been before.

Later that evening, as she once again sat propped against the pillows of the half-tester, she sent a brief follow-up to her earlier email.

Susan called. I'm meeting Elizabeth and her first thing Saturday morning. Can't wait to learn what it's all about. Glad to be of help!

Take care of yourself.

Adrianna

Discovering an email from her college roommate awaited her, she took a few minutes to read it and then sent a reply, surprised to find a response from Chase already in her Inbox when she finished. Clicking it open, she read:

Thanks for help. Don't know if I can pull this off. Larry's great!

Counting on you more than anyone – more than you know!

C

Closing her computer a few minutes later, Adrianna switched off the bedside lamp and settled against her pillows, thinking as she did so that waiting to see Chase until mid-July was going to be hard.

Just as her mind had all but drifted to sleep, though, another thought hit her. What if he had decided to shake the dust of Captain's Point from his feet and move to Boston?

CHAPTER LVII

Adrianna's alarm clock awakened her way too early for her liking on Saturday morning. She had gone to bed early in an effort to insure a good night's rest before she accomplished whatever task Chase had set her, but a bolt of lightning striking somewhere nearby had disturbed her sleep around two in the morning. Afraid of the storm, Max had then refused to settle, until finally she had gone down to the kitchen and brewed a cup of chamomile tea to sip on in the library, where she had finished reading *Emma* and exchanged it for *Persuasion*.

Finally falling back to sleep around four, she had dreamed of sailing first with Chase and then with Brad, each dream ending as a large white boom had swung rapidly towards her. Now her eyes felt full of grit, and she was afraid to look in a mirror.

Stumbling to the shower, she stood under the steamy water for longer than normal, hoping against hope that it would somehow revive her.

"You!" She glared at Max when she discovered him waiting for her in the dressing room. "How could you?"

Sensing her displeasure, he immediately hung his head, which made her feel worse.

"I'm sorry." She scooped him up. "It's not your fault that storms scare you."

At which point, he reached up from the comfort of her arms and licked her chin as a sign of his forgiveness.

Returning the dog to the floor, she slid into an old pair of jeans and a bright Chester's T-shirt that Jim had purchased for her on the day of the regatta, then headed downstairs.

Promptly at eight, she rang the doorbell at The Cove, wondering if anyone would even hear the chimes above the co-mingled sounds of dogs barking and children running and screaming, surprised when Susan opened the door almost immediately.

"Sorry about the racket." Her friend indicated she should go into what had once been a formal second parlor. "I'll be just a minute."

Now a casually decorated family room, Adrianna found the space not filled by a herd of wild elephants, but rather containing only a golden retriever, a small mixed breed terrier, a sturdy blonde-haired boy she recognized as Susan's son Daniel and an even younger auburn-haired girl who she knew to be his cousin. Immediately, she made a mental note to ask Otis if he thought Silver Queen would be up to letting the children ride her.

"And what, may I ask, is going on in here?" A giant of a man, whose platinum blond hair and blue eyes clearly reflected his Nordic origins, filled the archway that led into what Adrianna supposed to be the original morning room, seemingly unaware of his visitor.

"We're making a racket 'cause we're fighting a war," Daniel announced proudly, but this statement having been met with silence and a boring stare, he then lowered his voice and finished with, "Maybe we should be quieter."

"Ah…" The edge of the Nordic god's mouth twitched. "A man of sense."

"We're sorry, Grandpa." The little redhead whispered as she looked up with wide eyes.

"I trust, miss, that you are the princess on the winning side." Her grandfather advanced three steps and bowed deeply. "Please ask your minions to lower their voices."

"I knew you weren't really angry!" She ran forward and threw her arms around the giant's knees, at which he lifted her high into the air before hugging her to him.

"Goodness! I didn't know you were there," Anders Chesterton greeted Adrianna, having glanced her way in the process. "You must think we live in a madhouse here at The Cove, and frankly, you wouldn't be far off the mark. Elizabeth and Susan must be around somewhere."

"Susan said they would be ready in a minute," Adrianna replied. "In the meantime, I thought it best to remain silent so as not to become a casualty of war."

"Wise woman." He returned his granddaughter to the floor and encompassed the battlefield with a wave of a strong arm. "Why don't you and Daniel see if you can't pick up at least half of these toys, Lizzie?" he suggested.

"I think we're ready to go." Elizabeth Chesterton chose this moment to enter the room, her athletic body belying her years. "Are you sure you'll be all right with them for the whole day?" She glanced at her husband.

"You may find me a mere wisp of my former self when you return, but I'm sure we'll survive." He landed a kiss on her cheek. "Although I must say I'm beginning to rethink my opinions of Chase and our Larry."

"Well, I'd lay odds that they haven't both simultaneously lost their minds, so at this stage I'm willing to go along with their wishes," his wife said as she lifted a backpack from beside one of the comfortable looking armchairs. "Come on, girls, time's a wasting." She led the way through the home's front doorway and towards a path through a small pine woods that would take them to Sheffield Place.

"What exactly are we going to do?" Adrianna asked Susan as they followed along.

"Chase didn't fill you in?" Her friend sent her a surprised look. "We are to measure and draw plans of all the rooms in Chase's house, indicating doors and windows. We've also been charged with producing some sort of general inventory – room by room – of main items, making note of anything that one or more of us believes should be kept, may be intrinsically valuable or might have sentimental value."

"But why?" Adrianna asked, surprised.

"We don't know," Elizabeth tossed back over her shoulder as she turned a key in the front door. "We're assuming that Chase is hoping to replace some or most of the furniture with his aunt's, but wants to know what will fit before he moves any or all of it here. I know the original plans for the house were destroyed when Chase's father set his study on fire, the result of his having fallen asleep drunk while smoking a cigar."

Susan rolled her eyes, and indicated for Adrianna to precede her into the house.

"That was in the seventies, and Chase's mother got even with his dad by redoing the whole shebang, so prepare for some time travel." Elizabeth set her backpack on a round glass-topped table that filled the center of what Adrianna imagined had once been a wood paneled foyer similar to the one at Montgomery House, but now was lined with mirror from floor to ceiling.

"You've got to be kidding," she said, and then wished she hadn't.

"Don't hold back on our account," Susan assured her. "We both think it's hideous."

Remembering the traditional style of Chase's office at his firm, Adrianna wondered how much living in such a house had affected his innate sensibilities.

"Yes," Elizabeth said as if reading her thoughts. "Chase hates it, too."

"And yet, this is his home," Adrianna pointed out.

"It is, and it isn't." Susan accepted a clipboard and automatic pencil from her mother. "I'm not sure Chase has ever felt at home here."

As she, too, accepted a clipboard and pencil, Adrianna felt a cold, hard knot form in her stomach, knowing full well that if Montgomery House had looked like this when she had inherited it, she would have turned tail and run. Perhaps now that his aunt had died, Chase had his first real opportunity to do so.

CHAPTER LVIII

"Who would've thought when you boarded that plane in Chicago and chose the seat beside mine that not quite three months later you would be moving into the Montgomery House dependency?" Adrianna smoothed a length of shelf paper into the corner of one of the kitchen cabinets.

"Certainly not me." Edwina cut off another length and passed it to her only slightly taller landlady. "I still have to pinch myself."

"No regrets about moving to Captain's Point?" Adrianna's face sobered.

"No regrets."

"Paul's gone for another load, and your movers just turned into the drive." Otis joined them. "I'll remain here, so they'll know there's a man around."

"I'm so glad you're willing to help." Edwina smiled up at him. "Jason can't be here for another hour, because he's leading a webinar, and I told Ginny not to bother herself or put Lucy through this."

"They're here!" Penny appeared in the kitchen doorway. "I was dusting the second parlor and saw them turn in."

Knowing that Maggie Daniels did all the dusting, Adrianna refrained from commenting as she closed the last cabinet door, glad to see Edwina receiving such a warm welcome.

"You'll want to wash all of your dishes before putting them away," Penny said. "I can start working on that for you, once they bring in a dishpack if you want."

As the two older women continued chatting, Adrianna joined Otis on the front sidewalk, where she noticed that Nip was keeping an eye on things from the shaded entrance to the vine-covered tunnel.

"Well, boss…" Otis gave her a quick hug. "You've done it."

"No, we've done it." Her dark eyes twinkled back at him. "Today marks the end of the first round of renovations with four checks deposited in the new account – two rental deposits and two monthly rent checks. Does Paul seem pleased with everything?"

"He's thrilled with both the cottage and the new parking arrangement."

"I wish Chase could be here today," Adrianna said wistfully, but then the corner of her mouth twitched. "I bet, though, that Great-aunt Martha is turning over in her grave."

"I'm not so sure of that." Her property manager sent her a grin. "Martha always did love a good profit, and you'll be raking it in."

Between helping Penny to unpack and wash Edwina's dishes and deciding with Paul the best arrangement for his comfortable furniture, Adrianna was relieved when Otis showed up hours later with sliders and fries from Patrick's as she had ordered. Presiding over Montgomery House's breakfast room table, she raised her bottled water in a toast. "To Edwina and Paul. On behalf of Montgomery Properties may I be the first to formally welcome you to your new homes." She glanced from one of her tenants to the other.

"Here, here!" Otis raised his chilled can of beer.

"I third that!" Penny lifted a glass of iced tea.

"Thank you for the help and the housewarming gifts." Paul referred to a basket of fresh vegetables from the garden and a vase of roses that had been left on the kitchen counter of each new home by Jeff earlier.

"They were a lovely surprise," Edwina agreed, "and your help with the unpacking has meant the world to me."

Later, her new tenants having retired to their own homes, Adrianna slipped into a warm bubble bath and relaxed as her mind flitted from one thing to another.

It had been a busy three months filled with ups and downs, but the hard work would now begin to pay off. What would Brad have thought of her accomplishments with Montgomery Properties? There were times now when she wondered if he had ever cared for her beyond her filling the role of a reasonably good looking, professional woman on his arm at social events.

She had been surprised when Susan had stopped by on her way back to the office after lunch to check on them. Frankly, her friend had looked tired, and when asked if she had heard from Chase or Larry had merely responded, "Chase and Larry who?"

Adrianna reached for an oversized bath towel, wishing Chase could've been with them today, able to see the fruition of all her hard work. For a moment she wrapped herself tightly in the fluffy towel, closed her eyes and called forth his face in her mind – his deep blue eyes full of the soft look she had grown to love and need in her life, despite her best efforts not to.

Slipping into her soft cotton pajamas, she made her way to a window seat in her bedroom where Max joined her as the last rays of colored light disappeared from the July sky. "What is our Chase doing?" she asked. "Why hasn't he called me? Why hasn't he shared with any of us what Larry and he are up to?"

For some time, she relaxed against the window seat's pillows, stroking Max's back, enjoying the quiet, and watching the twinkling lights of the larger boats as they sailed past Captain's Point, bound towards Baltimore or New York or, perhaps, even to Boston.

"Sometimes I wonder if, like Brad, I'll never see Chase again," she shared with Max, whose tiny face wrinkled with concern at her sad tone.

The dog set upon the duvet, she slipped beneath the half-tester's covers, settled against the pillows and then debated with herself for a moment before succumbing to curiosity and reaching for her laptop.

Not bothering with the other emails that awaited her, she opened the one titled CONGRATULATIONS! and eagerly read:

Susan says moving day went well. Martha would be as proud of you as I am.
E will call you.
Need you here with me.
Please come to Boston!

C

For a moment, her mind was filled with first one thing and then another – Chase had remembered what day it was, he was proud of her, he needed her, he wanted her with him in Boston, and then her computer screen blurred as Adrianna burst into tears.

CHAPTER LIX

Elizabeth had called, but the earliest they had been able to secure convenient tickets on a flight to Boston was Monday the 4th of July, and Mrs. Chesterton had been unwilling to drive. Adrianna had been of two minds about the delay. On the one hand, it had meant two more days before she would find out what Chase's plans were, and on the other hand, it had meant that she hadn't had to disappoint Edwina.

The new art gallery was larger than Adrianna had anticipated and was situated in a row of shops that had been created by blocking off a small dead end side street in the downtown area. Having created a large free parking lot on one end, the developers had then replaced the short street with stone pavers, benches, and large flower pots, thus creating a pleasant area for shoppers.

The Fosters had excused themselves so they could thank Jason's employer for the tickets, and Adrianna had soon found her elbow grabbed by Jill, who had taken it upon herself to introduce the now embarrassed Montgomery heiress to half of the people in the already crowded room.

Claiming she was thirsty, Adrianna had extricated herself from the unwanted situation as soon as she noticed her acquaintance making doe eyes at a buff young man who stood alone in a corner. Now, as she selected a glass of champagne from the serving table, she couldn't help but overhear the conversation to the side of her.

"Dr. Chesterton," the middle-aged woman's voice boomed. "I know you're as devastated by the loss of our dear Ruth Stanford as I am."

Surprised to hear the prefix used in the context of Elizabeth Chesterton, Adrianna turned to find her way blocked by Arthur

Stern – the quiet, unassuming gentleman from whom she was now used to accepting her weekly church program.

"I didn't know you were an art lover, Miss Montgomery." Arthur beamed at her.

"Mr. Stern," she greeted him. "I was surprised to hear Elizabeth addressed just now as Dr. Chesterton."

"Oh, yes. Our Elizabeth is the foremost expert on the Underground Railroad as it existed here in Maryland," the older gentleman said. "Her books are filled with interesting stories and tidbits as well as being written in a way that's equally enjoyable for the non-scholar. Tell me, though, did I understand that Ruth Stanford has died?"

"The Ruth Stanford in question is Chase Sheffield's aunt and attended Vassar in the same class as Elizabeth." Adrianna felt herself being steered towards a quieter spot.

"You do mean Ruth Stanford of Beacon Hill, Boston, I presume." Arthur's right eyebrow rose in a questioning way. "Because, if so, that's going to send shockwaves through part of the art world."

"Really?" Adrianna found herself full of curiosity. "Why?"

"Almost forty years ago, I had the audacity to believe I was the next Gauguin." The older man had the decency to look sheepish. "Of course, I wasn't, but no one could dampen my spirits as I made plans to live a starving artist's life and paint my way around the world."

"How romantic!" Adrianna smiled.

"How absurd!" Arthur shot back. "My father's family had housed a Brazilian exchange student for a year, and Dad contacted his old friend. The long and the short of it is that two months later I found myself living in a high style apartment on Ipanema in Rio de Janeiro. A young man who really was a starving artist, Luciana Oliveira, had been lent the neighboring apartment by his aunt. Ruth and Mike Stanford were honeymooning and had rented the next apartment along the row of balconies for a month. We were all near the same age, and as we sat on our respective balconies in the evenings, we got to know one another."

"What an amazing coincidence."

"Ruth and Mike were polite about my feeble efforts, but they fell in love with Luciano's work," Arthur continued. "Once I saw his paintings, I wasn't even jealous. I knew that his was the true talent. He was a large brawny fellow, but his paintings were bright, detailed jewels full of color and the vibrant life of the Rio beaches. It was agreed before they left that Ruth and Mike would become his patrons."

"But Mike was killed only a few years later," Adrianna pointed out.

"Yes, but Ruth continued to buy his work," Arthur stated. "I believe only five paintings from his early period have been seen since they were shipped to the Stanfords. Then in the early eighties, Luciano shifted his style, and those works were offered to the wider market and earned him a great deal of success. Oliveira died three years ago of a brain aneurysm, so the value of his earlier paintings will have skyrocketed."

Adrianna's mind filled with possibilities. Could this be why Chase and Larry had been so circumspect?

"Do you paint as well?" Arthur asked.

"Not for many years." Adrianna felt a pang of longing as she remembered hours spent with her mother sketching or working with watercolors. "I've been thinking of beginning again. There are so many wonderful scenes and interesting faces that inspire me here in Captain's Point."

"There certainly are." Arthur chuckled and embraced the others in the room with a subtle wave of his hand. "Why these folks alone would provide one with a lifetime of work. But tell me, Miss Montgomery…"

"Adrianna, please," she interrupted him.

"Certainly, but you must call me Arthur," he obliged her. "So tell me, what have you been up to over there at Montgomery House? Every time I drive by I discover some sort of construction vehicle pulling into your driveway."

Quickly, Adrianna explained her plans in the briefest of terms and was surprised by the extent of his interest. Then she noted Ginny approaching.

"Arthur, this is Ginny Foster, the granddaughter-in-law of one of the tenants I was telling you about. The Fosters were nice enough to invite me to be the fourth in their party today, and I'm afraid I've been neglecting them."

"Not at all," Ginny assured her. "We could tell that you were connecting with friends and having a good time."

"Still, if you'll excuse me, Arthur, I'd better get back to Edwina," she said.

"Certainly, you ladies enjoy yourself," he replied. "I'll call you next week, Adrianna, about that other matter we discussed."

Working their way slowly through the growing crush of art lovers, the two young women finally managed to rejoin Jason and Edwina in front of a small painting of a single orange and a sprig of jasmine that had been placed on a blue bandana directly in the path of a ray of sunshine.

"Believe me, it took more talent to create that piece than you're giving the artist credit for," Jason stated as he indicated the curved outward edge of the fruit. "Look at that shadowing."

"Now don't get me wrong," Edwina protested. "I didn't say I didn't like the piece, but I wouldn't pay over $10.97 for it at a flea market."

Her eyes filled with laughter, Ginny met Adrianna's gaze over the diminutive older woman's head as each strove to maintain their composure. Gradually, the foursome completed a tour of the room, at which point Ginny whispered her relief that Jason hadn't discovered anything he loved enough to buy, Edwina stated that it had all been overpriced, and Adrianna was ready to go.

"Who was that nice looking elderly gentleman to whom you were speaking?" Edwina asked as Adrianna steered her Elantra into Montgomery House's front drive a few minutes later.

"Arthur Stern." She brought the car to a halt in front of the dependency. "I'd met him at church, but that was our first real conversation. He's a retired math professor and an artist."

"If I don't see you before you leave for Boston, have a safe trip," Edwina wished her landlady well as she disembarked.

Forty-eight hours later, seated beside Elizabeth Chesterton, Adrianna hoped she had packed everything that she would need – the black dress that Chase had liked, a pair of dress pants plus two tops, jeans, a pair of shorts, T-shirts and her traveling clothes. Surely, she had covered all of the bases in the one suitcase.

"Did you enjoy the gallery opening," Elizabeth asked as their plane taxied into position for take-off.

"Yes, I did," Adrianna answered, "and Arthur Stern indicated an interest in renting one of my retail spaces. He wants a place where he can showcase his work and give art lessons."

"Arthur's a good man, and he'll make a good tenant," Elizabeth assured her.

The sun having now set over Baltimore, Adrianna turned to the window, her thoughts filled with what lay ahead at their destination. Perhaps she had read too much into Chase's email. Perhaps he didn't need her, but only her help. Perhaps she was once again, like she had been with Brad, putting herself into a position to be hurt.

But then, the engines roared, she was thrust against the back of her seat and the plane lifted, just as the tiny window to her right filled with 4th of July fireworks that had been set off all over the city below and her spirit soared with anticipation. Chase was only a short flight away.

CHAPTER LX

Adrianna was disappointed at first to find only Larry waiting at the baggage claim area at Boston's Logan Airport, but his effusive greeting soon lifted her spirits.

"You two are a sight for sore eyes!" He planted a kiss on his aunt's cheek and then wrapped Adrianna in a bear hug. "Your luggage should be coming along any minute now." He steered them towards the second station in the long row.

"Where's Chase?" Elizabeth asked.

"John Mason arranged for the two of us to attend their family's 4th of July cookout, so he could introduce us to a friend of theirs who may be able to help with a key component of Ruth's estate," he explained. "It turned out that the man flies back to New York first thing in the morning, so he agreed to meet with Chase then and there. They weren't quite finished, so I came to pick you up. He'll probably beat us to the house."

Flashing lights on the baggage return station announced the luggage would appear shortly and effectively drew their attention. As she watched for her black bag that would surely blend in with all of the others, Adrianna couldn't help but wonder how much events of these past few weeks had changed her attorney. His cryptic emails certainly hadn't provided much of a clue.

A little while later, Larry having skillfully driven them through the Boston traffic, Adrianna disembarked from his Mercedes SUV, delighted by the lit façade of the Beacon Hill mansion. "It's exactly like you imagine one would be when you read about them in books," she said in an aside to Elizabeth as their chauffeur placed their suitcases onto the sidewalk.

Edmund opened the door as they approached, and Larry introduced him and Marissa, who was waiting behind her husband, to the new guests.

"Let me show you to your rooms, so you can freshen up," the older gentleman led their way up the curved stairway.

As she lifted her black dress from her suitcase a few minutes later, Adrianna turned to find Chase standing in the doorway of her room and greeted him with a smile.

"You look much better than the last time I saw you," she said, as he crossed the short space between them, and then lifted her fingers to touch the tiny scar just below his left temple, only to draw back her hand at the last moment.

"Does it bother you?" he asked, concern replacing the soft look that had been in his eyes.

"That little thing?" She laughed lightly. "Hardly. If anything, it adds character, although given that it was just two stitches, it probably won't show at all after a few months."

"It was three stitches, and believe me every one of them counted when they started to itch," he set the record straight with a relaxed grin.

"And your bruising is all gone," Adrianna pointed out.

"Actually, I'm still a little yellow in better light." He took her hand in his good one. "I'm so glad you were willing to come."

"I had forgotten how lovely Ruth's home is," Elizabeth's voice announced her approach.

"Larry and I'll have to take you two out on the town tomorrow evening, since you brought your best dress." Chase released Adrianna's hand and nodded towards her basic black. "Have you had a tour of my second home yet?"

"No." Adrianna slipped her dress into a mahogany wardrobe and turned back to him. "I'd love for you to show it to me, especially if the rest of it is furnished in similar style."

"I don't think you'll be disappointed." He stepped back and allowed her to lead the way to the hall, where they followed Larry and his aunt downstairs.

The tour starting in the kitchen, they surprised Marissa as she popped a pastry-covered Brie into the oven for them to enjoy with some wine. A pleasant looking breakfast room came next, as the floor plan appeared to closely mirror that of Montgomery House.

"This is the morning room." Chase showed them into a room that was furnished more formally than the one Adrianna so enjoyed in her own home. "The dining room…"

"Goodness, how many people does that table seat?" Adrianna asked.

"Do we know?" Larry looked to Chase. "It's set up for eighteen as it is, but I imagine it has several leaves stored away somewhere."

"No telling." Chase shrugged. "The main foyer and both parlors are through that archway, but if we go along this short hall we can access the study and music rooms first."

Adrianna recognized a piece by Liszt as they interrupted Edmund at the piano.

"Let's give the gals a taste of what we've been working on as a tension reliever," Chase suggested.

"Sure." The older man agreed as he shifted to the right on the piano bench.

"Ready?" Chase asked, now perched on the bench to Edmund's left.

"Ready," the older man confirmed as his right and Chase's left hands plunged to the keyboard and began jointly playing what had been written as a one person piece.

"Bravo, bravo!" Elizabeth and Adrianna exclaimed in unison as each applauded and the two men gratefully stood from their precarious positions and, arm in arm, performed a deep bow.

Adrianna thought she had never seen Chase look so relaxed, once again filled with gratitude for the rarefied environment and wonderful people that filled the new life to which her great-aunt's will had led her.

"Second parlor." Larry took over the role of docent as they moved on a few minutes later. "This room catches the morning light and leads into the conservatory."

The group entered the foyer, and Adrianna paused to admire a small bronze of a man and a woman dressed in Edwardian clothing. Standing on grass bent by a light breeze, a Springer Spaniel accompanying them, they had been caught as the man drew his love into his arms.

"Do you like it?" Chase remained with her as Larry and his aunt disappeared into the formal parlor.

"Very much." She raised her eyes to his just as Marissa entered the foyer from the back hallway, bearing the warmed Brie and other canapés on a tray.

"I'm glad." He escorted her through the next room. "It's one of the pieces I'm keeping."

Taking this as a sign that Chase wasn't planning to remain permanently in Boston, Adrianna felt her steps lighten as he indicated for her to go first into what proved to be the library.

"What a beautiful room!" She paused for a moment so as to take it all in – the floor to ceiling bookcases, the long table Chase and Larry had obviously been using as their headquarters, the massive desk at one end and the comfortable seating area for reading in front of the fireplace at the other. "I love the library at Montgomery House, but this one puts it to shame."

"I'm certainly going to miss it." Larry indicated for her to join his aunt, who was already seated in front of the fireplace. "One for you, and one for you." He handed a glass of chilled chardonnay to each of the ladies. "And for you?" he addressed Chase.

"I'll go with the wine tonight, too." Chase joined Adrianna on the sofa.

"Would you like for me to serve you," she asked, eyeing his still swollen wrist.

"Please." He settled back and let her help him.

"Mike loved this room," Elizabeth commented once they had all sampled the fare, "and Ruth never changed a thing."

"I'm glad she didn't." Chase popped a canapé in his mouth.

"So tell me…" Adrianna set her wine glass on the marble-topped coffee table. "Where are Luciano Oliveira's paintings stored?"

At which point, Chase and Larry exchanged shocked glances.

CHAPTER LXI

"How did you...?" "When did you...?" Larry and Chase sputtered simultaneously.

Unprepared for the dramatic response her simple question about Oliveira's paintings had drawn, Adrianna sought to ease their minds. "Arthur Stern told me about them two days ago at the opening of the new gallery in Captain's Point," she explained.

"Arthur Stern?" Larry's face reflected his exasperation. "How in the world did he find out about them?"

"Oh, that's easy." Adrianna proceeded to tell the tale of the chance meeting that had resulted in Mike and Ruth Stanford becoming Luciano Oliveira's patrons.

"And now he's spreading the story all over town." Larry rolled his eyes.

"I doubt seriously that Arthur Stern will tell his story to the world," Elizabeth stated firmly. "He's such a quiet, unassuming man. Are the paintings still hanging in the old ballroom?"

"You've seen them?" Chase asked.

"Only five...no, six of them," Elizabeth replied. "Ruth showed Anders and me the first five when we stopped and visited with her the year after Mike's death, and I believe she had purchased another one when I attended a conference in Boston and she invited me to the house for dinner."

"What did you think of them?" Chase leaned forward eagerly.

"I thought they were stunning. How many are in the collection now?"

"Seventeen, most of which will be sold at auction," Chase replied. "We can take you up there now if you want, but I would recommend that you wait until morning. They show better in the light."

"Then I'll wait," Elizabeth said.

"Me, too," Adrianna agreed. "I'd prefer to see them at their best."

"In the meantime, tell us what's been going on up here," Elizabeth addressed Chase as Larry stood and refreshed their wine glasses.

"I've spent hours signing papers." Chase laughed. "And, believe me, it hasn't been easy with this hand. Larry's gone over Aunt Ruth's investments, and I've been knee-deep in discussions with architects, auction house representatives and John Mason."

"So where do you stand, if you don't mind my asking?" Elizabeth separated a portion of Brie and placed it on a cracker.

"Let's just say that Aunt Ruth made good use of her master's in finance," Chase obliged her. "My plan is to sell this house and restore mine, which is part of the reason I asked you two here. Once the house is sold, I've arranged for an estate sale, but I want to refurnish Sheffield Place with what's here as much as possible. Once we've satisfied your curiosity about the paintings in the morning, I would like to go room by room with the two of you and get your opinions as to what I should keep and what should go."

"Won't the estate sale firm do that for you?" Adrianna asked.

"They will." Chase turned to face her. "But I would like your opinions. You two will both recognize value in the pieces and understand my tastes, and you won't have any other interests but mine. You've seen what my mother did to The Place. Think Montgomery House, and you'll have a much better idea of what it should be. Larry's made copies of the room plans you've already sent, and I'm hoping we can go so far as to establish placement of the main pieces."

"What about the Robinsons?" Elizabeth asked. "Did Ruth leave any provision for Edmund and Marissa?"

"She did," Larry confirmed, "as well as making several generous charitable bequests."

"Still, I imagine this came as quite a shock to the couple," Adrianna pointed out. "Their whole world has been turned upside down."

"It has." Chase sent her a look of approval. "This has been their home for the better part of forty years, and leaving it will be a wrench for them."

"Which is why Mr. Soft-Hearted here has asked them if they would like to move to The Place," Larry teased.

"But that's a wonderful idea!" Adrianna voiced her approval. "It won't be their home, but they'll still be surrounded by familiar things."

"They'll also have plenty to keep them busy." Larry grinned and indicated that Chase should finish the story.

"I'm hoping to turn The Place into an upscale B&B with Edmund and Marissa running it," Chase finished outlining his plans. "There are plenty of D.C. professionals who are looking for weekend getaways, and Captain's Point offers boating, deep sea fishing and the new artist community as a draw. I'll still keep a suite of rooms at my end of the upstairs hall, and I'm having the old servants quarters reconfigured into an apartment for the Robinsons that will be similar to what they've been used to here. The Place is too big for just me as it is, and like Montgomery House, it's a money pit as it now stands."

"Sounds to me like you've found a solution to your problems," Elizabeth said. "Augustus would be glad. I know he was worried about you toward the end."

"Do you think he would approve?" Chase asked.

"I'm sure he would," Adrianna spoke up, having heard the eagerness in his voice. "Like Otis told me when I started our renovations and said my great-aunt was turning over in her grave, Augustus Chesterton was a man who appreciated profit."

"You're right!" Chase threw his head back and laughed. "I hadn't thought of that, but he always had his eyes on the main chance when it came to money."

"I think you young folks will have to excuse me." Elizabeth placed her wine glass on the marble-topped table and stood. "It's time this old woman went to bed."

"Me, too." Adrianna rose from the couch and began placing their plates on the large tray that had been left on the library table as Larry gathered their glasses.

"I hope I didn't ruin anything when I mentioned the paintings," she said to her broker as the two of them headed to the kitchen with the tray and leftover food a few minutes later, leaving Chase to turn off the lamps in the library.

"I'm sure you haven't," Larry assured her. "You're asking about them like that just came as a shock, because the auction house is planning a news conference to announce their sale. Arthur and Aunt Elizabeth have known about them for years, and I'm sure we can count on you to keep their coming out party quiet."

"Of course." She set the plate of remaining canapés on the counter, and then met his gaze. "I'm glad you've been here with Chase."

"So am I." Larry's face sobered. "He isn't a complainer, but at every turn that hand and wrist have frustrated him. He can only type one-handed, signing all the necessary documents has been hard not to mention painful and, while Edmund would've helped him with some of the things I've been doing, he's more comfortable with me. He's using his hand more, though, so it should strengthen fairly quickly, and it's been handy to have him on call as I've worked at determining which of his Aunt Ruth's investments should be liquidated and what would be best to keep."

"I'm sorry his aunt passed away, but Susan told me Chase has been carrying a horrendous workload," Adrianna said. "Hopefully, all of this will relieve some of the stress he's been under."

"It will," he assured her. "In more ways than one. This time spent away from Captain's Point has given him an opportunity to step back and gain a new perspective as he's been forced to reconfigure his life going forward and to reflect on his priorities." Larry paused and appeared to her as if he wanted to say more, but instead he began putting the leftover food away.

"I can appreciate what you mean," she filled the void. "It's the reason I drove back from Seattle on my return trip to Captain's Point. I wanted to give myself a similar gift."

"And Chase will enjoy overseeing the renovations at The Place," Larry continued. "He's always wanted to take it back to its former glory as his grandfather would've said. Now you get to bed." He nodded towards the doorway. "I'm going to rinse off the dishes, so Marissa doesn't find too much of a mess in the morning."

Adrianna made her way back to the foyer, where she found Chase lounging against the bannister.

"I wanted to thank you again for coming," he said as they both started up the stairs.

"I told you I would help," she reminded him.

"Yes." He took her hand as they reached her bedroom doorway. "But you meant it, where others would've just said it, and I'm glad you're here. I've..."

"Do you need any assistance getting undressed?" Larry asked as he joined them, and Adrianna burst out laughing as Chase let go of her hand.

"No," she gasped as she regained control of herself. "I can manage fine on my own."

"Know that we both aim to please," Chase assured her, working hard to keep a straight face in view of Larry's embarrassment.

"See if I offer to help you again." Larry grinned as he mock-punched Chase's upper arm.

"Boys, boys," Adrianna stage-whispered. "You're going to disturb Elizabeth."

"It's good to have you both here." Larry gave her a quick hug.

"Be ready to start first thing in the morning." Chase threw his good arm around her and drew her close, holding her to him a minute longer than Larry had and dropping a kiss onto the top of her head before releasing her. "Sleep well, my favorite client."

CHAPTER LXII

The next morning found the four of them in what had once been a splendid ballroom, but had been converted by Ruth Stanford after her husband's death into a gallery for the Oliveira paintings. The drapes had been drawn from the tall windows at either end of the room, and Larry and Edmund were busy tying back the velvet curtains that protected the individual paintings and flipping on their tiny overhead lamps.

"How many of them do you plan to place in the auction?" Elizabeth asked.

"Probably ten," Chase said as he turned to Adrianna. "So what do you think?"

"They're fantastic." Her dark eyes as they met his deep blue ones reflected her pleasure. "The colors are so vibrant, and the way he has instilled them with so much motion is amazing. He must have used only a one or two strand brush to apply some of the paint. I see what Arthur meant when he spoke about a large man taking such pains with the tiniest details. And yet, even though they are clearly reflective of the Rio beach scene, they portray everyday events and facial expressions you could find anywhere and should have a wide appeal."

"I knew you would appreciate them in the same way that I do." Chase beamed at her as they moved on to the next one, Elizabeth having already made her way to the other side of the room to join Larry. "I want you to help me decide which ones I should keep."

"Me?" She didn't hide her surprise. "I've been exposed to fine art from all sorts of civilizations throughout my life, but I'm not an art expert."

"Exactly," Chase said. "You have been bred and trained for just such decisions as this. I could hire dozens of experts, and they would all tell me the same thing – Oliveira was a modern master. His paintings obviously speak to you, though, on a very visceral level, and I want to know which ones speak to you the most."

"I see..." For a moment, she studied the painting before her – the overturned vegetable cart, a barking dog, a child running after a ball - then she turned back to him. "Have you thought about where you plan to hang them?" She looked around the room. "For instance, six of them are large enough to hang singly over a mantel or a buffet, while the others are somewhat smaller."

"That's a good point," he agreed as they moved on to the next one. "They also divide into subject groups – sophisticated beachgoers, children dressed almost in rags, family scenes."

In the end, they settled on two of the larger paintings, two quite small ones, and four that centered around a group of sophisticated bathers enjoying a beach party as the ones Chase would keep.

"It's a relief to have that settled," he told Adrianna as they followed Larry and Elizabeth back downstairs. "The auction house has recommended a firm that will crate and ship them either to New York or Captain's Point as soon as we contact them. I want to know that they're safely out of the house before too many people traipse through here."

For a moment, Adrianna was struck with the enormity of the task before him, glad she was being allowed to help.

"So where do we start next?" she asked.

"I'm not sure." He paused at the foot of the curved staircase. "What do you two ladies think? Would it be best to go room by room, or do you know the place well enough to start from the plans of Sheffield Place and try to find pieces that would fill individual needs?"

"Why don't we begin with the plans," Elizabeth suggested. "Then, at some point, we'll probably want to switch gears when we get to the smaller pieces, lamps, etc."

Everyone in agreement, Larry left Chase and the two women to soldier on, while he contacted the auction house to apprise them of the decisions that had been made and to arrange for shipment of the paintings.

Except for a brief lunch break, they worked steadily through the day, finding places for most of the larger pieces as well as many of the more utilitarian items that would be useful once Sheffield Place was opened as a B&B. As they made their way through the rooms, Adrianna caught a glimpse of what a life beside Chase Sheffield would be – centered around meaningful work and thoughtful giving back to the community, generously peppered with rich cultural pursuits and way more laughter than she would have anticipated.

"Look at these!" She called Chase over to where she was seated on the carpet in front of a wall cabinet in the library as the afternoon drew to a close. "They're playbills and programs going back over a hundred years. This one's from an Oscar Wilde lecture here in Boston, and it's signed:

To Lavinia –

At whose table I would dine every night.

Oscar Wilde

"Isn't it wonderful!" Her dark eyes sparkled.

"Are you a fan of Wilde?" He sat on his heels and flipped through some of the others with his good hand, then stood, holding the signed Wilde notice by one corner.

"Definitely!" She smiled up at him. "He and Noel Coward are two of my favorites, but of course, they're from different periods. No telling what other treasures you have here."

"I'll mark these boxes for shipment to Captain's Point then," he said. "If you'll promise to go through them with me once things are more settled."

"Absolutely! I'd love to," she agreed and returned the aged materials to the cabinet before moving to the next one.

As Edmund had pulled strings and secured reservations for the four of them to eat at one of Boston's finest restaurants, they soon separated to dress for dinner, after which they had all agreed to call it a night as the women were scheduled to catch an early flight back to Captain's Point the next day.

Descending the curving staircase a while later in her black dress, Adrianna found the others already gathered in the foyer. Catching a glimpse of her as he finished sharing an anecdote, Larry whistled his approval while Chase kept his thoughts more to himself, revealing them only through the approving look in his eyes.

"Let's get going." Larry threw open the front door. "You two beautiful ladies shouldn't keep Boston waiting."

Adrianna found she was glad to have the support of Chase's good hand on her elbow as she made her way in heels along the original brick walkway to the sidewalk. "That dress really does suit you," he commented as he held her door open. "I'm glad you brought it."

The restaurant living up to its reputation, they all relaxed over the fine meal, tired after a busy day.

"Larry's driving us back to Captain's Point a week from Friday," Chase told Adrianna as they waited for the valet to return the Mercedes. "Would you be free if I dropped by around eight that evening to see you? There are some papers you need to sign that pertain to Martha's estate."

"Sure," she agreed. "Max and I will look forward to seeing you."

Later, as she was pulling her pajamas from her suitcase, she looked up to find him once again watching her from her bedroom's doorway.

"I have something for you." He strode forward and handed her a sealed, book-sized cardboard box. "It's the Wilde lecture program. Edmund called in a favor from a friend for me and worked a miracle while we were at dinner this evening. It's been framed and matted appropriately for an historical document, and it's packaged to make the trip if you think you can carry it on."

"Oh, but I couldn't accept…" she started to object, but then saw the hurt in his eyes.

"Yes, you could," his voice had taken on a hard edge, but then softened. "Please. I'll enjoy it much more knowing that it's giving you pleasure."

"Thank you." She set the package on her bed and then raised her face to his, her body fully sensing his presence so near as she willed him to break through the paper-thin barrier he had so carefully maintained between them throughout her visit.

For a moment, he read her face as his own expression reflected an inward struggle.

"You're so beautiful." He held her gaze as his finger traced the line of her jaw before he slid his hand down her bare arm and found the small of her back.

"Chase…," she whispered as he drew her forward and she molded her body to his, for the first time aware of the strength of his desire.

Then the tension left his face and he lowered his lips to hers, kissing her gently at first and then more passionately as he brought his other arm around and crushed her to him.

CHAPTER LXIII

Friday morning found Adrianna back in Captain's Point, still wondering at the ability of one simple kiss to change her life in such a marvelous way. How would she get through this next week with nothing more than a few cryptic emails from Chase?

She headed downstairs with Max at her heels, but paused in the foyer and drew in the scent of the long-stemmed roses that had arrived the previous afternoon accompanied by a simple message:

Until I return...

Yours,

Chase

But then her thoughts sobered. Chase had been hurt by those who should have cared for him at a time when he was most vulnerable. It had cost him to trust her with his innermost feelings, and he would give far more meaning to her having submitted to his passionate embrace than someone like Brad would have.

Shaking away such concerns, she surprised Max by detouring into the formal parlor where she selected a piece of sheet music from the cabinet that stood between two of the bay windows before taking a seat at the baby grand. Gingerly, she picked out the first lines of a Broadway tune as she quickly recognized two things – the piano badly needed to be tuned and she would have to hone her skills if Chase and she were ever going to enjoy playing duets together.

"Let's see if we can arrange for the first one and organize the second," she suggested to Max, whose tail wagged his enthusiastic agreement as he followed her into the kitchen where Penny provided the names of both a piano tuner and a teacher.

Time having turned into her enemy by Saturday evening, she called Susan.

"Let's have lunch at Montgomery's tomorrow and go shopping," Adrianna suggested, wanting to buy a few more hot dresses before Chase's return.

Monday seemed to pass more quickly as Otis and she worked hard to finalize details of the carriage house's renovations, which they had noted on their respective calendars should begin no later than the end of July. Tuesday, though, would have stretched long, if the piano tuner hadn't kept his appointment, filling the house with his repetitive tones.

By late Wednesday afternoon, having finished *Persuasion* and moved on to *Northanger Abbey*, Adrianna was finding herself hard pressed not to throw the novel aside when Penny announced that a package had arrived for her and was waiting in the foyer.

"It weighs a ton," her housekeeper explained as they hurried to open it, "so I've left it on the floor by the table where the deliveryman placed it. It's from Boston."

"Wonder what he's done now." Adrianna thoughts flew to the framed Wilde program that Otis had hung for her in a small grouping beside the fireplace in the formal parlor.

Once opened, the larger box was found to contain another one that had been carefully surrounded by packing material. Having quickly cut through the smaller carton's tape, Adrianna withdrew a heavy ball that appeared to be comprised solely of bubble wrap.

"What are you two doing?" Otis joined them, as she removed the last of the plastic and revealed the statue of the Edwardian lovers she had admired at the Beacon Hill home.

"How lovely!" Penny exclaimed as Adrianna centered the vase of roses on the table and placed the bronze to its left, where it provided a balance to the carved wooden box that normally filled the space on its own.

"He must have really appreciated your help," Otis teased her as Adrianna removed a small card that had been taped to the statue's base and read to herself:

Remembering...

Hope you are, too.

Chase

She slipped the card into her shorts' pocket, wondering how much it had cost him to write those few simple words with his injured hand as she glanced up just in time to see Otis and Penny exchange a meaningful look before they both turned and grinned at her.

Friday having arrived, Adrianna chose first one and then another outfit to wear when she welcomed Chase home that evening, finally deciding on a pair of black slacks and a shimmery, low-cut black and gold top shot with chartreuse accents that would set off her dark eyes and hair.

The doorbell chimed forth a few minutes before eight, as she secured the clasp on a simple gold chain she had placed around her neck.

"Thank goodness I'm ready," she said to Max as they both hurried down the broad staircase. "I'll take this as a sign that Chase has missed me as much as I've been missing him."

Quickly, she threw open the door and stepped onto the front porch, surprised to hear Max emit a deep growl in the background.

"Adrianna!"

For a moment, her mind didn't take in that it was Brad and not Chase who had stepped forward, drawn her to him and was now kissing her in the light beaming through the open doorway. Struggling against her ex-fiancé's embrace, she was only dimly aware of Max barking excitedly and the sound of a car driving up, pausing for only a moment and then pulling away, just as she gained her release.

"How dare you!" she vented her pent-up anger.

"Whoa!" Brad took a step back and held up his hand. "I thought you'd be glad to see me."

"You thought wrong," she made her position clear, even as memories of their time together vied for position.

"You can't mean that." His tone softened. "I know that I've hurt you, but I also know that you love me and have done so for the better part of six years. Surely, I deserve at least a hearing before you throw away what we had."

"You've already done that." She matched his calmer tone.

"A few minutes, that's all I'm asking for, Kitten," he used his pet name for her.

Realizing it was starting to sprinkle and they were still standing on the porch, she capitulated and led the way into the house, bending to reassure Max as Brad closed the door behind them.

"We can talk in here." She indicated the formal parlor, not wanting him to settle in.

"My, you have come into a nice place," he commented as he took a seat on a couch that Adrianna knew was no more comfortable than the hard chair she had chosen for herself.

"How did you find me?" she asked.

"Mary Ellen gave me your address and filled me in," he named a former roommate of hers who lived in Seattle and then leaned forward. "I made a mistake, Adrianna, the biggest mistake of my life."

"But why? What had I done to deserve such a betrayal?"

"Nothing." He met her gaze squarely. "That was the problem. You hadn't been actively engaged in our relationship for a long time. Instead of making plans for our wedding, you spent all of your time talking about this or that office intrigue at your work, and you no longer seemed interested in what was going on at the hospital like Pamela was."

"Pamela was…?"

"It was just sex. I didn't love her, but I needed someone to care."

So she had no one but herself to blame for what had happened, Adrianna thought as she examined his face that now seemed like a stranger's.

"I'm sorry." She stood and noted that Max did the same beside her.

"There's someone else, isn't there?" Resignation filled Brad's eyes. "Whoever it was who drove up as I was kissing you." He seemed to take in for the first time that she was dressed to go out.

"I'm sorry," she repeated, not knowing what else to say.

"There was no reason for you to see yourself as a nun because I'd done a jerky thing." He waved her apology away. "Let's leave it like this. I'm staying at the Captain's Point Inn just as you come into town. I'll be checking out around eleven in the morning unless I hear from you before then, at which point I'll stay until we can work everything out."

Not trusting her voice, she led the way to the front door and opened it.

"I made a mistake, Adrianna, but I love you." He lifted her chin with one finger. "I always have, and I always will." He turned and left her.

Adrianna closed the door and leaned her back against it until she heard Brad's car pull away. Clearing her mind completely, she let Max out one last time, locked up the house and turned off the downstairs lights.

"Come," she said to her furry companion, who followed her like a tiny brown shadow as she headed upstairs where she changed into her pajamas and got into bed, her heart filled with a torrent of mixed emotions.

CHAPTER LXIV

Several hours later, having tossed, turned and cried into her pillow, Adrianna threw back the covers, turned on the bedside lamp and reached for her cell phone.

Not what you think. Can explain. Please call later today.

She sent the brief text message to Chase, feeling that the rest of her life might possibly be ruined.

"I've made a mess of it," she admitted to Jebediah's portrait, almost expecting him to frown back. "Who knew that I had done that to Brad? And now, I've pushed Chase away from me, too."

Receiving no reply as expected, she switched off the light and finally drifted to sleep - Max curled beside her, his ears alert, guarding her against the night and possible further intruders.

Her phone's ring jerked her awake to the full light of mid-morning, and she fought to clear the fog from her head as she answered it.

"I'll be there at eight, unless it would disturb you," Chase replied brusquely to her greeting.

"Max and I will be here alone," Adrianna agreed to wait until evening, not wanting to push her luck as she heard a sharp click that announced he had terminated the call.

"That doesn't bode well," she admitted to Max who had removed himself to his bed in front of the fireplace, his attempt to open one sleepy eye his only response in acknowledgement.

For a moment, she considered returning to bed herself, but instead reclined against the pillows in her favorite window seat and half watched the sailboats come and go before her on the ocean, her mind working overtime until finally she dozed.

More refreshed when Max nudged her hand and awakened her, she let him out and then realized with a start that Brad's eleven o'clock deadline had already passed.

Determinedly, she made her way through the day, at one point forcing herself to eat a container of yogurt.

Six o'clock having finally arrived, she took a long bubble bath and then dressed in a pair of jeans and a comfortable shirt, thinking that clothes wouldn't help her in this instance, but still taking care with her hair and makeup.

"Once again, it looks like I'm ready too early," she admitted to Max as she headed downstairs and made her way to the study, where she checked her email on the off chance that Chase had sent her a message.

Disappointed, she answered a friend in Seattle before she swiveled the desk chair around, but then realized that Max must have left her to get a drink as her eyes fell on the intricate frieze that ran along the top of the five foot high wainscoting.

The answer is in the garden... She once again gazed upon carved flowers that she hadn't yet found the time to investigate and, rising from the chair, began working her hand along the roses and peonies until a muffled click preceded one of the flat panels sliding open to reveal a stone staircase going down as it let the scent of salt air into the room.

Grabbing a flashlight from the desk drawer, she made her way carefully down the steps until they ended at a narrow tunnel that led, if she was right, toward the sea. Flipping on the flashlight, she stepped forward and then grabbed a metal ring embedded in the rock wall as she slid on something slimy that had remained unseen in the dimness, her flashlight falling against the rock floor. To her horror, she then watched as the panel behind her closed shut.

Panic grew within her as she fumbled in the dark for the flashlight, which refused to turn on once she found it. Reconnecting with the metal ring, she did everything she could think of to open the panel, finally making her way back up the stairs and running her hands all around what she thought was the aperture from the sound of Max barking on the other side of the wall.

Believing herself to have no choice, she carefully made her way down the steps and along the tunnel, which seemed to ramble this way and that as she discovered what felt like openings to rooms going off of it and attempted to stay on what she thought was the main path. Then she perceived a lighter area up ahead as the sound of crashing waves became stronger to her ears and she reached a point where the path split – one way widening before it headed into the water and the other more slippery one turning sharply left to where she could see the opening to yet another room or tunnel.

Holding on to first one and then a second metal ring that hung from the rock wall, she made her way safely into what proved to be a room – only to be disappointed when she discovered that the light within came from a root-filled grate in the ceiling that was at least ten feet above her. To make matters worse, a bolt of lightning now shot across what little dark cloud-filled sky she could see overhead, the thunder effectively drowning out her shouts for help as she felt the water that was now lapping against her ankles.

A glimpse out to where the path had once been failed to convince her that she would now be able to make it back to the tunnel without the tide pulling her out with it.

"Help!" She called again, grateful for the slight slope of the room's floor. "Help! Someone please help me!"

But the room steadily darkened, and no response to her repeated shouts came save for the increasing noise of the now aggressive waves battering against the rock wall beyond where she stood.

"Help!" She screamed. "Help!"

"Adrianna, it's Chase. Are you in the room?"

"Yes!" she called back as relief surged through her.

"Are you hurt?"

"No!"

"Stay where you are! I'm coming to get you!"

"Don't! The walkway's too dangerous! There's a grate in the ceiling."

But she received no reply, and her mind filled with fear that he would do something foolish trying to reach her. Then the beam of a flashlight bobbed along the wall to her left, and a moment later Chase appeared in the doorway - a coil of rope slung over his shoulder, more wrapped around his waist.

"Hurry!" He reached out his hand and drew her towards him, and in that moment, she recognized the young scout from her childhood memory and knew with surety that she would be safe.

Working rapidly, he folded a beach towel into a narrow strip and wrapped it around her waist. "Hold that in place." He then passed a length of rope three times around over the towel, finishing it with a sailor's knot that effectively tied her to his side.

"Here." He passed her the large flashlight. "Whatever happens try to keep that over your head with one hand and hold onto the rope around my waist with your other. We may only have one shot at this. The tide's rising rapidly in this storm."

Wrapping his right arm around her, he waited until the water level lessened and then waded onto the walkway where he grasped the metal ring closest to the room with his right hand and the other ring with his left one, crushing her between him and the wall as he took the brunt of the next angry wave.

What level of strength and personal courage it was taking him to hang onto the ring with his injured hand, she didn't know. She was only grateful as he managed to do so until the water retreated from the wall and the rip current overcame his grip, sucking her away with it as her feet were pulled from the floor before she was jerked back by the rope that attached her to him.

"Now!" He screamed in her ear over the enhanced noise of the surf as he somehow found the strength to drag her all but dead weight towards the safety of the tunnel as she fought to regain her footing.

Reaching the dry rock of the path, her knees gave way beneath her and she sagged against his body, her head resting on his chest above the strong beat of his heart.

"You really must stop getting into positions from which I have to rescue you." He held her tightly to him. "This was a close one."

"How did you do that?" She gazed up at him, her eyes filled with admiration. "How did you keep us from being drawn out to sea?"

It was then that he raised his chafed and bleeding left wrist around which he had wrapped several times the rope that he had secured to a third ring a few steps along the tunnel before he had made his way to her in the room.

"Can you get us back into the house?" She found the strength to go on. "We have to attend to that so you don't get an infection."

"You're right," he agreed, "but if you'll pull my knife from my right pocket, I believe it would help if we removed ourselves from the rope first."

"It was Brad you saw me with last evening," she strove to explain what had led them to this point as she cut the rope from the ring."

"I know. I had forgotten to stop the surveillance on him that your great-aunt had requested and received a call late this afternoon. I also know that he's gone."

"How did you realize there was a room where I was with the walkway under water?" she asked.

"I had been there before, but from the other direction," he told her. "Augustus and I rowed in and explored once when the tide was out years ago. Your great-great grandfather probably used these side rooms to store contraband liquor during Prohibition. It might be worth checking to see if there are bottles still left in any of them."

"Perhaps another time," Adrianna stated firmly and led them away from the sea.

As they made their way towards the staircase, she could hear Max's shrill bark growing in strength and then Otis's voice as well. "Adrianna? Chase? Is that you?"

"We're almost there," she called back as they rounded a bend, and she could see her property manager up ahead in the study, holding a squirming Max under his arm.

"That little guy saved your life," Chase told her as they started up the stairs. "I could hear him barking, and when Otis let us into the house he was scratching frantically at the paneling in the study."

"No." She sent him a shy smile. "You saved my life. I'll never forget what you did back there."

"You – upstairs and into a hot bath," Otis commanded once he could see Adrianna clearly. "And you…" He pointed at Chase. "You seem to have taken everything you needed, but now you're coming with me to let Penny look at that wrist."

In the light of the room, Adrianna saw immediately that her property manager was right, as she glimpsed the tight lines around Chase's lips for the first time and realized how the salt-filled wounds must be hurting him.

"Thank you both again." She turned to leave, suddenly feeling depleted by her experience, but her attorney grabbed her wrist and kept her with them.

"I'll be back in one hour – no more," he said as Otis and he walked with her towards the foyer. "Leave the front door unlocked for me."

"One hour." She smiled at him as her heart filled with anticipation and then closed the door behind them, before rushing up the stairs faster than she would've thought possible a few minutes before.

CHAPTER LXV

Half an hour later, showered and dressed, Adrianna stood by her bedside table, her attention drawn to the photo of her great-aunt reading to her in the kitchen garden that had been in the envelope with the clue.

The answer is in the garden, the clue had read, and then she recognized what she hadn't paid attention to in the photo before.

"Of course, Max! It's been right here all along, propped against the base of the lamp that I've turned off every evening when I've gone to bed. Let's see if I'm right."

She hurried downstairs to the library, where her finger ran along the rows of children's books until she found it – a worn copy of Frances Burnett's novel, *The Secret Garden.*

"This is the book Great-aunt Martha was reading to me in the photo," she explained to the dog, who wagged his tail eagerly at her feet. Quickly, she pulled the volume from the shelf and then held its spine loosely in her hands, whereupon it fell open and revealed one of her great-aunt's signature blue envelopes.

Withdrawing a single piece of paper, she was aware of Max deserting her as she rapidly read the text of the letter, confirming what she had already learned:

Adrianna -

You are now surrounded by your Montgomery heritage and the fine old traditions of our family. There is no more that I can give you beyond that which you already carry within yourself. Look around you at the people of Captain's Point - search their eyes, know their hearts, welcome them into your life - for therein lies the world's true wealth.

Know that I love you and always have, although there surely have been times when you would have thought not. Believe me, and understand that I loved you enough to force you along the best path.

Forgive me if I was wrong.

Martha C. Montgomery

Then she heard Max bark a greeting in the foyer and looked up.

"Adrianna?"

She heard Chase's footsteps approaching.

"In the library," she called out to him. "You won't believe what I've found."

"I don't care what you've found." He strode across the room and pulled her into his arms, planting a firm kiss on her lips. "Don't ever…" His face clearly showed that he meant what he said. "And I mean *ever*, do that to me again."

"Promise." Her expression sobered. "I was scared to death, but you were amazing. How's your wrist?"

"It'll do," he waved her concerns away, but she was glad to see that Penny had bandaged it for him. "Do you have a pen?"

"Right here."

"Then sign these." He set the file folder he was carrying onto the library table beside them and opened it to reveal several legal-sized documents. "Here, here, here and here."

"You must be sick to death of dealing with me as my great-aunt's administrator," she joked as she applied her last signature.

"That I am," he agreed. "Which is why I am telling you here and now that you have met the unreasonable terms of Martha's will."

"I disagree," she argued her point, tapping with her pen the piece of blue stationery she had discovered. "My great-aunt knew me and the way I had been raised better than I knew myself. If she hadn't forced me to return to Montgomery House and Captain's Point, I would still be focused on earning money and getting ahead instead of all the wonderful people that now surround me. I would never have grown as a person enough to effectively fill the role of the last remaining Montgomery in the way that she knew was best. The house would never have unveiled its secrets to me or made my family real again."

"Still," he maintained, "it's over and behind you now."

"But a year isn't up yet," she insisted, not wanting to break even this link to him.

"Trust me, it's been long enough," he said gruffly. "You've shown yourself perfectly capable of sustaining Montgomery House and its various assets, you're taking an active interest in community affairs, and you have put down roots. It would be totally unreasonable to expect any more of you."

"So the estate is now mine, and you're freed of your responsibility?"

"So the estate is yours, and I'm freed of my responsibility for overseeing Martha's wishes, which means that I can now speak about my feelings for you in a way that I wouldn't have been comfortable doing before." He drew her to him. "I love you Adrianna Montgomery. I love everything about you. I have ever since you arrived back here in Captain's Point although, looking back, it may have all started when I first looked into the large, trusting, dark eyes of a little girl who had fallen in the woods behind your gazebo."

"You've been rescuing me for a long time, haven't you?"

"Yes, and I've hit on a way that I can hopefully limit such episodes in the future." He smiled down at her. "Marry me, my love. Tell me that you will sit beside me on this wild and crazy ride that's destined to be our lives and will take me to be yours."

"Yes." She slid her arms around his neck. "Yes, I will. I've never wanted anything more than to belong to you, Chase Sheffield, but promise me one thing."

"Whatever your heart desires." Her betrothed threw caution to the wind.

"Promise me that we can be married soon."

"The sooner the better, if it will keep you out of trouble." He laughed and then once again lowered his lips onto hers.

You Are Invited
to
The Wedding
of

Chase Augustus Sheffield
and
Adrianna Maria Montgomery

in

A Man for Susan

By

Charlotte Kent

The second novel in the Captain's Point Stories
series

Available August 1, 2013

A Special Treat for You!

From

Annie Acorn

Chocolate Can Kill

Chapter One

Here she comes! What if it doesn't work? What if she doesn't die?

No! Don't think about it. Concentrate. Focus on the crowd.

Why now, so long after the careful planning and firm decision? Why these questions in my mind?

They don't matter – nothing else does now. It's just another of life's challenges - made to be overcome. A few minutes, seconds really, and it'll all be over.

It's a shame I have to do it. Everybody loves her, even me, but like killing a chicken to eat a drumstick, it's a necessary evil.

Why these shivers? I should be hot. When did mind and body separate – one determined and in control, the other jumpy and unpredictable? Sweaty palms, clumsy fingers, churning stomach. These could cause mistakes. Flesh is weak, but I am strong!

Good. She hasn't noticed. Time to go.

No! Wait a moment, let her pass. Remember, nonchalant. Blend in. Look around, expecting someone up ahead.

A single thrust, a second to end a nightmare. Make it quick and true. It's you or the chicken - a matter of survival, nothing more.

* * *

Too rushed to notice anyone else around her, Emily Harris focused on the moving tread of an arrivals' escalator, slid one foot forward and quickly followed it with the other. Secure, she adjusted the strap of her shoulder bag, heavy with paraphernalia of travel.

As her father's farmhand, Uncle Reuben, had always said, the best part of any trip was coming home. His stories, told to her as a child so many years ago, had sparked the flame that still shone brightly as her career. As with all his wise old sayings, Uncle Reuben had been right. It felt good to be home. Birmingham had never looked better than when they had flown over Red Mountain and circled their approach.

How long would it take to grab her luggage and get to the house and Warren? Twenty minutes? Thirty? Anticipation washed over her.

Behind her the crowd pressed closer as a boy and girl rushed past her. A push, followed by a sharp jab, and suddenly she was falling.

Someone screamed. Was it her?

Startled faces and clutching hands registered in her mind as she grabbed for support, felt rubber rail beneath her fingers, but failed to get a grip. Relentless stairs descended, taking her feet with them, and she lost her hold again.

Unable to gain control, her shoulder blade slammed against a wall, and an elbow cracked as it met metal, bouncing her forward as she desperately grabbed at something, anything that would stop her fall. Finally, her head struck the bottom of the escalator, and she jolted to a halt just beyond the flow of passengers.

A rush of noise filled her ears and a swirling blackness tried to overtake her senses. Somewhere to her left, she heard a man ask, "Is she dead?"

She focused on the circle of worried faces that hung above. Was her mind playing tricks? Warren was supposed to be home with dinner waiting, but he stood amongst the crowd instead. Had he followed her on the escalator?

"What are you doing here?" she tried to ask, but darkness came again.

* * *

"Oh, my God!" Warren knelt beside his wife's prostrate body. "Let her be okay. Oh, God, just let her be alive!"

Was she breathing? Yes, but her right arm extended at an awkward angle and a large bump had risen at her hairline.

"Em, it's me, Warren. Can you hear me?" Frantically checking her pulse, he wondered what he should expect to feel, and relief surged through him as her eyelids fluttered open.

"Warren?" Her brown eyes seemed unfocused.

"I'm here." He tugged her skirt into a more modest drape. "You're back in Birmingham, but you fell down an escalator. Remember? You're going to be okay. I promise."

"My arm hurts, and my left knee, too." Emily struggled to rise.

"Shouldn't you lie still?"

"No." Her voice was firmer now. "I've made a spectacle. Just get me to a chair somewhere."

"Call 911!" Warren shouted at an airport security guard who was running towards them. "I want an ambulance and some privacy! Stat!" Then, belatedly, he added, "Please."

"I don't need...," Emily argued, but her husband interrupted not wanting her to waste her breath.

"Don't worry," he patted her shoulder. "I'll take care of everything. Hold that arm tight against your waist." He helped her rise. "It'll all be over soon."

* * *

Embarrassment gave way as Emily mentally withdrew from activity around her, sensing a slow motion world. What was causing this reaction? How hard had she struck her head? Maybe it was the pain. No, she felt surprisingly little pain, just a weird numbness in various spots along her body.

A huge shudder shook her as Warren half carried her to a bench. There they remained, her head resting on his shoulder. Thank goodness he had fetched her, despite the gulf that had grown between them recently.

Trying not to move, she took stock. Her head and knee both throbbed, and a jab of pain shot up her arm as numbness from initial shock wore off. She cautiously ran a finger along her forehead. Yes, a knot protruded there. So much for her crowning glory as her husband called her brown hair, which was probably a mess.

"Warren, about my fall..." She straightened and looked into his face.

Under strain, Warren's features had assumed a fragile, brittle quality beneath his flyaway, sandy-colored hair. A worried expression superseded his normal boyish optimism and his familiar gray-green eyes held what? Concern or fear?

Frustration rose within her. A wife should recognize her husband's reactions like her own. Still, there were times when...

Emily supposed it was asking too much for a couple to get along perfectly day after day for thirty years. But this time was, well, worse. Her mind reviewed a list of things they shared - their boys, their home, their memories - things worth fighting for.

"Don't worry about your fall now." Warren's words interrupted her thoughts and brought her back to here and now. "We'll go over everything when you're all fixed up."

"But I want you to know..." She tried again, needing to regain control of her life, but he withdrew his arm and stood as the unmistakable wail of an ambulance drew nearer.

"There they are." He smiled, near and yet removed.

Emily let out a sigh. There was no use talking when his mind was elsewhere, but the sharp poke and then the fall... Given the state of their relationship these past few weeks, would he even care? Perhaps, she shouldn't bother him.

"That didn't take long." Warren glanced at his watch with satisfaction. "I'll stay right behind you in the car," He assured his wife as he waved the EMTs in their direction. "We'll soon have you back together again."

The line, "all the king's horses and all the king's men," danced through Emily's head. Could they put her together again? After all, it wasn't just her injuries that demanded healing. Her whole comfort zone had been destroyed by actions of another.

More and more, the world had morphed into an often ill-mannered and sometimes dangerous place as she had reached middle-age. Still, she wouldn't have believed that someone could shove her down an escalator and then calmly walk away.

Well, she was an intelligent, capable, professional woman, and somehow, someway she was going to find this person and give them a piece of her mind. The proverbial buck would stop here – no, it would come to a screeching halt, she determined as the stretcher was readied and she noted its lowered position with gratitude.

"It's mainly my right arm and left knee," she explained as the younger EMT helped her up. "I fell down an escalator."

"Dangerous things escalators." He exuded calm, but his eyes held concern. "You hang on, ma'am. We'll get you to the hospital in a jif." He indicated his partner with a nod. "Buddy here races at Talladega on the weekends, so don't you worry."

True to their promise, the men completed the trip to the hospital in record time.

Frank Zenni, the Harris's next door neighbor, was leaving work as they approached. With amazement, Emily watched as Warren whirled their friend around without an explanation and shoved him through the open emergency room doors into the glaring lights and staring faces of a waiting room beyond.

"What the heck?" The orthopedic surgeon's blue eyes widened in his normally calm, bedside manner face, as he looked from her to Warren then back again, concern having replaced his initial surprise.

With difficulty, she again subdued a laugh. Perhaps she was hysterical, or maybe this was shock. Didn't people die of shock? Emily thought they did.

"So that's what happened." Warren's words returned her to the emergency room around them.

"Bring those forms in here," Frank ordered a surprised intake clerk as he indicated an examination room and then proceeded to speed them through hospital routines of paperwork and x-rays, staying with them until her results were in.

"Your right arm's cracked at the elbow, and your left kneecap's badly bruised." Their neighbor's calm tone reassured her, as he applied a necessary splint and sling himself. "That was a nasty fall."

"Tell me about it," Emily agreed.

"You're lucky you didn't break your neck," the surgeon glanced up. "We have to slow down as we get older, you know, so you take care. I don't want to see you like this again."

She ignored his comment about her age, as more important thoughts of makeup and curling irons filled her head. How would she manage with no right hand? There would be no way.

One thing Emily knew for sure, though. No matter what she looked like or how she felt, she would find whoever had robbed her of her dignity and left her bruised and broken before too much time had passed.

"That should do it." Frank examined his work with satisfaction. "These'll help both the elbow and the knee." He handed a small pill packet to Warren. "Now let's get you out of here." Frank offered Emily a hand.

"I'll fetch the car." Her husband hurried ahead of them along a busy corridor as their friend pushed his patient's wheelchair forward.

"Here you go." Warren opened their car's passenger door a few minutes later.

Carefully, Emily eased herself onto the front seat as her husband saluted their friend goodbye.

Warren's face, usually so kind and familiar, appeared sinister in reflected red tones from the dash as they cleared the parking lot, and she couldn't help but wonder. Who was this man beside her?

Her husband, her mate - the answer came clearly in her head.

After all these years, her pulse still quickened when he entered a room, but no matter how deep and visceral a connection she felt to him, there were no guarantees. For a moment, as a darkened world rushed past beyond their car's windows, she felt they were strangers in an icy land and shivered despite the warmth outside.

"Let's get you upstairs." Warren brought the car to a halt in their driveway.

With her husband's arm around her, leading always with her right leg due to growing stiffness in her left, Emily forced herself, one step at a time, upstairs and along the hall.

"Made it." She limped into their bedroom, and restful ambience of dark wood furniture and a chintz-covered chaise lounge washed over her. All she wanted now was to lose her pain in sleep.

"Take it slowly." Warren assisted with his wife's gown and then pulled the bedcovers back.

Carefully, Emily edged herself onto the mattress, unwilling to move too much even for more comfort.

"Here." Her husband tugged on the sheet from where he remained beside their bed. "You're all scrunched up somehow." His fingers, long and thin like himself, shook slightly as he fumbled with the covers.

Was he so tired, or worse could he be ill? Maybe that was why he had seemed so distant recently. Worry filled Emily, but then resolved.

After all, she had barely recognized herself in the dresser mirror on her way to bed. Pain and fatigue had defined a tight, pinched expression, and dark circles beneath her eyes had produced a haunted, raccoon effect. Even her short, rounded body had acquired a bloated appearance that wasn't flattering.

"It's good to have you home again, even if it is in pieces," Warren returned to her side, having closed the drapes. "You were unconscious for a moment at the airport, no matter how much you deny it."

"You would think I had a broken neck the way you're carrying on." Emily didn't hide her pleasure at his words.

What had affected them so adversely these past few weeks, she wondered again in the face of his concern? Simply stated, something small and intangible, but nonetheless important, was wrong with Warren. She sensed it, even reacted to it, but she couldn't identify it.

A knock down, dragged out fight would have been better, but that had never been their style. Instead, tension grew and he withdrew as whatever it was remained beneath the surface, a boil coming to a head.

She needed to do something, but she couldn't defeat an unknown enemy. And so, it simply lay between them.

Still, as Uncle Reuben had always said if something didn't seem right, it probably wasn't. Her friend's uncle had been an old man when she was a girl, but even as a child, Emily had recognized wisdom in his trite words.

Perhaps Warren and she could talk things out now that Matt was gone. Memory of their youngest son's excitement the previous Saturday morning, when he had left for computer camp, lifted Emily's mood. Now she and Warren had the house to themselves – a golden opportunity.

"That's a nasty bump along your hairline," Warren interrupted her thoughts. "You can't imagine how I felt when you were flying towards me."

Again Emily felt she was viewing a stranger as she watched her husband reach his fingers toward the ceiling, stretch and then head to their bathroom. Exit stage left, she thought and then realized lines from nursery rhymes and plays seemed to be filling her head, even as a vague memory from her rush along the airport concourse that she wanted to remember remained elusive.

"Take this." Warren dropped one of the tablets Frank had given them onto his wife's palm and handed her a glass of water. "You'll need it before the night is through."

"Thanks." She washed down the pill, returned the glass and sagged against her pillows.

A soft mound beneath the covers defined her body except where her splint protruded as if pointing at her husband to go. Sharp pain met her attempt to adjust her arm, and Emily ceased her efforts as he placed the glass on the bedside cabinet, looking like her same old Warren. A wave of love passed through her, and yet, tension lay between them like an elephant in the room.

She needed to tell him about the jab before her fall, but now was not the time. Closing her eyes, she pulled the sheet over her face against the light and her concerns, then listened as he moved about.

"I'll sleep in the guest room." Her husband's voice indicated he faced her again. "That way I won't roll into you. Anything you need before I go?"

"No." She peeked from beneath the sheet. "I missed you while I was gone. I always do."

He paused in the doorway. "I missed you, too."

"I'm sorry I've made such a mess of things."

"It's nothing we can't work out." Warren shrugged and sent her a smile. "The arm will mend. Arms do. Everything'll look better in the morning," he promised and switched off the light. "Call me if you need anything, anything at all."

Emily listened as footsteps carried him along the hall. Then slowly, so as not to disturb her injured arm, she reached her other hand around and carefully probed a large bruised area on her lower back.

Someone had changed her life forever. They had violated her space and stolen her security. An umbrella? An elbow? She didn't know, but whatever object they had used, someone had deliberately pushed her down the escalator. Of that she was sure.

But who? And why? And how could she abstract them from a world filled with strangers? She must marshal her thoughts and figure out the answers now while the memory of her fall was fresh.

But against her will, her eyelids sagged, and she realized her plans were not to be, as the little white pill Warren had dropped into her hand took control and closed her eyes for one last time.

A Special Treat for You!

From

Juliette Hill

Pink Lemonade Diary

Chapter One

Thirteen year old Victoria Gray, Vicki to her friends, fumbled through the pockets of her school uniform jacket for the key to her family's Manhattan apartment.

"Finally!" she exclaimed, as the key turned in the temperamental lock. Brushing her long, blond hair from her eyes, she opened the door. "Summer vacation! Freedom! No more homework!"

Her Siamese cat, Spice, and Pom-chi, Cinnamon, welcomed her with enthusiasm. Spice meowed loudly for attention, while Cinnamon ran circles around her in his little dog way.

The apartment felt comfortably cool after the walk from school in the June heat and humidity.

"Hey, guys, wait a second. Let me put my backpack down!" Dropping her pack where she stood, Vicki kicked off her shoes and removed her jacket from her long, slender frame, before she headed along the hall to her bedroom to change into more comfortable clothes.

Jess, her BFF since first grade, was waiting on a call about getting together later, both girls anxious to celebrate. Her friend, though, would just have to wait.

"Mom…Dad?" Vicki called out as she looked through her closet for something to change into. "Anyone home?"

Suddenly, despite her excitement about summer vacation, a sense of impending doom that had hovered all day overwhelmed her.

Last night, her parents' muffled voices from the living room had mentioned her name several times as she drifted off to sleep, and this usually meant something unpleasant - a dentist appointment, perhaps, or a stint at a summer camp.

"All I want to do this summer is hang out with my friends," Vicki muttered to the dog, who looked back with a slight tilt of his head. "They never tell me anything until the last minute!" She pulled on a pink tank top and matching shorts.

Picking up the cat, she rubbed her cheek against his soft fur. "Let's get a snack." Vicki strode to the kitchen, where she discovered some of her favorite homemade chocolate cupcakes. The fridge, though, revealed nothing but pink lemonade, and she turned back to the dog. "Mom knows I hate pink lemonade as much as I hate eating brussel sprouts!"

Cinnamon barked in agreement as he followed her around, begging for a treat.

Taking a seat at the marble-topped island, Vicki heard the rattle of the front door.

"Sorry I'm late," her mother called out. "I had some last minute shopping to do."

"I'm in here, having a snack. Why the pink lemonade?" she shot back. "I can't stand the stuff, so what's up?"

Having set down her shopping bags, Vicki's mother joined her in the kitchen. "I guess I felt nostalgic for the 'good ole' days."

"Huh...the what?"

"Last night, your father and I were discussing summer break, and I was reminiscing about a vacation I spent with my Auntie M on that barrier island off the Georgia coast, when I was about your age. "I'll never forget that special summer."

"You're so sentimental sometimes." Vicki's feeling of dread returned. "I thought I heard my name mentioned when I was falling asleep," she added.

"Why don't the three of us go out for Italian, and we'll talk."

"Oh, no, what have I done now?" Vicki's mind raced as she swallowed hard. "Jess and I want to get together later and celebrate. It's Friday, so you know how crowded the restaurant will be."

"Your father will be home any minute. I'll make a reservation, and you go text Jess."

"Whatever," Vicki said in a bored tone, and headed into the family room where she turned on the TV.

Left alone, Sophia Cassandra Gray, Cassy to her friends, tapped a manicured fingertip on the marble countertop, as her mind drifted back to conversation of the evening before.

"I'll never forget those carefree days." She had handed her husband his customary brandy. "We spent hours lying under the magnolia tree sipping Auntie M's ice-cold pink lemonade."

"Urban living is harsh, unforgiving and competitive." Max had met her gaze. "I want Vicki to have a variety of experiences like you did - a quieter, gentler alternative to the glitz and glamour of fast-paced city life."

Now, again, her memory returned to Auntie M's barrier island. Once, there had even been a boy that she had liked in a way she had never felt before, but they had only shared a few glorious weeks and then he was gone. Years later, when she had met Max, something in him had reminded her of that long-ago love. How lucky she had been!

Bringing herself back to the present, Cassy peered into the family room. As usual, her daughter had the television blaring, cell phone in hand. Some things never change," she thought, or could they?"

Now, all they had to do was break the news to Vicki.

OTHER TITLES AVAILABLE FROM ANNIE ACORN PUBLISHING LLC

By Annie Acorn

Chocolate Can Kill

Murder With My Darling

A Stranger Comes to Town

The Young Executive

When to Remain Silent

On the Road

The Magic Sand Dollar

One More Christmas Past

One Last Gift To Go

A Haunting Christmas

Too Busy for Christmas

An Afghan of Many Colors

A Tired Older Woman: Loses Weight and Keeps It Off!

How to Survive Your New Home Purchase

How to Survive Your 203K Mortgage

Annie Acorn writing as Charlotte Kent

A Clue for Adrianna

A Man for Susan

A Christmas Kiss

By Beverly J. Crawford

A B-17 Christmas

The Christmas Child

The Best Homemade Christmas

While Shepherds Watched

The Stockings Were Hung

Towards the Sun

By Peggy Teel writing as denise hays

Niki Knows the Dirt – A Niki Edgar Mystery

Monkey Business – A Niki Edgar Mystery

Merry Christmas Minus One

Walking for Weight Loss

By Peggy Teel

God and Grandma

Christmas in Tartan Glen

The Best Worst Christmas

A Merry Mary Christmas

Twelve Bells for Christmas

By Juliette Hill

Pink Lemonade Diary

Two Beaux for Christmas

Christmas Shoppe Magic

The Christmas Spirit of Starlight Cove

Country Cabin Christmas

Annie Acorn

Annie Acorn is the pseudonym of a prolific, internationally published author, whose readership recognizes her mainly for her women's fiction, cozy mysteries and richly woven stories with a warm southern flair. She is a founding member of From Women's Pens – A Cooperative of Women Writers.

Annie is the mother of two sons, one of whom is married to the best daughter-in-law in the world. She lives in the Washington, D.C. area, where she has done extensive technical writing as a contractor.

She owned a tri-state medical outsourcing business for a number of years and was the Director of a behavioral healthcare firm. She once flipped a comic book and collectible retail company comprised of five stores, and she has managed cemeteries and funeral homes. She is the owner of Annie Acorn Publishing LLC.

Ms. Acorn has published in *The Inspirational Writer*, and she edited an in-house publication for the State of Mississippi. She is a contributor of ezine articles.

In her spare time, Ms. Acorn enjoys reading, writing mysteries, listening to classical music, playing cards, and spending time with her family and friends – often at a restaurant serving delicious food.

Annie is the author of the blog at annieacorn.com. You can friend her on Facebook and tweet her at Annie_Acorn. She will respond to your email sent to annieacorn11@gmail.com.

Juliette Hill

    Juliette Hill is the pseudonym for a creative writer who is passionate about all things vintage, traveling with her husband and exploring family history. She enjoys treasure hunting at local antique markets and estate sales, searching for her next great 'find' that will spark her imagination. Her desire to discover the story behind each treasure motivates the writer within.

    Juliette's other interests include planning family gatherings, scrapbooking, cooking, shopping and dining out, to name a few.

    Her works, including *Pink Lemonade Diary, Christmas Shoppe Magic, The Christmas Spirit of Starlight Cove,* and *Two Beaux for Christmas* involve multi-dimensional characters and generational plots which bridge the gap between the past and present. She is a founding member of From Women's Pens and is currently working on several projects for Annie Acorn Publishing.

www.ingramcontent.com/pod-product-compliance
Lightning Source LLC
Chambersburg PA
CBHW060733180626
46819CB00001B/8